Praise for Joe Gores's

SPADE & ARCHER

"A respectable piece of work. . . . [Gores] captures Hammett's razor-sharp dialogue and his lovingly detailed portraits of the streets of San Francisco."

—*The Washington Post Book World*

"Gores's voice is a pleasure. If it isn't seamless ventriloquism, it's the sound of a writer professing his love for the master who came before." —*Newsday*

"Absorbing. . . . Readers with an appetite for Hammett can feed it with this new novel. . . . A fine reimagining."

—*The Plain Dealer* (Cleveland)

"Gores does a bang-up job. . . . [He] knits together a clever and appropriate backstory for the iconic detective that makes for a nifty period potboiler all on its own."

—*Rocky Mountain News*

"[Gores] is a master storyteller. . . . [*Spade & Archer*] engages and flows with creepy atmosphere, crisp dialogue and multiple plots." —*The Dallas Morning News*

"Gores is far and away the best candidate to pull off such a risky endeavor. . . . *Spade & Archer* [is] never less than entertaining." —*Los Angeles Times*

"A prequel that honors and enhances the legendary volume it enshrines. . . . This novel feels pre-aged more than dated—as vintage Hammett often does to today's readers. . . . Respectful, but too mindful of the source to be reverent—*Spade & Archer* exalts Dashiell Hammett, codifies his life's work and decorously affirms the master's serious intent."

—James Ellroy

"No one understands Dashiell Hammett better than Joe Gores, and no one but Joe Gores could have produced such a masterful and faithful rendering of the prequel to *The Maltese Falcon*. *Spade & Archer* stands on its own as a taut, engrossing existential crime saga set in San Francisco's vibrant 1920s, and its evocation of Hammett's style and plots is a triumph. Gores's wondrous talent shines and the shadow it casts of Hammett is smiling." —James Grady

"Seventy-nine years after *The Maltese Falcon* was first published, the other (gum)shoe drops. It's called *Spade & Archer* and it's fabulous." —Michael Harvey

"*Spade & Archer* is a triumph—intricately plotted, deft and strongly written, and perhaps most exciting, he shows us Sam Spade at the beginning of his career, deepening our appreciation of the character. I loved it."

—Robert Ferrigno

"I was amazed at Joe Gores's *Spade & Archer*. He's got Hammett's style down, and the story he tells is every bit as engrossing as anything Hammett ever wrote. I adored it."

—Joe R. Lansdale

JOE GORES

SPADE & ARCHER

Joe Gores, formerly a private eye, is the author of sixteen other novels, including *Hammett*, which won Japan's Falcon Award. He has received three Edgar Awards—one of only two authors to win in three separate categories: Best First Novel, Best Short Story, and Best Episode in a TV Series.

Dashiell Hammett, the author of *The Maltese Falcon*, was born in St. Mary's County, Maryland, in 1894, and grew up in Philadelphia and Baltimore. He left school at the age of fifteen and held various odd jobs before he became an operative for Pinkerton's National Detective Agency at age twenty-one. World War I, in which he served stateside, interrupted his sleuthing and injured his health. After being discharged from the hospital and making sporadic attempts to return to detective work, he turned to writing, and in the late 1920s he became the unquestioned master of detective fiction in America. During World War II, Mr. Hammett again served in the army, most of which time he spent in the Aleutians. He died in 1961.

SPADE & ARCHER

SPADE & ARCHER

The Prequel to Dashiell Hammett's
The Maltese Falcon

JOE GORES

VINTAGE CRIME/BLACK LIZARD
Vintage Books
A Division of Random House, Inc.
New York

FIRST VINTAGE CRIME/BLACK LIZARD EDITION, MARCH 2010

 Published in the United States by Vintage Books, a division of Random House, Inc., New York, and in Canada by Random House of Canada Limited, Toronto. Originally published in hardcover in the United States by Alfred A. Knopf, a division of Random House, Inc., New York, in 2009.

The Library of Congress has cataloged the Knopf edition as follows:
Gores, Joe, [date].
Spade & Archer / by Joe Gores.—1st ed.
p. cm.
"The prequel to Dashiell Hammett's The Maltese Falcon."
1. Spade, Sam, (Fictitious character)—Fiction. 2. Private investigators—California—San Francisco—Fiction. 3. San Francisco (Calif.)—Fiction. I. Title.
PS3557.O75S63 2009
813'.54—dc22 2008048288

Vintage ISBN: 978-0-307-27706-0

www.blacklizardcrime.com

Printed in the United States of America
10 9 8 7 6 5 4 3 2 1

For Dori

The Candle whose glow
Lights my way through life

1921

I

Samuel Spade, Esq.

The victor belongs to the spoils.

—F. Scott Fitzgerald

1

Spade's Last Case

It was thirteen minutes short of midnight. Drizzle glinted through the wind-danced lights on the edge of the Tacoma Municipal Dock. A man a few years shy of thirty stood in a narrow aisle between two tall stacks of crated cargo, almost invisible in a black hooded rain slicker. He had a long bony jaw, a flexible mouth, a jutting chin. His nose was hooked. He was six feet tall, with broad, steeply sloping shoulders.

He stayed in the shadows while the scant dozen passengers disembarked from the wooden-hulled steam-powered passenger ferry *Virginia V*, just in from Seattle via the Colvos Passage. His cigarette was cupped in one palm as if to shield it from the rain, or perhaps to conceal its glowing ember from watching eyes.

The watcher stiffened when the last person off the *Virginia V* was a solid, broad-shouldered man in his late thirties, dressed in a brown woolen suit. His red heavy-jawed face was made for joviality, but his small brown eyes were wary, constantly moving.

The passenger went quickly along the dock toward a narrow passageway that led to the city street beyond. The watcher, well behind, ambled after him. The first man had started through the passageway when he was jumped by two bulky, shadowy figures. There were grunts of effort, curses, the sound of blows, the scrape of leather soles on wet cobbles as the men struggled.

The watcher announced his arrival by jamming his lighted cigarette into the eye of one attacker. The man screamed, stumbled unevenly away holding a hand over his eye. The second attacker broke free and fled.

"'Lo, Miles."

Miles Archer, holding a handkerchief to his bloodied nose, said thickly through the bunched-up cloth, "Uh . . . thanks, Sam."

"Wobblies?" asked Sam Spade.

"Wobblies. Who else?"

They went down the passageway toward the street. Archer was limping. He had the thick neck and slightly soft middle of an athletic man going to seed.

"They finally made you as undercover for Burns?"

"Took 'em long enough," Archer bragged. He looked over at Spade. "Back with Continental, huh? Uh . . . how'd you find me?"

"Wasn't looking. Was staked out for a redheaded paper hanger out of Victoria."

"I saw him miss the ferry in Seattle."

Spade nodded, put a smile on his face that did not touch his eyes. "Belated congratulations on your marriage, Miles."

"Yeah, uh, thanks, Sam." Something sly and delighted seemed suddenly to dance in Archer's heavy, coarse voice. "We're living over in Spokane so's she can keep working at Graham's Bookstore, even though I'm down here most of the time. Tough on the little lady, but what can she do?"

Spade was at a table set for afternoon tea when the fortyish matron entered from Spokane's Sprague Avenue. The Davenport Hotel's vast Spanish-patio-style lobby was elegant, with a mezzanine above and, on the ground floor, an always-burning wood fireplace. When the woman paused in the doorway he stood. His powerful, conical, almost bearlike body kept his gray woolen suit coat from fitting well.

She crossed to him. She had wide-set judging eyes and a small, disapproving mouth.

"I am Mrs. Hazel Cahill. And you are . . ."

He gave a slight, almost elegant bow. "Samuel Spade."

Mrs. Cahill set her Spanish-leather handbag on one of the chairs, stripped off her kidskin gloves, and slid them through the bag's carrying straps. Her movements were measured. She turned slightly so Spade's thick-fingered hands could remove her coat.

She sat. She did not thank him. She said, "Three o'clock last Monday afternoon he and two other men came from this hotel, laughing about their golf scores. My husband, Theodore, and I just moved here from Tacoma a month ago, and it's been five years, but I know what I saw."

"I didn't say you didn't."

"Theodore does. Constantly." Her head shake danced carefully marcelled curls under her narrow-brimmed hat. "You men always stick together."

Spade nodded with seeming indifference.

"Theodore and he were great cronies—golf and tennis, drinks at the club. When he abandoned poor Eleanor five years ago and didn't turn up dead Theodore called him the one who got away. Eleanor is my best friend. She never remarried."

The skylight in the high vaulted ceiling laid a slanted bar of pale afternoon sunlight across one corner of their table. Spade's raised brows, which peaked slightly above his yellow-gray eyes, encouraged confidences.

"Did Eleanor's husband recognize you?"

"No. And only when they were past did I recognize him, from his voice—a distinctive tenor I'd always found irritating." She pursed thin lips and something like malice gleamed in her eyes. "Of course I immediately called Eleanor in Tacoma to tell her I had seen her missing husband here in Spokane."

"And she believed you. Even if your husband doesn't."

"My husband never believes me."

"If the man's here I'll find him."

After she had gone Spade remained, rolled and smoked three cigarettes in quick succession, muttered aloud, "What the hell?" and left the hotel.

John Graham's Bookstore was on the corner of Sprague Avenue and West First Avenue, hard by the Davenport

Hotel. Spade entered with long strides, slowed as if looking for a particular volume on the crowded shelves. There were a half dozen browsers and an almost pleasant smell of old books in the air.

Graham himself, a thin bespectacled man with a trim white mustache and wings of silver hair swept back from either side of his face, was ringing up a sale on the front register. A female clerk was selling a customer a book halfway down the store.

Spade went that way, his eyes hooded. The clerk was a blonde of about his age, pretty verging on beautiful, with an oval face, blue eyes, and a moist red mouth. Her silk-striped woolen rep dress, too fashionable for a shopgirl to wear to work, clung to an exquisite body.

The big round blue eyes lit up when she saw Spade. She hurried her sale to just short of rudeness, came up to Spade, raised her face for his kiss. Instead, he put an arm around her shoulders, turned her slightly, kissed her on the cheek.

"You didn't tell me you were in town!" she exclaimed in a slightly hurt voice.

"Just for the day," he lied easily. "On a case."

"And you came into Graham's for old time's sake," she said. "Because we met here." In that light her eyes looked almost violet. "That first time, you came in to get a book and instead you got . . ."—she opened her arms wide—"me!"

Spade grunted. "Just as a rental."

"That's a nasty thing to say to a girl, Sam."

"Not a girl anymore. Not Ida Nolan anymore."

"What did you expect? You ran off to be a hero in France."

His eyes hardened between down-drawn brows. He said in a sarcastic voice, "I love you, Sam. I'll wait for you, Sam."

"I got lonely."

"And married Miles Archer three months after I left."

"Miles was here. Miles was eager to marry me. Miles—"

"I saw Miles in Tacoma a couple of nights ago," Spade said. "He thanked me."

She said almost cautiously, "For what?"

"Going into the army. Leaving him an open field."

"He isn't due back from Tacoma until tomorrow . . ."

"I'm booked on the four oh five stage to Seattle."

"To hell with you, Sam Spade," Iva Archer said viciously.

The engines growled and shook; white water boiled up around the stern of the *Eliza Anderson* as she backed away from the ramshackle Victoria, British Columbia, slip. Fog, wet as rain, already had swept most of the passengers off the darkening deck into the cabin for their three-hour trip down Puget Sound to Seattle.

A dark-haired man just shy of forty turned from the coffee urn with a steaming mug in one hand. He had a trim mustache over a wide mouth, narrow, amused eyes under level brows, a strong jaw, a small faded scar on his left cheek. Before exiting he set down his coffee and cinched up the belt of his ulster.

Sam Spade, who had been leaning against the bulkhead midcabin, sauntered out after him. Moisture immediately beaded Spade's woolen knit cap, the turned-up collar of his mackinaw.

The man was standing at the rail, mug in hand, staring down at the wind-tossed water. A glow came into Spade's eyes. His upper lip twitched in what could have been a smile. He leaned on the railing beside the other man.

"Mr. Flitcraft, I presume?"

The man dropped his mug overboard.

Charles Pierce slid warily through the doorway like a cat entering a strange room. He relaxed fractionally when he saw a bottle of Johnnie Walker whiskey and two glasses on a tray on the table. Spade was at the sink running water into a pitcher. The room was simple, comfortable, homey, with a private bath.

"I want to get this over with," said Pierce in a high, clear voice. "Not that I have anything to feel guilty about."

They touched glasses. Spade said, "Success to crime."

"There's no crime involved here. Nothing like that."

Without obvious irony Spade said, "Five years ago, in 1916, a man named Robert Flitcraft did a flit in Tacoma. Before leaving his real estate office to go to luncheon, he made an engagement for a round of golf at four o'clock that afternoon. He didn't keep the engagement. Nobody ever saw him again."

Pierce downed half his drink. Spade's hands had been rolling a cigarette. He lit it, looked through the drifting smoke with candid eyes.

"The police got nowhere. Flitcraft's wife came to our Seattle office. She said she and her husband were on good terms, said they had two boys, five and three, said he drove a new Packard, said he had a successful real estate business and a net worth of two hundred thousand dollars. I was assigned to the case. I could find no secret vices, no other woman, no hidden bank accounts, no sign Flitcraft had been putting his affairs in order. He vanished with no more than fifty bucks in his pocket. He was just gone, like your lap when you stand up."

"What he did makes perfect sense! He—"

"When I went into the army in nineteen seventeen he was still missing. Last week his wife came in to tell us a friend of hers had seen him here in Spokane."

Spade rubbed his jutting chin as if checking his shave.

"Now we have Charles Pierce living in a Spokane suburb with his wife of two years and an infant son. He sells new cars, nets twenty-five thousand a year, belongs to the country club, plays golf most afternoons at four o'clock during the season. His wife doesn't look like Flitcraft's wife, but they're more alike than different. Afternoon bridge, salad recipes . . ."

Pierce was fidgeting. "What are you getting at?"

"I was sent here to find and identify the man our informant thought was Flitcraft. I've done that. Charles Pierce is Robert Flitcraft. No definite instructions beyond that, but there's the bigamy question. Wife here, wife in Tacoma. Kids from both marriages . . ." For the first time Spade addressed Pierce directly as Flitcraft. "Of course since you left your first wife extremely well fixed you could claim you thought that after all this time she would have divorced you *in absentia*—"

"I was on my way to lunch." He paused. "A steel beam

fell from a new office building and hit the sidewalk right beside me."

"A beam." Spade's voice was without inflection.

"A chip of concrete flew up . . ." His hand absently touched the faint scar on his left cheek. "I was more shocked than scared. I was a good husband, a good father, I was doing everything right, and none of it meant a damned thing if a beam could fall off a building and kill me."

"As if someone had taken the lid off life and let you see how it really worked?" Spade pinched his lower lip, frowned, drew his brows together. "No logic, no fairness, only chance." His frown disappeared. "Sure. By getting in step with what you thought was life you got out of step with real life."

"You do get it! I decided that if my life was merely a collection of random incidents, I would live it randomly. That afternoon I went to Seattle, caught a boat to San Francisco. For the next few years I wandered around and finally ended up back in the Northwest. I got a chance to buy into an auto dealership here in Spokane, met my wife, got married, had a son . . ." He grinned almost sheepishly. "I like the climate."

"Three things not in my report," said Spade.

Ralph Dudley, resident supervisor of Continental's Seattle office, was in his seventies, fifty years on the job, white of mustache, pink of face. His kindly eyes behind rimless spectacles were misleading; they never changed expression, not even when he sent his ops out to face danger, sometimes death.

"First item," said Spade. "Nobody's said so, but before Flitcraft disappeared Mrs. Cahill made a play for him. An affair wouldn't have fit in with his view of what the good citizen-husband-father did so he turned her down. She didn't like that. So when she spotted him in Spokane she couldn't wait to try and make as much trouble for him as she could."

Dudley said in mild-voiced skepticism, "I see."

"Second item. Flitcraft was afraid his first wife wouldn't get what he did. She didn't. She just figures he played a dirty trick on her so she's going to get a quiet divorce." Merriment lit his face. "Flitcraft doesn't get it either. He adjusted to falling beams. When no more beams fell he adjusted back again."

"You mentioned three things, Spade."

"Flitcraft is my last case."

Dudley turned his swivel chair to stare out the window. Half a dozen mosquito-fleet ferries were churning their various ways across Elliott Bay between the Seattle waterfront and the distant irregular green rectangle of Blake Island.

Dudley told the window, "In nineteen seventeen you couldn't wait for us to get into the war. Disregarding my direct order, you went over the border to enlist in the First Canadian Division." He turned to look at Spade. "While training in England you took up competitive pistol shooting. You made some records."

"The pistol made the records. All I did was point it and make it go bang," said Spade. "Eight-shot thirty-eight Webley-Fosbery automatic revolver. Only three hundred of them ever got made because they jammed in combat, but they were so accurate on the firing range they got banned from competition shooting."

Dudley went on coldly as if Spade hadn't spoken.

"You were assigned to the Seventh Battalion of the Second Infantry Brigade and saw action in the trenches of the Lens-Arras sector of France. You were wounded. You got a medal. Upon your return, against my better judgment, I took you back." His voice took on a nasty edge. "A competitive pistol shot, a war hero, and suddenly you don't like guns. Suddenly you're quitting the detective trade. Do you mind telling me why? Or have you just lost your stomach for real man's work?"

Spade stood. He did not offer his hand.

"I think if you need to use a gun you're doing a lousy job as a detective. As for resigning, I don't like the work here much since the war. Too much head knocking, not enough door knocking. And who says I'm quitting the detective trade?"

2

Samuel Spade, Esq.

San Francisco's summer fog was in. Sam Spade's Wilton was pulled low over his eyes, his hands were jammed deep in his topcoat pockets. He walked past the United States Mint on Fifth, turned right past the secondhand store on the corner. Remedial Loans, at 932 Mission Street, had venetian blinds on the ground floor, a high arched window above them, and an elaborate second-story facade with incised decorative heraldic designs.

The wind had crumpled the front section of that morning's *Call* against the recessed street door of the shabby office building beyond Remedial. Spade's left hand scooped up the newspaper while his right hand opened the door. He climbed a narrow flight of stairs, turned left, started down the second-floor hall. The boards creaked under his steps.

The door of the second office down popped open. A dark dapper thirtyish man in a brown suit that matched his eyes stuck out his head. He brought the smell of cigar smoke with him. His tired oval face, olive skinned, was dominated by a big nose. A gold watch chain glinted across his vest. Dandruff speckled his already thinning hair and the shoulders of his suit coat. His voice was high-pitched, almost shrill.

"I'm Sid Wise. You the new tenant?"

"Yep. Sam Spade. You got a wastebasket?" Spade thrust the crumpled-up *Call* into Wise's hands. "Thanks."

He went on to the next office. A man in a white smock was blocking out letters on the opaque glass of the propped-open door. The letters, when filled in, would spell out SAMUEL SPADE, ESQ.

"Two more hours, Mr. Spade."

"That's the stuff," said Spade.

A shadow moved across the floor of his outer office. He stopped short, jerked his head slightly sideways.

"A girl," said the sign painter. "I had the door open, she went right in. I thought she was your new secretary. When three more women showed up she told them the position was filled."

Spade squeezed his shoulder, went by him. The office was a ten-by-twelve uncarpeted cube without a window. An open door in the far wall led to an inner office. On the plain golden-gloss oaken desk were a telephone, a steno pad, and a Remington Standard typewriter, nothing else. An office chair was behind the desk, another against the wall beside the door. Beside it was an end table with a single magazine on it. Nobody was in the room.

Spade hung his overcoat and hat over a double hook on the coatrack beside the door. He was wearing the same suit he had worn in Spokane. A girl came from the inner office with a water glass full of fresh daisies. She was so shocked at the sight of Spade she almost dropped the flowers.

"Oh! I—you startled . . ."

Spade beckoned, went by her through the connecting door to the inner office. The girl put the flowers on the desk and followed, hesitantly. The inner room was larger than the other; it had a window looking out over busy Mission Street, open far enough to stir the curtains. In one corner were a sink and a towel rack. The inside of the sink was wet.

Spade sat down in the swivel armchair behind the desk. It was a larger version of that in the outer office, with a deep drawer on the left side for the upright filing of long ledger books and letter files. It bore a blotter, a pen set, an ashtray. No framed photographs. No papers. No files.

The girl sat down hesitantly on the very front edge of the oaken armchair across from him. She was ten years younger than Spade, with an open, almost boyish face and direct brown eyes that didn't meet his frankly appraising yellowish ones. She was wearing a woolen skirt and a tailored jacket and a spotless white blouse with frilled cuffs. A bejeweled locket on a thin gold chain glinted on her shirtfront. Her right hand played with it.

She said nervously, "Your ad in the *Chronicle* didn't specify what sort of business you're in, but it was for a part-time receptionist-typist to answer your phone and keep your files in order. My shorthand is still pretty slow, but filing and typing I can do. And I'm a quick learner."

From his vest pocket Spade took a packet of brown papers and a thin white cloth sack of Bull Durham with a drawstring on top. He sifted tan flakes onto the paper, spread them evenly with a slight depression in the middle, rolled the paper's inner edge down and then up under the outer edge, and licked the flap, using his right forefinger and thumb to smooth the damp seam, twisting that end and lifting the other end to his lips.

He lit the cigarette with a pigskin and nickel lighter, drew deeply, spoke to the girl through drifting smoke.

"Private investigations."

Her face lit up. "Like in *Black Mask*?"

Spade said to the universe at large, "Sweet Jesus, she reads the pulps!"

He leaned forward to tap ash into a nickel-plated tray on the desk. Beside it was a glass cigarette holder with a brass top, empty, and an attached matchbox holder.

"No, not like *Black Mask*. Jewel thefts and bank robberies and handling security at racetracks are jobs for the big agencies. For the one-man shop it's searching records, catching cashiers stealing from their employers, finding people who have disappeared, guarding the gifts at fancy weddings. Sitting around and waiting for a client and smoking too many cigarettes." He put both hands flat on the blotter. "The sign painter said three other women showed up in answer to my ad."

"They . . . left." She raised her chin almost defiantly. "I told them the position had been filled."

"Why the flowers?"

"I—I bought them for my mother. She loves daisies. But this place looked so drab I thought— Oh! I don't mean . . ." She colored. "I can come in after school for the next month, until I graduate from the St. Francis Technical School for Girls. Then I can be full-time."

He said in a sort of singsong, "Shorthand, typing, filing, and comportment for young ladies in an office environment. Right now I only need part-time. How old are you? Seventeen?"

She tried to prepare a lie, but her face couldn't bring it off. In one breathless burst of words, again with that chin raised, she said, "Yes, seventeen, but I'm very mature for my age and I'm a quick learner and—"

"Ten dollars a week," said Spade. "If you make it through the first month maybe you'll get a pay raise. If you earn it."

She said in an astounded voice, "You mean that I—"

"If you know how to roll a cigarette."

"I'll learn."

Spade stood to come around the desk, saying, "I'll just bet you will, sister," and stuck out a thick-fingered hand. He said, almost formally, "Samuel Spade."

She pushed her chair back and stood to take the proffered hand with a formality matching his own.

"Effie Perine. I think you should leave the 'Esq.' off your door. "Just Samuel Spade is more elegant."

"Comportment for young detectives? OK, scoot out there and tell the sign painter to leave it off. He's still blocking in the letters; it should be easy for him to do."

She bobbed her head, turned to leave.

"Then bring in that steno pad from your desk. If I'm going to be paying you all that money, we've got to get out a stack of client solicitation letters."

3

This and That

Effie Perine stood aside so the stocky, redheaded man with the squirrel-cheeked florid face could get by her, then went in to Spade's inner office. Spade was behind his desk getting out his Bull Durham and his papers. She stopped in front of him, eyes bright.

"So, did he hire us?"

"I shooed him away. I forgot to tell you, sweetheart, your Sammy doesn't do domestic. Find out before you send them in." As she hooked a hip over the corner of his desk, took papers and tobacco from him, and began expertly rolling his cigarette, a sardonic light, quickly quelled, came and went in Spade's eyes. "He's on the road a lot, his wife gets lonely."

Effie Perine held the rolled cigarette out to him, end up.

"And he thinks she's cheating on him."

"He's right."

"I graduate tomorrow, Sam. Will you come?"

"I'll try to make it if you'll keep your mother away from me."

"Samuel Spade, I never once said Ma—" Seeing the smug look on his face, she stopped, almost giggled. "Greek women are great at business. Of course she wants to size you up."

"I've got a maybe client named Ericksen coming in at noon. Get him to sign a standard contract. I'll show up tomorrow, just to convince your mother that I don't keep a tommy gun in my desk and that I can't pay you more than ten bucks a week."

She said in a soft voice, "Thanks, Sam."

At 8 a.m. a week later Spade trotted up the stairs carrying that morning's newspaper. The doors of both his and Sid Wise's offices were standing open. Wise's office was one room only, unoccupied. The desk had no typewriter on it. As Spade cat-footed past, his big shoulders hunched under his blue topcoat and a perhaps-delighted light came into his eyes.

He stopped short of his own office so his shadow would not be cast inside by the hallway light. Overriding Effie Perine's expert typing was Sid Wise's voice, less shrill than usual, more resonant than might have been expected from such a slight man.

"We hereby submit the moving papers, already examined by the respondent. The moving papers consist of the accusation, the statement to the respondent sent by certified mail, a signed copy of the notice of defense, a notice of hearing—"

Sam Spade spun around the doorframe and into the

office. Sid Wise was in the middle of the room, a declaiming finger pointed at the ceiling.

"What a God-damned lawyer trick, using my secretary on the sly because you're too tight to hire your own girl."

Wise's finger dropped very quickly to his side. "Don't blame Effie. I talked her into it."

"You've been out of the office all week on the Ericksen case, Sam." Effie Perine's voice was small. She was sitting up very straight, red with embarrassment. "You didn't leave me any work to do and I wanted to practice my skills."

"You defend him sneaking in here like some midnighter to steal the silverware?" Spade clapped his hands together, gave a sharp bark of laughter. "My work comes first and as of last Monday, Sid, you're paying Effie five bucks a week."

"You're a son of a gun, Sammy," said a shamefaced Wise.

Spade was sitting behind his desk smoking a cigarette when Effie Perine came in with a pen and steno pad, all efficiency.

"Were—were you really mad, Sam?"

"Hell no, sweetheart. I've known you've been doing his work this past week; I just wanted to catch him at it. I'm going to start needing a good lawyer one of these days." He pointed at a folder on his desk. "Close and bill on Ericksen."

For the next twenty minutes Spade talked in even, well-formed sentences as Effie Perine's pencil covered page after page of her shorthand pad with his closing report. He never stumbled, never went back to correct some fact.

Sven Ericksen and his partner, Paul Lembach, had the Ericksen-Lembach Complete Home Furnishers at Seventeenth and Mission.

"Strictly a working-class neighborhood," said Spade. "Credit up to fifty dollars, nothing down, a dollar a week."

Ericksen was a widower with two small children, so Lembach stayed late most nights to count the cash, make out a deposit slip, and put the money in the Bank of Italy's all-night depository at Mission and Twenty-third.

"Sales are level, but their gross has been slipping for the past six months. Ericksen took Lembach on right out of business school, taught him the trade, made him a partner. He can't admit to anyone, especially himself, that the man's a thief."

"So you concentrated on Lembach without telling him?"

"Mmm-hmm. About six months ago Lembach started betting heavily on the ponies, and losing even more heavily. For five nights, through a hole in the wall of the storeroom next to the office, I watched him count the cash. He coffee-canned ten, fifteen, twenty, and forty bucks and gimmicked the bank deposit slips to correspond to the cash he was depositing. The third day his horse came in, so he didn't steal anything."

Effie looked up from her pad, excitement in her face and voice. "Did you confront him with it?"

"He'd just deny it and our client would side with him. So last evening just after closing I secretly counted the cash. This morning I gave my total to Ericksen."

"Which he'll check against Lembach's deposit slip total

and find a"—Effie Perine looked down at her pad—"a forty-dollar discrepancy for last night."

The corners of Spade's mouth drew up in a grin. "You'll make a detective yet, sweetheart. I'll advise Ericksen to dissolve the partnership and demand restitution over a six-month period for Lembach's defalcations. He won't be sore at me and he'll pay our invoice without a squawk."

"Ericksen will need a lawyer for that, won't he, Sam?"

"Yeah." Spade grinned sardonically. "And yeah, I'll recommend Sid Wise for the job. Then Sid'll really owe us."

4

Enchanted with These Islands

Golden Gate Trust was located between Bush and Pine in the heart of San Francisco's financial district. Three of its plate glass windows looked out on Seaman's Bank across Montgomery; in the fourth was a massive vault with a gleaming brass locking mechanism as big as the steering wheel of a Duesenberg.

Sam Spade approached a bank official whose desk was angled so he could watch the tellers at work even while serving a customer. His desk plaque read TOBIAS KRIEGER.

"Samuel Spade to see Charles Barber."

Krieger wore a high starched collar and gray spats over shiny black oxford dress shoes. He had the wispiest of pencil mustaches over a pink upper lip. He led Spade through a maze of hallways to a door of solid teak that bore the legend

CHARLES HENDRICKSON BARBER
President

25

Krieger knocked, opened the door, and stood aside while announcing, "Mr. Samuel Spade."

The banker stood up behind a ten-foot-long teakwood desk that had stacks of files on each end and three telephones and an ashtray and a leather-edged blotter with a pen set. The two framed portraits on the desk faced Barber.

"That will be all, Krieger."

Barber was a vigorous sixty, white-haired, with dark, piercing eyes. He was as tall as Spade, heavier, thicker in the middle, with the muttonchop sideburns and walrus mustache favored by those in the San Francisco power structure. He did not offer to shake hands. His voice was brusque.

"Sit down, Spade. Do you know why you're here?"

"Sid Wise said, 'a confidential matter.' "

"Can you keep it confidential?"

"Keep what confidential?"

Barber reared back in his swivel chair, eyes snapping, then gave a bark of laughter and came forward again.

"Hah. I think you'll do. Wise and Merican is the law firm on retainer by the bank, but I can't use them for this. Old man Wise wanted young Sid to join the firm, but Sid's out to prove he can make it on his own. He's hungry, he's close-mouthed, and he's a Jew. Jews are shrewd. I need a shrewd man on this."

Barber turned one of the framed portraits on his desk to show Spade a striking blond woman of about forty with an oval face and warm eyes.

"My wife. My second wife. She has a position in the community so she abhors publicity."

Spade was frowning. "Sid said this was not domestic."

"It isn't." Barber turned the other portrait toward Spade. "Our son, Charles Hendrickson Barber III."

It was a snapshot of a well-built boy of seventeen grinning at the camera in front of the exclusive Pacific Heights School in Jackson Street. He had a shock of black hair and dark eyes that looked soulful and dreamy.

"Popular with the girls," Spade said with assurance.

"It's not girl trouble. He's an excellent student and reads a lot and is impossibly romantic. He gets that from his mother. He disappeared two nights ago."

Spade leaned forward, focused. "Phone calls? Ransom message? The police?"

"None of those. He left a note." Barber handed Spade a folded sheet of paper from his middle desk drawer.

Dear Mother and Father:

I am enchanted with these islands. Don't try to find me.

Love to you both,

Henny

"Henny?"

"Family name. Short for Hendrickson."

Spade's frown drew deep vertical lines between his brows. "This means something to you?"

"His mother and I made the mistake of taking him on a cruise to Hawaii as a high-school graduation present and he fell in love with the South Seas. He started reading Jack London, Joseph Conrad, Robert Louis Stevenson . . ." He looked almost suspiciously at Spade. "Have you heard of any of them?"

Spade had a momentary faraway look in his eyes. "Yeah. I read a book once. I know who they are."

"My wife tells me that the quotation is from a character in a Joseph Conrad novel, a man named Axel Heyst."

"So," said Spade, "Hawaii. Or Tahiti. Or maybe American Samoa—Stevenson was called Tusitala, Teller of Tales. He's buried on a mountain called Vaea on Apia." He was on his feet. "Henny'd have the money just to book passage, but that won't be romantic enough for him. If no ships have sailed for Australia via those ports of call since he disappeared, he'll probably be hanging around the docks looking to stow away."

Barber waved a well-manicured hand. "Find him. My wife is delicate, and she's frantic."

"I suggested to Barber that there's nothing so wrong with the kid trying to stow away on a freighter, getting it out of his system, instead of going straight to college."

"Not Barber. Strictly financial," said Sid Wise. "He wants Henny to do just what he himself did when his father retired—step into his shoes at the bank at the proper moment."

"The boy's mother is calling the shots, and she's afraid that Henny might actually stow away, or might run into some real trouble if he's hanging around the docks. She's probably right. I did when I was his age."

"What did your folks do about it?" asked Effie Perine.

"My ma moaned a lot. My old man was a longshoreman, what could he say? He'd done the same in his day."

Sid Wise checked his watch. "I've got a client coming."

Effie Perine moved Wise's chair back into the outer office. When she returned Spade said, "Get an afternoon *Call,* angel. Leave a rundown on my desk of all the freighters and liners expected in from Australia during the next few days that will be making stops in the islands on their way back."

"Hawaii, Samoa, Tahiti?"

"Yeah. Maybe Aitutaki in the Cooks, too."

"Maybe I'll stow away with him," she said almost wistfully.

"You'd stow away alone. I'm going to nab our Henny before he can clear the Golden Gate."

Spade walked the three long blocks to his one-room efficiency in Ellis Street, changed into a denim jacket and pants, gray chambray work shirt, and heavy work shoes with five-ply leather heels. None of the clothes were new.

Paddy Hurlihey's was a waterfront bootleg joint at Pier 23 on the Embarcadero. It smelled of stale beer, was wreathed in cigarette smoke, was crowded with loudmouthed stevedores. Spade, dressed like any other longshoreman, bellied up at the bar beside a wiry lean-faced twenty-year-old.

"Let me buy you a drink, Harry."

"I'll be damned. Sam Spade." Harry's large direct eyes, under brows turned down at the outside edges like a bloodhound's, were too old for his chronological age. His voice had an Aussie twang. "I heard you was with Continental up in Seattle."

Spade caught the barkeep's eye. "Got back a month ago to set up on my own here. I know this town."

"Towns is all the same," said Harry morosely. "I bet it's as bad for the workingman up there as it is down here."

"One of the reasons I left. Too much strikebreaking."

"See? The same. Since the old Riggers' and Stevedores' Union went down after the strike of nineteen the shipping companies have set up something they call the Blue Book union. It's supposed to be independent, but we don't got no contract no more and it's a closed shop for guys like me who was active in the strike. I get some work over in Richmond. Tramp steamers, the Alaska Packer Line, the Japs, the Aussies—they don't gotta go along with the company union. Ship's there a week, a man can make fifty, sixty bucks. But ships is few and far between."

The burly Irish bartender came down the stick. Without asking, he poured two shots from a bottle with an Antiquary label, then clamped his hand on Spade's forearm. Spade jerked free, his hand already closing into a fist. The bartender stepped back quickly with both hands raised, palms out.

"I just need your brass check before you gents can drink."

Harry took a round brass disc from his pocket, tossed it on the bar. "The shape-up bosses pay in these instead of cash. The number on it shows that it's legit. Only places you can cash 'em is gin mills like this here one, the bookie joints along the waterfront, and Sly-Pork's pool hall up the street.

You gotta buy two drinks at two bits each. Then you get one on the house."

Spade put a dollar on the bar next to Harry's brass check and held up four thick fingers. "And two on the house."

The bartender hesitated, poured, departed. They fired down their shots.

"You still a betting man, Harry?"

Harry nodded. "Between ships I stay alive with the whores, the fours, and the one-eyed Jacks."

"I've got ten bucks says you can't get me a lead to a seventeen-year-old kid hanging around down here until he can find a freighter to the South Seas to stow away on."

"Maybe I oughtta stow away with him—go back home to Australia where I belong. I ain't doin' so hot here."

Spade described Henny Barber, gave Harry a ten-dollar bill.

"Hell's sake, Sam, I ain't found out nothing for you yet."

"You will," said Spade. His grin made him look pleasantly satanic. "I can always find you over in Richmond if you welsh. Kid might be staying with a friend somewhere nights and hanging around the docks days, and talking about stowing away. He's called Henny. Anything you can find out about him will help."

5

Missing Gold Sovereigns

Spade hooked a hip over one corner of Effie Perine's desk while fishing papers and tobacco from his vest pocket. She looked up from the *Chronicle*'s shipping news.

"Harry called to say that the hen is sleeping in the henhouse but pecking around Pier 35. He's betting ten bucks that what you want is the Oceanic Line's *San Anselmo,* newly arrived from Sydney via Honolulu and due to go back to Australia after a two-day turnaround here." She rattled her newspaper in frustration. "Who's Harry? What's he talking about?"

"Harry's a longshoreman when he can get work. He helped lead the strike by the Riggers' and Stevedores' Union back in nineteen. Trouble was it broke the union instead of the shipping companies. He was only eighteen then, but they've got him down as a dangerous radical—maybe a Commie."

Her eyes were bright. "So you gave him some work."

"Ten bucks worth. It ain't charity, sister. He's found out

that our boy Henny—the hen he mentioned—is bunking in safely with buddies but was hanging around Pier 35 waiting for the *San Anselmo* to dock. Any other messages?"

She took his cigarette makings from his fingers.

"Sid said that Charles Hendrickson Barber"—she drew out the word *Hendrickson* in a la-di-da voice—"wants you to call him at the bank when you get in."

"String him along for me, darling." He jabbed his lighted cigarette toward her. "*Don't* tell him about the *San Anselmo.* I want to hold off grabbing Henny until just before he tries to stow away." He winked at her. "Run up the charges."

"Samuel Spade, never mind about your charges! What about that boy's poor mother? She thinks he's in mortal danger—"

"What would your ma do if it was you?"

Effie Perine giggled. "She'd be down on the docks herself raising blue blazes."

"There's your answer," said Spade.

The *San Anselmo* was a rakish one-stack steamer that had come through the Golden Gate under pilot the night before, too late for quarantine anchorage. That morning early it had docked at its home pier, 35. Spade, carrying a clipboard, looking vaguely official in a watch jacket and a yachting cap with gold braid on the visor, went up the gangplank with authoritative strides. Aft, on the poop deck, stevedores were unloading brown-leafed hands of Hawaiian bananas from between latticed frames.

"Port Authority," Spade told the seaman standing gangway watch, a blond, clever-looking man with vivid blue eyes.

"Quartermaster Kest, sir."

"I have to examine your lifeboats for—"

"Christ, man, are we glad to see you!" Advancing on him with outstretched hand was a hard-bitten man with his share of gold braid on his uniform. "Tom Rafferty, first officer."

"Daniel Gough, Port Authority."

"How'd you get here so quick? We only just called the International Banking Corporation five minutes ago."

Spade said blandly, "I was here on another matter."

"Well, c'mon down to the strong room so you can see firsthand what they did to our specie tank. You'll have to tell us proper procedure. We've never had anything like this before. The officials of the I.B.C. were already planning to come with armed guards and trucks to take the treasure to their vaults, so they shouldn't be over half an hour getting here."

Spade wore his poker face. "How much is missing?"

"Captain Ogilvie will want to show you for himself."

Kest said, "Should I get another quartermaster up here to relieve me, Mr. Rafferty, in case Mr. Gough has any questions?"

"Do so," said Rafferty. As they descended a series of ladders to the strong room he said over his shoulder, "When the passengers started disembarking, the captain said we'd better open the first two of the three strong room locks."

"Standard procedure?"

"Not really. The three keys are held by Captain Ogilvie, Purser Abbott G. Battle, and myself. Usually we'd open all three, but because the *San Anselmo* was going to be carrying such a huge number of gold sovereigns, Captain Ogilvie had his lock replaced with a new one in Sydney."

Rafferty led Spade through the door from the first-class staterooms to the baggage room. There was a loading port at each side. The room was virtually empty.

"The first-class passengers have gone and their luggage has been taken off. During the voyage they had access to this room for two hours each day. Under guard, of course."

A door in the opposite wall led to what Rafferty called the extra-mail room. It was empty. Straight ahead was a bulkhead door, closed. To their right was a steel door, open.

"That's the vault. The other door leads to the messroom. This is the most secure location on the ship." Rafferty stepped to the strong room door and sang out, "Port Authority's here."

Two uniformed men came out. The one introduced as the purser, Abbott G. Battle, had a face shiny with perspiration. The other man was big and hard and fifty, reeking of authority, with a hand made hard by calluses and the deeply tanned face of one who has spent his life at sea.

"Captain Floyd Ogilvie," he said.

"Daniel Gough," said Samuel Spade.

The shrewd blue eyes took Spade in. "Where's your usual man? Frank Petrie?"

"Off sick. What do we have here?"

"A hell of a mess. Three of us have to be here for the vault to be opened because we each hold one of the keys. This morning when we got to port I gave Tom here my key to open up the vault while I was overseeing the passengers' leaving."

"My lock and Abbott's opened up, but the captain's key wouldn't fit," said Rafferty. "I called him down immediately."

"You keep the keys in your cabins?"

"We do. Abbott and I share quarters. Of course the captain has his own cabin."

Purser Battle spoke for the first time. He had a husky voice edged with belligerence. "The thieves must have made impressions of our keys so they could get in here and remove the gold between Honolulu and Frisco."

Ogilvie said, "I saw immediately that the lock's shackle was brass. The one I had put on in Sydney was steel. We had to get the ship's carpenter down here to saw it off. When I got the door opened and switched on the light this is what I found . . ."

Ogilvie led them into the strong room. Quartermaster Kest had shown up to crowd in behind them. Battle mopped his face with his handkerchief and stayed behind in the mail room.

The strong room was a compact armored chamber, cold and clammy. It held ten locked and steel-bound money chests.

"So what's missing?"

"Five chests just like these. Each chest contains ten thousand sovereigns—five thousand pounds worth of British gold. Seventy-five thousand pounds in gold specie in the fifteen chests, consigned by the Commonwealth of Australia to the International Banking Corporation here in San Francisco."

Spade gave a low whistle. "Three hundred and seventy-five thousand American, total. Twenty-five thousand bucks in each chest. No wonder you had your lock changed in Sydney."

"For all the good it did me," said Ogilvie sourly. "I can't believe any of my men were involved in something like this. We have a veteran crew of loyal seamen. A *union* crew."

"And the looters got what—a third of it? One hundred twenty-five thousand bucks. What do these chests weigh?"

"Including the boxes themselves, eighty pounds each."

Spade looked at his watch. "Four hundred pounds in all, and clumsy to move. I make it a four-man job, three crewmen to do the work and a first-class passenger who planned it and set it up. Probably boarded the ship at Pago Pago or Honolulu."

"The master criminal," said Kest in an awed voice.

"Given the keys, the theft's easy. Getting the loot off once the ship docked is what's tough." Spade paused. "You came in too late to go through quarantine and anchored off until morning?"

"That's right," said Ogilvie. "We usually do."

"So, maybe a fifth man ashore. When the I.B.C. and the customs officers and the cops and the detectives get here, they should run down all of the passengers and their luggage and not let them leave the jurisdiction. Tell 'em to concentrate on anyone who came aboard at Honolulu. Search all crew members before they go ashore, then search the ship itself."

"You think the gold is hidden aboard?"

Spade checked his watch again, shrugged. "Could be. Are the mail sacks unloaded by hand or handled by machine?"

"By machine," said Rafferty.

"So you could take the gold from the boxes, wrap it in small packages, and hide it in mail sacks consigned to some direct-delivery address." Spade nodded. "Yeah. If the mail hasn't already been cleared at the customs shed you might want to open the sacks and check them—if you can do it legally."

"You Port Authority people can," said Ogilvie.

"I'll go set that in motion right now," said Spade quickly.

Topside, he took a quick five minutes to check the canvas-covered lifeboats hanging from their davits beyond the railings, left when he heard the approaching police sirens.

6

Continental

"It's the purser," said Sid Wise. Effie Perine had brought in an extra chair from Spade's office, was working the steno pad balanced on her knee. "In his position he could move around the ship at all hours without anyone thinking anything about it."

Spade shook his head. "Uh-uh. Our inside man on the heist is Quartermaster Walter Kest. I'd have liked twenty minutes alone with that bird. Tap him, he'll crack like an egg. Trouble is I shot my mouth off, telling them the investigative steps to make, which they'll pass on to the International Banking Corporation and the cops. I had to beat it before some smart flatfoot recognized me."

"They should just be grateful for all the work you did."

"You've got a lot to learn about the coppers, sweetheart. I saw a sergeant named Dundy going aboard. He'd love to get me between floors at the Hall of Justice with a couple of other cops and rolled-up newspapers for some kidney work.

I stuck my finger in his eye once too often when I was with Continental."

"Sometimes I think you just like to make people in authority mad at you."

"It keeps things stirred up." Spade stood. "The cops and Continental and Burns will be all over that boat for the next couple of days looking for the loot."

"What about my client's son?" demanded Wise. "How will you know he hasn't stowed away if you can't get back aboard?"

"I'll get aboard all right. Meanwhile, no other vessel's scheduled out of San Francisco for the South Seas this week."

In the hallway Spade said to Effie Perine, "You're having the time of your life, aren't you, sweetheart? Be an angel, while I'm gone run down and get the newspapers to see how they're handling the story."

The round ornate pillar clock in front of Samuel's Jewelers in Market Street showed just shy of 2 o'clock when Spade entered the triangular-shaped Flood Building. He took the stairs to the third floor, walked down a quiet linoleum-covered hallway. Light from a pebbled-glass fire escape window at the far end of the hall showed CONTINENTAL DETECTIVE AGENCY on the door to suite 314. Spade entered without knocking.

In the reception room a secretary he didn't know was banging on a typewriter as if it were a faithless lover. Spade pointed a forefinger at her with his hand closed behind it, worked his thumb like the hammer of a gun, said, "Samuel Spade to see Phil Geaque. I'll be in the operatives' room."

She started to her feet, protesting, but by then Spade had slid through the door in the left-hand wall and closed it behind him. The big boxy tan three-windowed room held a couch, seven chairs, four desks, and a conference table. On the desks were messy stacks of paper, typewriters, unwashed coffee mugs. On one wall was a notice board plastered with WANTED posters from other Continental offices around the country.

Lounging on the couch under the windows was a hulking Irishman with an ingenuous face and big ears that stuck out a mile. Beside him was a tall lean man with lank brown hair and a big head thrust slightly forward on a surprisingly thin stalk of neck. Sitting in a turned-around straight-backed chair was a medium-size youngster with a narrow face and quick eyes. His chin rested on forearms crossed on the back of the chair.

The Irishman was saying, "I'd of had the chance of a one-legged man in an ass-kicking contest if that boogie'd had a shiv on him," when Spade interrupted with, "Hi, Mickey."

Mickey Linehan sprang to his feet, grinning, exclaiming in a bogus Irish brogue, "Faith an' be-Jaysus an' they let you out early. For good behavior, is it?" He said to the other two men, "Samuel Spade here was the best shadow man Continental ever had."

The tall lean man switched his store-bought cigarette to his left hand and stuck out his right. "Woody Robinson.

Pleased t'meetcha, mate." He had bad teeth and a marked Australian accent. "This bird here is Phil Haultain, with us a week today."

"Woody and the kid just got back from a shadow job down in Calistoga," said Linehan.

Haultain said, "The Frisco D.A.'s office was hiding two witnesses down there until they could get on the stand. They were at the party the night that Virginia Rappe got dead."

Spade hitched his hip over the edge of a desk, began rolling a cigarette. "Hell of a town to do a tail job in, Calistoga. Everybody knows everybody."

"We found that out," said Robinson. "Fatty Arbuckle's lawyers wanted us to get a line on the witnesses—a couple of good-time girls named Bambina Delmont and Alice Blake—though they're calling themselves models and actresses now. Their chaperone, a woman from the D.A.'s office, made us dead quick."

"The jury'll set Arbuckle free," said Spade around his cigarette. "She didn't die until four days after he took her into that hotel room at the St. Francis. The D.A.'d as lief charge the two ladies with manslaughter as Arbuckle."

"Their sticking her in that cold bath because they thought she'd had too much to drink probably ruptured her bladder and killed her right enough," nodded Mickey sagely.

Spade shook his head. "I figure her torn bladder grew out of some chronic condition aggravated by bootleg hootch. But I hear this assistant district attorney Bryan likes to win cases so much that he pretends the law is what he says it is."

"You mean it ain't?" said Robinson.

The receptionist stuck her head in. "Mr. Geaque can see you now, Mr. Spade."

The superintendent's triangular corner office had windows overlooking Powell and Market Streets. Phil Geaque, standing up behind his littered desk, burst out laughing. He was bald headed and sharp-eyed and came just to Spade's shoulder.

"Daniel Gough indeed! As soon as Pearl told me you were here I remembered you always liked to use street names for aliases, so I knew it had to be you who'd been nosing around the *San Anselmo* this morning."

They shook hands as if they liked each other, sat down on opposite sides of the desk.

"I figured you'd already be on it, Phil, so I came by to pick your brains."

"Slim pickings so far. It's a good heist, Sam. But how'd you get on it so soon? Looking to collect the reward they'll be offering?"

"Why not? You boys can't touch it. Actually, I was down there on something else and just ran across it."

"And told them how to conduct their investigation. Not that you weren't right. If they weren't looking to arrest you they'd be looking to hire you. I can give you some cover by taking you on at the usual pay, backdate the start of employment, and say you were there on a case."

"Six bucks a day, twenty-four hours a day, three hundred

sixty-five days a year?" Spade chuckled and shook his head. "No, thanks. I've had my fill of that. They know who I am?"

"No, but Sergeant Dundy thinks Daniel Gough might have been involved in the heist and was making a 'daring foray' to see what the authorities had discovered. He says he thinks he recognizes Gough's description. Now run it down for me, Samuel."

Spade did, finishing with, "I like the quartermaster, Kest, for the inside man, with a couple of crewmen from the graveyard shift at sea. But whoever planned it is the key."

"You're giving away a lot of weight here, Sam." Geaque had a twinkle in his eye. "We're going to beat you to the gold *and* the glory if you're not careful."

"You'll be out in front of the coppers and Burns, Phil. I figure I can stay out in front of you without much trouble." Spade mashed out his cigarette. "Somebody'll spot me if I hang around down there, so I need tin mittens to get me my information. Way I see it, now you owe me so you'll feel guilty if you don't keep me up-to-date on the official investigation."

Effie Perine looked up from the messy stack of newspapers she was rifling when Spade came through the door. She grabbed up her shorthand pad from the desk blotter.

"A police sergeant named Dundy was by. He told me I'd better let him know whenever you show up or it'll go hard on me."

Spade smiled without showing any teeth. "That's our Dundy, all right."

"He had a patrolman named Polhaus with him."

"Tom Polhaus?" Spade's eyes had brightened. "That's a break. If Dundy gets too snotty go to Tom. Anything from Sid on how our client is behaving? Sid's office is locked up."

"Nothing. No other calls."

"Just make sure he pays you for any work he dumps on you."

"Of course I'll get paid!" She sounded shocked. "Sid is your friend and the man who brought you the job you're—"

"*And* he's a lawyer." He lit a cigarette. "The papers have anything we don't know, snip?"

Effie Perine began sorting through the stack of newspapers with slim, efficient fingers, pausing at this or that article.

"The *Chronicle* says, 'When the theft was discovered, guards were immediately placed on the pier and aboard the liner. Search of the large vessel was immediately begun by a special detail of customs officials, accompanied by police and detectives from the Continental and Burns agencies. All members of the crew were searched before they were allowed ashore.' "

"They had to go through the motions even though it was way too late to do any good."

She blurted, "They're doing all the things you told them to do, Sam!"

He didn't react, so she returned to her papers. "The *Call* says, 'After an all-day search by police and private detectives, the disappearing gold remains an inscrutable mystery. An inside job involving several members of the *San Anselmo*'s crew is suspected . . .' "

Spade gave a derisive snort as she selected another paper.

"The *Examiner* says, 'An international ring of specie robbers, including either members of the crew or persons who frequently travel on the liners across the Pacific, is thought responsible for the crime.' "

"Next they'll be saying it was the Commies looking to finance another revolution."

"The *News* says, 'The baggage still on the pier and the mail that had been stowed adjacent to the strong room were searched without result.' Gardner Matheson, Oceanic's general manager, is quoted as saying, 'The gold unquestionably was removed in Pago Pago or Honolulu before the *San Anselmo* sailed on to San Francisco. All passengers have been queried—' "

"*All* passengers?"

" 'Except those of unquestionable reputation.' " She frowned, scanning further. "There's something . . . Here it is. The *Daily Herald* says, 'Two passengers were not immediately contacted. One disembarked and disappeared with only a single suitcase. The other had made several voyages on the *San Anselmo* and had been seen in close communication with several members of the crew. He left the vessel with two trunks each weighing one hundred eighty pounds and checked into the Palace Hotel but never occupied his room. The police are still seeking him.' "

She looked up at Spade, eyes shining, voice excited. "What sort of luggage weighs three hundred and sixty pounds, Sam? He hid most of the gold in his trunks in the baggage room and was among the first passengers off so he could get away before the theft was discovered."

"How did he get into the strong room? How did he get the gold into the trunks when he only had two hours in the baggage room, and that with guards watching his every move?"

"You said yourself that crewmen were involved."

"Yeah. Look, I don't know if the police are looking for him, but try to find out everything you can about the man with the single suitcase. If he came aboard at Honolulu he's our meat. Also, get everything you can on the quartermaster, Kest."

Effie Perine was making shorthand notes on her pad.

"You're going to have to keep the office running and keep Dundy off my back," he told her. "Tell Sid I'm working full-time on our stowaway. Tell everybody else you don't know where I am."

"Oh, Sam, all that gold!"

"We'll see. I have an idea of how they might have gotten at least some of the gold off, and I need to check places aboard where they might have hidden the rest of it."

"The police and the detectives—"

"Are thinking big and complicated. I'm thinking small and simple." He touched a finger to the tip of her nose. "Simple is always best, sweetheart."

7

The Plot Thickens

Sam Spade, in his longshoreman's getup, was in the morning Blue Book shape-up for a job unloading the rest of the *San Anselmo*'s cargo. As expected, he was passed over.

"How d'ya get a job in this burg?" he complained.

The burly stevedore next to him in the shape-up, who said his name was Tingly, looked Spade over carefully. He had a two-day growth of beard, hard eyes, and a weary air.

"You don't, less'n you offer a kickback on your wages."

"Hell with that stuff. That's why I left Seattle."

They strolled, stopped to roll cigarettes. Tingly stood on one foot with the other leg bent, his shoe flat against the wall of Pier 35. He gestured with his cigarette and laughed bitterly.

"Looks like the flatties got somethin' on what they call their minds."

Dundy and Polhaus and two other uniformed policemen were striding purposefully up the ramp to the *San Anselmo*, where Quartermaster Kest awaited them at the head of the gangway.

"Maybe they're gonna arrest somebody," said Spade, drifting that way. Tingly drifted with him.

"Or bust some heads. That one in the front, Dundy, busted mine during the strike in nineteen."

They were standing near the foot of the gangplank when the policemen descended with four manacled seamen between them. Both men turned away to draw on their cigarettes as the officers and their prisoners passed. When Spade and Tingly turned back, the first officer, Rafferty, and Quartermaster Kest were at the head of the gangplank to watch the procession to the squad cars. Their voices carried.

"I bet those four let that passenger put all the stolen gold in his steamer trunks in the baggage room," said Kest.

Rafferty shook his head almost belligerently.

"Don't you believe it. They're all good union men and they've been with us for six voyages now. They'll be back. Then whatever s.o.b. pulled this job, he'd better haul ass. The cops will be out for blood for sure."

"I s'pose you're right." Kest added casually, "Can you get Phillips to relieve me here while I get some chow?"

Rafferty went in search of Kest's replacement. Spade said, "Let's play some pool. Penny a ball?"

"Why the hell not?" said Tingly. "There sure ain't gonna be no work today for the likes of us."

As they strolled down the Embarcadero, Kest roared by them on a green motorcycle with a sidecar.

. . .

It was 11 p.m. The two seamen pulling graveyard watch, Hans Grost and Shelly Grafton, were on the boat deck checking the gas-vent pipes from the fuel tanks. Grost was thick and slow with pig eyes, Grafton lean and lithe, knife eyed. Their movements were surreptitious. They descended quickly and silently to the promenade deck, which had been roped off so it could be re-covered with gray rubberized paint before the vessel departed San Francisco. After quickly checking the bottoms of the scuppers—drainpipes—from the boat deck, they set off toward the smell of fresh coffee wafting from the galley.

Sam Spade, still in his longshoreman's denim jacket and pants, a blue knit navy watch cap pulled down hard on his head, emerged from an alcove beside the doorway to the passengers' cabins. He crossed quickly to the drainpipes. The bottoms of all of them were plugged pending the paint job. Spade lightly tapped each in turn with the rounded steel end of his Flylock pocketknife. The first three gave off a hollow metallic clang. The fourth emitted a dull thunk.

Spade followed that scupper up to the boat deck. Its top was blocked. The others were not. He stared thoughtfully at it for a full two minutes, then went around tapping the vent pipes from the fuel tanks that Grost and Grafton also had been checking. Again, one of them emitted a thunk instead of a clang.

After looking into the lifeboats hanging from their boat deck davits, Spade departed the vessel. It was just midnight.

. . .

Fog was drifting in through the Golden Gate and the horns were busy, as well as the bells and whistles of the ferries crossing to and from Oakland and Sausalito, up in Marin County.

Spade strolled from Pier 35 down toward the Ferry Building. As he passed the intersection where Front and Union touch the Embarcadero, three bulky shapes emerged from the shadows. Their features were obscured by the heavy hoods of their jackets. The man in front had a baseball bat, brass knuckles glinted on the second man's fist, a knife gleamed in the hand of the third.

Spade backed up against the front of the Pier 19 warehouse. His body seemed to shrink, to draw in on itself as if to make him a smaller target. Terror was in his eyes, his head swiveled from side to side to keep all three men in view. His hands were out as if to ward off attack. The fear in his eyes was echoed in his voice; he seemed to have trouble getting words past a closed-down larynx.

"Chrissake, guys, don't—don't hurt me. I'll give you everything I've got. You don't have to hurt me."

The lead man gave a heavy laugh of triumph.

"A snoop, and a yellow-livered snoop besides. You've been sticking your nose into the wrong guy's business."

He swung the baseball bat at the cringing figure's head. But Spade had already charged inside the bat's arc. His right elbow jammed up into the attacker's exposed throat.

His charge was so sudden that the second man's brass knucks only grazed the side of his face, dropping him to one knee. But even as Spade went down, he was driving forward off his other foot.

The top of Spade's head crunched into Brass Knucks's chin. The man went backward with blood spouting from his ruined mouth as the first attacker, gasping and choking, hit the pavement with the back of his head. He was motionless.

Grunting like a wild boar, Spade whirled to drive his cupped hands simultaneously against both of the knifeman's ears. Howling with the pain of shattered eardrums, the man landed on his knees, tipped over sideways, and lay still, clutching both sides of his head, yowling.

Forty-five seconds had passed.

Spade looked quickly around, panting, holding his handkerchief to his scraped cheek. No pedestrians were in sight. No traffic passed on the Embarcadero. He bent over each man in turn, pulling back their hoods so he could see their faces. It was obvious from his expression that he didn't know any of them. He checked their pockets. No money, no I.D. He walked away.

At the turnaround in front of the Ferry Building, Spade jumped aboard an almost-empty Market Street Owl just pulling away. He took a seat close to the back door and kept his head down and the handkerchief to his face to mask the bleeding.

He left the car at Ellis Street, walked the block and a half to his apartment at 120 Ellis. His hands were shaking. The blood on his cheek was clotting. He took off his heavy woolen cap. There was a bloody tooth embedded in the fabric. He threw the tooth into the gutter, let himself in, trudged up the stairs, let himself into his room.

Spade pulled the chain of the bare overhead sixty-watt bulb, tossed his cap and coat on the davenport bed, and went around a counter with a tall stool in front of it. In the tiny cubicle behind it were a sink and a table with an Energex single-burner hot plate on top, two plates, and cutlery on the shelf below.

He washed his hands and face, wincing when the hot water hit his lacerated cheek, dried gingerly using the towel that hung on a rack behind the counter. From a narrow cupboard above the sink, he took a Johnson & Johnson first aid medical kit and liberally applied iodine to his cheek, again wincing, added a gauze pad and sticking plaster.

From the shelf below the bedside stand he got a wine glass and a half-full bottle of rum, opened the window to let in the cold wet night air and the smells and incessant night sounds of Market Street. He sat down in the room's only chair and drank rum and rolled and smoked cigarettes.

"The plot thickens," he finally muttered aloud.

He washed and dried his glass, put it and the Bacardi back in the nightstand. He undressed and put on the green-and-white checked pajamas he took from under the pillow, pulled the chain on the overhead bulb, and got into bed.

He slept.

8

Take It to the Bank

"Sam, what happened to your face?"

Spade wore a white shirt with narrow green stripes; his suit coat was over the back of his swivel chair. He stubbed out his cigarette, said, "Three muggers. We're making progress."

"Getting beat up is making progress?"

"You oughtta see the other guys."

"There was nothing in the papers—"

"I can't figure if they were warning me off or trying to kill me."

"Kill you?" Effie Perine's face was suddenly pale.

"Brass knucks, a shiv, a baseball bat. Easy to go too far. Someone's getting worried." He leaned forward, elbows on the desk. "I was on the *San Anselmo* last night and watched two seamen on graveyard watch checking out the drain-pipes."

"You mean they saw you and—"

"You think I'm a baby in diapers?" he snarled. "If I don't

want to get seen I don't get seen." Then he chuckled and patted her arm. "Don't mind me, sweetheart, my face hurts."

The door to the outer office was thrust open with such force it banged against the wall. Two men burst in. Effie Perine started to her feet. The shorter man, in front, wore a black bowler hat. He pointed at Spade in triumph.

"The man on the beat told me he saw you coming in!"

"Hello, Sergeant," said Spade cheerily. His only move had been to lean back in his chair. He gestured. "I believe you've met my secretary, Effie Perine."

Dundy was a head shorter than Spade, compact but strongly built, with a bullet head and a square face and green eyes. His short-cut brown hair and tightly trimmed mustache were starting to show glints of gray. He lowered his pointing finger.

"I've met her," he said harshly.

Spade lit the cigarette he had been rolling when Effie Perine came in, gestured lazily with it.

" 'Lo, Tom."

The big man behind Dundy jerked a nod. "Sam."

He was Spade's size but carried more weight, most of it in a hard-looking belly that stretched at the shirt buttons above his belt. His mouth was thick, hard-edged; he looked like he would always need a shave. His eyes were small and blue and shrewd, constantly shifting.

Spade clasped his hands behind his neck.

"So what are you two birds up to this morning?"

"Up to our necks in the manure you've been spreading around town," snapped Dundy, crowding the desk. "Wasting our days running around in circles trying to catch up with you."

"Well, I'm here now." He said to Tom Polhaus, "I hear you took the four luggage-room guards down to the hall and were grilling them until all hours."

"How did you know—"

"It's all over the docks, Dundy," Spade said mockingly.

"Had to let them go," said Polhaus in an almost apologetic voice. "Nothing to show they were in on the heist."

"I could have told you that"—said Spade. He unclasped his hands and lowered his arms and leaned his elbows on the desk. He grinned—"if you boys could have got hold of me."

"We've got you now," said Dundy with triumph in his voice. "Got you for impersonating an officer—"

"Prove it."

"I knew you'd say that, Spade. I'm going to take you down to the *San Anselmo* and show you to First Officer Rafferty and Quartermaster Kest so they can identify you as the man who went aboard just after the robbery claiming to be—"

Spade was on his feet, his movement so abrupt that his swivel chair crashed back against the wall under the window.

"You got a warrant for my arrest?" he demanded.

The veins were swelling at the sides of his thick neck. Dundy took an involuntary step back and Tom Polhaus started forward, alarm on his face.

"Take it easy, Sam, we're just—"

"Just busting in, making accusations without a warrant."

He put his left hand flat on his desk and leaned forward on that arm while pointing his right forefinger at Dundy's chest as Dundy had pointed a finger at him.

"If I impersonated anyone, it would have been a minor Port Authority official, not a cop. If you want to arrest someone, clap the nippers on Quartermaster Kest. If you can find him."

"Straight goods, Sam?" asked Polhaus.

"Take it to the bank." He jerked a thumb at Dundy. "And take your pal here with you when you go."

"How do you know Kest is involved if you weren't in on it yourself?" demanded Dundy doggedly.

"It's called investigating, Dundy. If you think you can prove anything on me, go ahead, take me in." He turned to Effie Perine, who was still standing back from the desk, white-faced and astounded. "Run next door, sweetheart, ask Sid Wise to come in—"

"We're going, Spade." Dundy's mouth worked beneath his mustache as he turned away. "But we'll be back."

Polhaus paused long enough to nod to Effie Perine and shake his head at Spade in exasperation. Then he went out behind Dundy. Only after the outer door had closed behind them did Spade drag his chair up to the desk again and sit back down in it. Effie Perine, still shaken, sank into the other chair.

"Sam! A police sergeant! He's going to—"

"He's going to try," said Spade. "What have you got to tell me about our missing passenger without any luggage?"

Her face fell. “Nothing. He boarded at Honolulu as you thought, slight and bearded, under the name St. Clair McPhee. Paid cash. Left the ship and just disappeared.”

“Good!” Spade’s face had brightened. “Then we can give odds forever that he’s the one behind the whole scheme.”

“But if he’s gone and the gold’s gone—”

“Some of it’s still aboard the *San Anselmo.* Give Tom Polhaus time to get back to the hall, call him, ask him to meet me at the Waldorf at noon. Those three mug artists who jumped me last night knew who I was. If Tom can bird-dog them for me through police records I’ll tail ’em until they lead me to this St. Clair McPhee.”

She started to speak, but he interrupted.

“They weren’t hired by Kest. He went on the lam yesterday. They weren’t hired by my graveyard-watch seamen because they didn’t see me. So it has to be our missing passenger.”

He shrugged into his suit coat and started for the door.

“And tell Sid Wise I’ve got the kid nailed down. I don’t know where he is minute to minute, but he’s OK.”

Spade was at a corner table in the Waldorf Café in Market Street, drinking a seidel of beer and eating a ham sandwich. Tom Polhaus sat down, tipped his hat back, and sighed.

“That beer looks good. I ain’t been in here before.”

Spade swept a thick, hostlike arm around the small, dim saloon. “Buy one and the sandwiches are free.”

Polhaus lumbered to his feet, went up to the bar, returned

with his own stein of dark beer and a big plateful of ham sandwiches on small hot biscuits. He started wolfing them down.

"Did Dundy really think those four seamen were in on the heist, or was he just trolling for headlines?"

Polhaus shrugged. "He tried hard enough to break 'em, that's the truth. Took 'em downstairs for a little session."

"Waltzing around a quartet of tough seamen who don't know anything in the first place does a lot of good." Spade blew out smoke. "What about the quartermaster? Kest?"

Polhaus drank beer, looked quizzically at Spade. "That on the up-and-up, Sam? You really think he's the one planned it?"

"Planned it? No. In on it? Yes." Malice glinted for a moment in his eyes. "Not that you're likely to find him even if you do look. Not him or his green motorcycle with the sidecar."

"Motorcycle with a sidecar?"

"Yeah, but here's another one for you. What's the story on those three guys got beat up on the Embarcadero last night?"

Polhaus stared at him with small, bright, suddenly suspicious eyes. "What happened to your face, Sam?"

"Cut myself shaving. Who are they? What's their grift? What tale did they spin for you?"

Polhaus drank beer and wiped the back of his hand across his mouth, his knuckles rasping the bristles on his chin. When he spoke it was slowly, thoughtfully, as if feeling his way.

"They were the ones got beat up, not the other way around."

Spade chuckled. "By a dozen Chinese highbinders with lathers' hatchets? Anybody want 'em for anything?"

"You sure you cut yourself shaving?"

"Out-of-towners? Local? Where are they staying?"

"No wants, Sam. They got patched up and walked away."

"I'd get more from the newspapers," said Spade irritably. "Let's talk about all the help you're giving us."

"I gave you Kest. What more do you want?"

"I want you to level with me about those three guys."

Polhaus finished his sandwich, scraped his chin again, sighed. "Well, might could it wouldn't hurt to take a look at Kest. That sidecar big enough to carry some of that missing gold?"

"Yeah, but it didn't."

"I wish I knew what you aren't telling me, Sam."

Spade put money down. "I might have something for you in a day or two. For *you*, Tom. Got it?"

"I got it," said Polhaus almost glumly. Then he added unwillingly, "Those three guys, they're Portagee fishermen out of Sausalito, maybe turned leggers. I ain't got their names on me but we couldn't hold 'em anyway. No wants or warrants on 'em."

9

The Portagee

The *Eureka,* one of several side-wheelers that made the thirty-two-minute run to Marin County half a dozen times a day, slowed to a crawl to slide between the massive wooden pilings of the middle of Sausalito's three ferry slips. The mooring lines were tossed out, and the gangplank was slid out and down. Spade followed the other passengers off, walked a hundred yards to a three-story pseudo-Mission-style hotel overlooking the meager downtown.

For now the hotel lobby was deserted. Dust motes danced in the air. The check-in counter was unmanned. From the room behind it came muted voices and the clink of chips.

Spade slapped the round metal bell on the counter several impatient times. A stooped man wearing a green eyeshade stuck his head through the doorway with a surprised look on his face.

"Yes, sir," he piped. "Can I help you?"

"Benny Ruiz back there?"

"Benny." He trailed off as if unsure of the name.

"Ruiz. Quit the clown act. Is the Portagee in the game?"

The face disappeared. Another took its place, square and meaty, wearing whiskers and a cigar. "Who's askin'?"

"Spade."

"Course it is. Long time no. Try the Lighthouse."

Spade nodded. "You up or down, Duke?"

"Down twenty berries."

"When you gonna learn not to draw to an inside straight?"

The head made a rude noise and disappeared. Spade went out into the street to walk north along the waterfront.

The Lighthouse looked like its name, a small white café with a fake octagonal wooden lighthouse on top. The windows were steamy. The clatter of cutlery, the jumble of voices, the smell of frying peppers and spicy Portuguese chorizo came out when Spade pulled the door open. A counter ran down the center of the room with stools in front and the grill behind. There were booths along the front and side walls. In four of them were lean, narrow men in rain slickers, some with missing fingers.

Three of the seven stools along the counter were taken, one by the Lighthouse's lone woman. When Spade entered all conversation in American ceased. The sweating cook abandoned the hash browns and sausage and eggs he had sizzling on the flat steel grease-stained grill to look at Spade. His shirt was open to show the top of a red union suit.

"Yeah?"

Spade walked through the silence toward the only man at the counter who had not turned to look at him, a wide and thick man with meaty arms and shoulders under a black sweater. His round face was slightly concave, with receding black hair and round brown eyes under thick brows. His nose was broad, open pored, his lips thick. A black peacoat draped the stool beyond him.

Spade took the nearer red vinyl stool. The man turned to look at him. "Hell's sake, Sam. What's it been?"

"All of five years," said Spade.

Conversation resumed. The cook slopped a mug of steaming coffee down in front of Spade. The Portagee had his elbows on the counter, was sucking heavily on a Fatima cigarette.

"New cook, new clientele. Place has changed, Benny."

Benny Ruiz nodded. "Lots of us Portagees is leggers these days. We get nervous-like when strangers show up."

"How about you, Benny? Dealing crab or liquor?"

"Both since Prohibition. Hell, Sam, bringing in booze beats working."

Spade blew on his coffee, sipped it, made a face.

"Dregs of the pot," said the cook without turning around.

Ruiz stubbed his cigarette out in the remains of his meal, picked up his peacoat, and dropped a quarter beside his plate.

"See you around," he said.

Spade made and smoked a cigarette, sipped at the vile coffee. After all of ten minutes he tossed a dime on the counter and went outside. Ruiz fell into step beside him.

"Didn't want to blow the gaff on you, Sam, if you was working a game on somebody for Continental."

"I'm out on my own now, Benny. Three leggers, Portagees, jumped me in the city last night. They work out of Sausalito. I don't have names. Maybe you could ask around, find out who's carrying scars. Find out if one of them took a boat out—his own or somebody else's—after midnight three nights ago and came back before first light with a load that wasn't hooch."

"I'll be damned. The *San Anselmo* gold heist?"

"Maybe, maybe not. But there's reward money out. Find out if he maybe met up with a man named St. Clair McPhee."

Effie Perine was on her way down the stairs when Spade came in the street door. She stopped, said eagerly, "I can come back up if you need me."

"Go on home, angel. I've been over in Sausalito."

"Why Sausalito?" She sounded surprised.

"Because that's where our three mug artists are from. And that's where the bootleggers keep their boats."

"I don't know what you're talking about."

"Neither do I, sweetheart. See you tomorrow."

"Sam, wait! A Phil Geaque—I think that's how you pronounced it—called. I left his message on your desk."

"You got it right. Gee-ack."

"And Sid says his client is getting up on his hind legs. Three ships are slated to sail for Australia with ports of call in the South Seas during the next week and Henny could try to stow away on any of them. Does that still hold what you told me this morning, Sam? That you have Henny nailed down?"

"I'll know where to find him when the time comes, if that's what you mean."

Effie Perine went down and out. Spade went up and in. By the illumination coming through the thin net window curtains he rolled a cigarette, picked up the phone, gave central Kearny 5330-1. He heard Geaque's voice in his ear.

"Still there, Phil? Scraping the bottom of the barrel?"

"You know us, Sam. We never sleep. Bottom of the barrel is right. The police had to let those four seamen go."

"There was never anything in that anyway."

"We wired our Honolulu office to check whether the replacement lock and hasp for Captain Ogilvie were obtained there by the thieves. We haven't gotten any word yet."

"And won't. The locks were changed in Sydney."

"Locks? Only the captain's was changed."

Spade shook his head impatiently even though Geaque could not see him. "All of the locks. The *San Anselmo* was there eight days with the strong room open and empty and the locks hanging on their chains and their keys hanging on hooks in the ship's officers' quarters. Everybody ashore except a seaman or two on watch? Go on with you. New locks, new keys, to replace the old."

After a long silence Geaque said slowly, "But then the captain replaced his lock with *another* one of his own, so they had to put on *another* lock that they'd have a key for."

"The quartermaster, Kest, is the bird who switched 'em."

Geaque's sigh came over the wire. "Kest failed to report for last night's midnight watch, and today the police found two gold sovereigns in a pawn shop. The man who exchanged them for American money fit Kest's description. But I find it hard to believe he had the brains to set this whole thing up."

"Nor did he. It was a passenger got on at Honolulu."

Geaque's voice was sharp. "Who is he? What's his name? Where is he right now?"

"Don't know, don't know, and don't know. He gave the name of St. Clair McPhee—surely false—to the shipping line, paid cash, was first off the boat, and disappeared."

"That's him for sure?"

"Sure as death and taxes."

"The authorities now hold the theory, and I concur, that the gold was stolen before the ship ever arrived in Honolulu, and was off-loaded and hidden there. The thieves'll be planning to pick it up when the *San Anselmo* passes through on its way back to Australia. I'll plant an undercover man aboard in hopes that he can identify them before Honolulu."

"Waste of time, Phil. The gold was stolen here."

"You're wrong, Sam. We've confirmed it's not hidden aboard and there's been no opportunity to smuggle it off the ship since it docked. It has to be in Honolulu." Another sigh. "Anyway, the point is moot. We're out of time here. The authorities can't hold the *San Anselmo* much longer."

Spade's voice betrayed urgency. "When will it sail?"

"They'll start loading cargo tomorrow, let the passengers aboard the next day, and sail that afternoon."

"Thanks," said Spade and hung up abruptly.

• • •

He locked the office and left, but did not go back to his apartment in Ellis Street. He caught a down car to the Ferry Building, walked out to Pier 35. When the loading started in the morning there would be lots of activity, but at midnight the *San Anselmo* was deserted. As it had been the night he'd gone aboard to watch Grost and Grafton, the gangplank was unguarded.

Spade easily vaulted over the gate across the head of the gangway, landed on the deck on almost silent feet, and cat-footed it across the boat deck to the lifeboats.

In the third one he checked he obviously found what he was looking for. He left the ship wearing a satisfied expression.

"Tomorrow night," he muttered to himself.

10

You're Worth Money to Me

At 6 o'clock the next evening Sam Spade strolled through the cigar store that fronted Sly-Pork Cunningham's pool hall across from Pier 27. He looked successful, dapper, almost dandyish in a blue woolen double-breasted suit, a hand-tailored blue patterned tie, and shiny black oxfords. He was smoking a cigar.

Able-bodied seamen Grost and Grafton were playing rotation at one of the six green felt tables. The pool hall was high ceilinged, noisy with the clack of balls and the voices of the kibitzers lining the walls in straight-backed wooden chairs. The overhead lights were filtered through cigar and cigarette smoke.

Grafton ran the three through nine before miscuing on the ten. Spade spoke in a flat, almost menacing voice.

"I play the winner. Dime a ball."

Grost took him in, almost sneered. "Private game, Mac."

"I play the winner, dime a ball," said Spade in that tone.

Grost was the heavy-bodied one, thick and slow in a faded tight-fitting middy and blue jeans that bagged on heavy flanks. His body looked poised for violence, but his chin was just going south and his piglike eyes could not hold Spade's stony stare.

"Ah, OK, sure. Ah, anything you want."

Rattled, he shot and missed. They played out their game hurriedly. Grafton won. Spade put aside his cigar and selected one of the cues held upright in the rack midway down the room, laid it on the table, and rolled it back and forth. It was bowed, rolled unevenly. The next one he selected rolled flawlessly.

As he chalked up he said, "Lag for break."

Grafton won the break. Spade set them up, tightly so they would break wide, hung the wooden triangle back up on the wall.

Grafton put so much force into his break that the twelve ball jumped off the table. Spade fielded it left-handed like a good shortstop, set it back on the green felt.

Grafton made the one and two balls, had to try a bank shot for the three, missed. Spade ran the rest of the table in order. He put his cue back in the rack, picked up his still-smoldering cigar. With ill grace, Grafton gave him a dollar.

"Close enough," said Spade. "Let's barber. Outside."

Grafton stepped up close, almost chest to chest. In sharp contrast to his fellow seaman he was lithe and lean, his work clothes almost tailored, his face bland but his eyes dark and blade sharp. Emboldened by him, Grost stepped closer too.

"Who the hell you think you're kidding, Mac?"

Spade touched his ear. "Too many lugs hanging out in

here." He leaned close, murmured without any apparent movement of his lips, "The sovereigns," then walked out.

He had thrown his stogie into the gutter and had started rolling a cigarette when the two seamen came up to him.

"This had better be good," said Grafton in an icy tone.

Spade hunched against the fog-laden evening wind to fire up his cigarette with his lighter.

"The *San Anselmo* boards passengers tomorrow morning and sails for Australia in the afternoon. You two only have tonight to get the rest of the gold off."

"We don't know what you're talkin' about," mumbled Grafton.

Spade dragged in smoke and looked around in exaggerated confusion. "Am I talking to the wrong people here? Kest must have told you to be on the lookout for me before he lost his guts and ran away and hid."

They seemed to struggle for what to say. Spade shrugged as if in disgust, started up Sansome Street. The two men hesitated, then hurried to fall into step with him.

"We knew there was someone, but Kest—he didn't say nothing," said Grost. "We been waitin' for him to—"

"Shut up, you damn fool!" snarled Grafton.

Spade chuckled. "What a smart pair you are! He'll rat you out to the cops to save his own hide. I got most of the gold off the night the *San Anselmo* arrived, but I told Kest a couple of hiding places aboard ship just in case. I figured it was safer for all of us if you two never met me face-to-face. But with the ship leaving tomorrow I have to chance it."

"We was promised a third of what we hid aboard, but now we want half."

Spade looked angry, then tossed away his butt, shrugged.

"OK, half it is, seeing as how we'll be splitting Kest's share. I've got a Chink merchant lined up in Chinatown'll give me seventy-five cents for every dollar of gold I bring him. But you boys don't see a dime unless you recover the rest of it tonight."

Grafton got a crafty look. "Look here, mister, how do we know you ain't just some grifter tryna cut yourself in?"

"You birds figure you can smuggle off the gold still aboard when you get to Honolulu." Spade shook his head. "You'll land in the brig for sure. I'll see to that. But if you move it here tonight you'll get your share. Tomorrow's too late."

Spade started walking again. Grafton hurried to catch up. "Maybe you don't have no idea if there's gold hidden aboard. Maybe you're just tryna con us into telling you things."

"Half's in a vent pipe from the fuel tanks, the other half's in a scupper from the boat deck to the promenade deck."

They stared at him in silence. Grafton got sly again. "Where are you gonna be while we're takin' all the risks?"

"Waiting for you on the dock with a car," said Spade.

Grafton shook his head. "Uh-uh. You're gonna be right there with us so you'll be in the can with us if anything goes wrong."

Spade sighed, shrugged. "You birds are too smart for me."

From the Pacific Telephone and Telegraph Office in Powell Street, Spade called Tom Polhaus in the Detective Squad Room at the Hall of Justice. "Dundy around, Tom?"

"Gone home." Polhaus chuckled. "So we can talk, if that's what you're driving at."

"That's what I'm driving at."

"I can't be goin' around behind my partner's back, Sam."

"He would behind yours. Bring him in after if that's what you want, but if he knows about the play beforehand he'll hex it for sure. And he'll hog the glory and the promotions. Do you want in on the *San Anselmo* gold-theft collars or not?"

"Damn, I just knew you had a line to that gold," said Tom.

Spade talked, hung up, called a Hertz Drive-Ur-Self station and said he would be by to pick up a car within the hour. At Bernstein's in Powell Street he had a plate of steamed clams, then walked to his apartment to change clothes.

An hour after midnight a 1920 Model T Ford went out along Pier 35 to stop at the wooden fence. Its streamlined hood and big radiator with nickel trimmings gleamed under wet-haloed dock lights. Beyond the fence the black curved side of the *San Anselmo* stretched up into darkness. In the bay Alcatraz was baying like an old hound, Land's End lighthouse was yapping back from beyond the Gate.

The car ka-chunked to a stop. The driver's door creaked open. Sam Spade stepped out. The salt tang of the bay filled his nostrils. He stood for long moments, his head swiveling like the head of a wary bear.

Satisfied, he put one hand on top of the wooden fence and

vaulted over. Stood again, listening, watching. At the top of the unguarded gangway two shadowy figures materialized, one heavy, wide, slouchy, the other tall, narrow, quick.

"Where's the gangplank guard?" asked Spade in an undertone.

"Down in the galley." Grost used the same low tone. "We put them drops in the coffee urn like you told us; he's sleeping like a baby. Last night in port, no one else is aboard."

"The chest's in the car. Let's go get it," said Spade.

The three stealthy figures hauled the obviously empty iron-bound chest up the gangplank, carried it awkwardly down to the promenade deck, opened it, set it under the bottom of the scupper that had clunked dully under Spade's earlier tapping.

Grafton's sheath knife dug out the plug. Down poured a shower of gold sovereigns. Spade grabbed the rope handle at one end of the chest, began backing toward the stairs, dragging it with him. The two seamen pushed from behind, then lifted it up step-by-step. On the boat deck above, Grafton unblocked the vent pipe. They hand-over-handed up a twenty-foot length of fire hose, its nozzle down. Spade tipped the open end of the hose over the chest. Another flood of gold coins poured down.

"Fifty thousand dollars in all," panted Grafton in triumph.

They dragged the chest over to the gangplank, Spade carrying one end by its rope handle, the two seamen carrying the other. Spade seemed to catch his heel on something, lost his balance. He dropped his end of the chest on Grost's foot;

his flailing elbow caught Grafton on the side of his jaw. The chest broke open, gold coins spilled out.

There were sudden shouting voices, pounding feet, light from wildly waving electric torches. Uniformed bulls surged up the gangplank and came from the shadows on the deck. Tom Polhaus was in the forefront, directing them, his small shrewd eyes alight.

"We'll have the devil's own time to gather up all them coins, Samuel," he said.

Spade growled, "What do you want, Tom? Pretty ribbon wrapped around 'em? Here's something else: if I were you, I'd put divers off the stern of this ship tomorrow morning early."

"Divers? What for?"

"To recover the two empty chests those birds dumped overboard after they hid the gold you just recovered by inspired police work." He gave a sardonic laugh. "Unless Dundy is back at the hall working out ways to grab the glory."

"Aw, c'mon, Sam," said Polhaus almost sheepishly. "You know the sergeant's a fair man in his own way."

Spade said, "I'll be in tomorrow to give my statement."

Polhaus led his shackled prisoners down the gangplank as police officers on hands and knees gathered up the scattered coins. Spade melted into the shadow of the cabin, unseen, until the police and dockside onlookers below had dispersed.

Only then did he jerk aside the already-loosened canvas cover on one of the lifeboats slung on davits above the rail.

He reached in and, one-handed, bodily hauled a squirming teenager out by his coat collar.

"Sorry to forestall your South Seas dream, son," he said to "Henny" Hendrickson Barber, "but you're worth money to me."

11

At the Blue Rock Inn

Sam Spade's left hand was about to replace the receiver when he heard Sid Wise's sleep-thick voice in his ear.

"If the city isn't on fire, I'm going to—"

"My office. Pronto." Spade hung up.

He looked at the disconsolate teenager slumped across the desk from him, arms hanging limply outside the chair arms toward the floor. It was cold in the office.

"How much trouble am I in?" asked the boy finally.

Spade licked the paper of one of his hand-rolled, twisted the ends, put one end in his mouth, lit it. "With the cops, none at all." He put a shrug in his voice. "With your folks—"

"How'd you find me?"

"I saw your clothes and food and books in a lifeboat."

The boy fell silent. Spade smoked placidly. Henny finally said, "You sound like you tried it once."

Spade chuckled. "I didn't get any farther than you did. My old man whaled the tar out of me."

"That'd be beneath Pater's dignity. My ma will yell at me and then start hugging me. She never lets me *do* anything."

Hurried steps pattered up the hall, came through Spade's outer door without slowing down. Sid Wise burst in.

"Sam, what the devil are you . . ." He ran down, seeing the boy for the first time. He exclaimed, "Henny!"

" 'Lo, Mr. Wise," said Henny despondently to the floor.

"Where'd you find him?"

"*San Anselmo.*" Spade grinned wolfishly. "Got the gold, too, fifty thousand worth. Seventy-five is still missing. So is McPhee, so the case isn't closed yet in my book."

Wise gestured Henny out of the chair, fell into it himself. "You'd better tell me all about it. From the beginning."

Spade pointed at the telephone.

"Call the Barbers. I'll fill you in while you're driving the three of us out to their estate to bring this desperado here home to his folks."

Henny couldn't hide his sudden grin at the description.

"You'll be fighting off the girls with a stick at U.C. Berkeley, son." To Wise he said, "I gave it to Tom Polhaus. The find, the takedown. By the time Dundy gets through shoving him aside, neither his nor my name will appear in the papers."

Sid Wise reached across the desk for the telephone, chuckling to Spade. "Even so, we're golden on this one, Sammy."

"Sure." Spade was on his feet. "I'll get paid, Geaque will know who found the gold, and he'll get the word out. It'll do me good in the long run with the movers and shakers."

. . .

When Spade entered the office at 7:30 the next morning, Effie Perine was already at her desk, the little jeweled gold locket she had been wearing on the day he hired her open before her. She had a wistful expression on her face.

Spade looked over her shoulder. Unfolded, the locket showed miniature photographs in a four-leaf-clover shape, each picture under a thin glass plate.

"Trouble?" asked Spade.

Effie Perine jumped, startled. "I—I didn't hear you come in, Sam. No. No trouble. Just . . . memories . . ."

On the left was the cracked, faded portrait of a handsome Greek man with piercing, soulful eyes. He was dressed in the high starch collar and cravat of the previous century.

Spade said, "Your father?"

"Yes. Tassos Perinos. He died in the nineteen eighteen flu epidemic."

The photograph across from her father's was of a young woman, older now, whose face Spade knew well. "And your ma." He looked at the lower one. "And their wedding picture."

The top photograph was a tiny portrait of a Greek woman of twenty-two or twenty-three. It too had been amateurishly cut with nail scissors to fit the oval frame. It was too small to show much detail.

Effie Perine said, "Penelope Chiotras. Penny. She's six years older than I am. Our parents came here together from Greece in nineteen hundred. Penny's always been like a big sister to me. She took care of me for a year when my mother sort of fell to pieces after Dad died. I haven't seen her for a year. I know she's all right; she makes regular deposits in her mother's account. But . . . nobody knows where she lives or works. I miss her."

"I'd miss her too," said Spade.

Decisively, she closed the locket and hung it back around her neck on its thin gold chain. Her mood had lightened.

"Did you find Henny? Is he all right?"

"Yeah," said Spade.

Effie Perine said, perhaps snidely, "You could at least have rubbed the lipstick off your cheek."

"The boy's mother was grateful to get her son back all in one piece, that's all. C'mon—you'll hear all about it."

An hour later they were eating ham, eggs, toast, and marmalade and drinking coffee with Sid Wise in the Palace Hotel on New Montgomery just south of Market. Where horse-drawn carriages had once stopped to drop off wealthy top-hatted and bejeweled patrons there was now an ornate roofed lobby with a fancy dining room.

Sid Wise had one of the morning papers braced against the silver coffeepot, folded open to the story of the midnight gold recovery aboard the *San Anselmo.*

"According to the newshawks, Sergeant Dundy has had his eyes on Grost and Grafton since the day the theft was discovered. Of course he figured they'd have to make their move on the night before the ship sailed, so he directed patrolman Tom Polhaus to have men concealed on the dock and aboard the ship. The thieves appeared with the gold in an iron-bound chest—"

"Sam isn't even mentioned?" demanded Effie Perine.

"I'm surprised Tom got mentioned," said Spade. "As for me, it isn't just Henny's ma who's grateful. His old man is happy his kid's escapade won't be making the newspapers, so he'll pay without a squawk. And plenty, too." Spade grinned. "The kid's taking no harm. Just getting caught was an adventure."

"How did you know where to look?" asked Effie Perine.

"One of the lifeboats had food and clothing and novels about the South Seas in it."

"But how'd you know *last night*?"

"The ship is sailing this afternoon."

"Then there's the reward money," said Effie Perine.

"The International Banking Corporation will make the point that total recovery wasn't made—seventy-five thousand worth of stolen gold is still missing," said Wise. "They'll say their policy is that the reward gets paid only on full recovery."

"It isn't fair!" exclaimed Effie Perine.

Wise popped the last piece of toast into his mouth, chewed, nodded. "But that's the way they'll play it."

"But all along Sam's been focused on the reward money!"

"So everybody else would focus on it, Effie. The two real questions have always been, who is St. Clair McPhee *really*, and how did he get the rest of the loot off the *San Anselmo*?"

"Is that why you went to Sausalito?"

Spade turned to Wise, who had tented his hands under

his chin and was staring judiciously at the ornate chandelier overhead.

"Hear that, Sid? I told you she was a smart Greek."

"Never knew one who wasn't. And that's a Jew who says it."

Spade said to Effie Perine, "Now the point is to find McPhee, and pronto. He has his gold, but he isn't through yet."

Effie Perine asked, "Is he the one who hired those men?"

"Yeah." Spade's face darkened. "He won't want *anyone* around who can identify him."

"You mean he might—"

"Kill people? Sure. Anyone who *helped* get him the seventy-five thousand dollars that he got away with, and me, who kept him *from* getting the other fifty thousand dollars. I have to take him down, and quick."

"But the papers are saying it was Dundy who found it."

"McPhee, whoever he is, will know better than that."

When they walked into Spade's office, leaving Wise behind, the phone was ringing. Spade hung his hat on the rack by the door; Effie Perine picked up. "Samuel Spade Investigations."

As he was crossing toward his private office she waved him to wait with the hand not over the receiver.

"A man calling himself the Portagee wants you to meet him at the Blue Rock Inn in Larkspur," she said. "He sounds tough."

"He is tough. Tell him I'm on my way." There was satisfaction in Spade's voice. "I've been waiting for his call."

Though it was noon there was no sun in Sausalito. The train to San Rafael would go through Larkspur, but not soon enough. After leaving the ferry, Spade hunted up the "Hamburger Line" taxi—"two Greeks and six cabs"—that had recently expanded from San Francisco into Marin, and climbed into the front seat beside the cabdriver of the line's lone Studebaker sedan. He pulled his topcoat tighter around him.

"Larkspur. The Blue Rock Inn."

The gap-toothed skinny driver had rheumy eyes and a tweed cap pulled down over his ears and fur-lined gloves on his hands. He looked over at Spade disconsolately.

"Cold old ride up over the mountain. Train'll be going in an hour," he said, as if reluctant to venture out of the relative shelter of town into the windswept lower reaches of Tamalpais.

"I don't have an hour," said Spade.

The driver nodded sadly and slammed the car into gear, and they took off with a jerk. The two-lane road ran from Richardson Bay to Larkspur, first out across the lowland tidal flats, then up and over the hill beyond Mill Valley. It was a corkscrewing, up-and-down nine-mile ride on gravel.

Air rushing around the edges of the windscreen made talk impossible, so Spade rolled and smoked cigarettes and stared out at the pines and redwoods and, on the steeper slopes, manzanita and Scotch broom. Black-crested Steller's jays flitted through the foliage. Once Spade looked back and could see the city gleaming white across the bay.

The taxi went down a winding decline through a final set of racetrack curves, past a farmhouse and a red barn with horses in the hillside pasture. Then they were back on level ground and chugging along Magnolia Avenue. Beyond more groves of towering redwoods the tiny town of Larkspur appeared. The driver pulled off the road opposite the newly refurbished Blue Rock Inn.

"Guess I better wait for you?" he asked in glum hope. A return fare other than Spade would be rare indeed.

"Yeah. And get yourself a drink. On me."

"Hey, you're all right, cap."

They crossed the street together and went into the restaurant. There was no traffic, few pedestrians. The bar, against the right-hand wall, made no pretense of abiding by the strictures of Prohibition. A sign in the dining room read:

$1.00—FRENCH AND ITALIAN DINNERS—$1.00

Under it was another notice, for the hotel on the top floors:

RATES
$2.00 A DAY
$12 & $14 A WEEK

The cabbie took a stool while Spade walked back through the empty dining room looking for Benny Ruiz. He found the Portagee at the farthest table in the rear, under a window looking out onto unpaved Ward Street. There was a bottle of cheap red wine and two filled glasses in front of him. He was sucking on a Fatima. He raised his glass in greeting. There was a dirty bandage around his left forearm.

"You made quick time, Sam."

"Hired a cab." Spade sat, picked up the second glass, drank. He didn't seem to see the bandage. "What are you doing out here in Larkspur?"

Ruiz shrugged heavy shoulders. "I asked around like you said, about someone going out the night before the *San Anselmo* gold heist was discovered."

"And?"

"Legger name of Fundão 'Fingers' Lisboa spread it around he had a load of hooch coming in that night. But when he went out at one a.m. it was in his dinghy. His motor launch is the fastest on the bay, even carrying thirty cases of Canadian, and he leaves it behind. Foggy night, nobody seen where he went."

"What time'd he come back?"

"Three thirty, four."

"Hmmm. Not long enough to go out through the Gate and back. Where does he hide the booze until it gets picked up?"

"Sometimes Angel Island. Sometimes below Yellow Bluff. Here in town is a couple places built on stilts so the water washes in underneath them, deep enough to bring a boat in. The booze can sit there above high tide until they can truck it out."

"He go out alone? Come back alone?"

"Out alone. Back with someone. Nobody saw 'em clear."

Benny Ruiz flicked ash from his Fatima onto the floor and screwed up his heavy face in a worried look. "You think maybe he was this St. Clair McPhee guy you're looking for?"

"Seems likely," said Spade. He drew on his cigarette, emptied his wine glass. Benny refilled it. "You talk to Fingers yourself after he got back?"

"Sure. He was half lit, talkin' 'bout a big bootleggin' syndicate they was gonna set up, playin' as if he'd actually been out on a liquor run. Then he shut up quick, like he'd said too much. He didn't say no more."

"Anything on the other two guys?"

"Second was Fingers's cousin Figueiro Mondego. The third was a tough bird named Villalba Berlingas. Fingers couldn't hardly talk. Big black-and-blue marks on his neck."

Spade nodded. "The ringleader. He had a baseball bat."

"Figueiro had a almost-busted jaw and missin' teeth."

"Brass knucks," said Spade.

"An' Villalba had busted eardrums. Still had dried blood down the side of his neck when I saw him."

"The shiv," said Spade.

Benny looked around, hunched toward Spade across the table.

"Thing is, last night I sat in at the game in the hotel, made a fin. After midnight I was climbin' up the hill to my rooming house when somebody jumped me. I figured it was 'cause I'd won at the game. But he tried to knife me." He held up his left arm. "Just a scratch, but if I hadn't of blocked it . . ."

"So you cleared out," said Spade.

"Well, I didn't see the guy cut me, but Villalba's good with a shiv. So this morning early I jumped the San Rafael train, hung on the outside of the caboose. Jesus, was it cold! Dropped off below the station here in Larkspur. Didn't nobody see me get on or off. Got a room. Called you."

"Smart man," said Spade. He finished his wine, got to his feet. He dropped a twenty-dollar bill on the table. "You hear anything, let me know. I hear anything, I'll let you know. You can use your time trying to figure out where the *San Anselmo* loot might be hidden. Find that, you'll get some reward money."

He left Benny Ruiz looking thoughtful.

12

Dead Men Tell No Tales

When Spade boarded the ferry in Sausalito for the return trip to the city, it was full dark and the fog was in, heavy and wet. The half a hundred passengers were all inside, crowding the seats near the engine-room wall, where the warmth seeped out.

He went to the stand-up counter next to the cigar- and newsstand. A dark-eyed girl with short frizzy red hair and a waitress uniform poured him black coffee without asking.

"Thanks," said Spade. He laid down his nickel. "Say, how about a roast-beef sandwich to go with it?"

She brought him the sandwich on a plate with mashed potatoes and brown gravy. Spade paid his forty-five cents, ate it standing. Then he pulled his hat low on his head, wrapped his topcoat tightly around himself, and started toward the door.

"You aren't going out into that weather!" exclaimed the waitress in a concerned voice.

"Cold air helps me think," said Spade, grinning.

The squat ferryboat was plowing through the waves with a lurching up-and-down motion. The engines seemed to be straining, off-key. From every direction came blaring horns and moaning whistles, the jangling of bells. Despite the lights above the deck, Spade couldn't see even the bow of the vessel.

Brief light was laid across the deck as another hearty soul emerged from the cabin. The door shut; again it was dark.

"Filthy night," said a man's voice full of tension.

As Spade started to turn toward the tension, he was struck on the side of his head with something blunt and hard. His hat partially absorbed the force of the blow, but it was what prizefighters call a quitter. He was still awake, trying to see the face of the man who had struck him, but when a foot swept his feet out from under him he went down hard on his side.

Quick hands tried to roll him off the deck between the railing stanchions. He caught one of the supports, wouldn't let go. A heavy boot drove into his side once, again. He felt a rib give. His feet were shoved over the side, his torso followed. No splash would be heard in the moan of wind and din of waves. Only his clinging hand kept him from dropping into the water.

Fingers tore at his fingers. Ripped them free. He was falling. He got the other hand hooked over the edge of the deck, hung on, invisible. The door swung open again, laying down light, emitting unconcerned voices. The door shut. He was alone.

Spade's volition was returning. He got the fingers of his other hand, strong as steel hooks, curved over the edge of the deck. Flexed his arms as if doing a pull-up on a gym bar. Shot his right arm out, gripped the base of the stanchion again. When he did the same with his left hand, pain shot through his torso from the cracked rib. He did not let go.

Spade began swinging himself from side to side. On the fourth try he hooked a shoe around another stanchion. Twisted his body, stifling a cry at the pain from his rib cage. But he had rolled himself up onto the deck once more.

He lay there for minutes, hatless, breathing harshly. He finally dragged himself to his feet by clinging to the railing. He shambled to the very bow of the craft, stayed there hunched in the shadows, where he could remain unseen until the boat had slid into its berth at the Ferry Building.

Spade, last off, found a corner in the echoing terminal. After twenty minutes without spotting any watchers, he went gingerly out to the streetcar circle and caught a car to the Sutter Hospital to get his ribs taped. From there he went to his apartment and drank enough Bacardi to put himself to sleep.

At 8 a.m. he sat up groaning, called the office, told Effie Perine he would not be in that day, and hung up without telling her why, or where he was.

He got central again, asked for the Blue Rock Inn across the bay in Larkspur. The connection took five minutes, which he spent hunched on the side of the bed, shivering, rolling and smoking a cigarette. Finally he got through, asked for Benny Ruiz by description instead of the phony name he was using.

Another two minutes, he had Benny's voice in his ear. He said, "Those three birds won't be bothering you anymore."

A pause. "Gotcha. I'll go back to town this morning."

Spade stubbed out his cigarette, lay back down groaning.

When Spade, pale but clean shaven, clear-eyed, and moving well, walked into his office at 11 a.m. on Friday morning a uniformed bull was standing outside the hallway door. Inside, Polhaus bulked large next to the door, arms crossed, dissociating himself from Dundy, who was leaning over a cowering, white-faced Effie Perine, jabbing a finger at her face.

"Quit stalling, sister. I want to know where your boss—"

Spade caught Dundy by the back of his suit-coat collar, winced slightly as he spun the sergeant around before Tom Polhaus could even get his arms uncrossed. The uniformed man was frozen in place outside.

Blood suffused Dundy's face and his fists clenched. His right arm started to move, but by then Polhaus had interposed his bulk between the two angry men.

"Get him out of here." Spade's neck was bulging; the whites of his eyes were limned in red.

"That's no way to act, Sam. He was just—"

"Get him out." Spade leaned over Effie Perine's desk to ask in a soft, very different voice, "You all right, angel?"

She gave Spade a wan smile. The color was coming back to her face. She nodded.

The tension was leaving Dundy's body. He stepped back a pace. "We're going, Spade. But you're coming with us."

Ignoring him, Spade said to Polhaus, "This a pinch, Tom?"

"Nothing like that, Sam. They just want to ask you some questions like, over in Sausalito."

"Sausalito? All you had to do was call. I'd of come running. This is what I've been waiting for."

"Sausalito! You admit you're involved!" trumpeted Dundy.

"Of course I'm involved. I've been pointing my finger at Sausalito for you birds all along."

"Now you can point it from the other side of the bay." Dundy raised a hand as if to grab Spade's arm, thought better of it, dropped his hand.

Still ignoring him, Spade asked Effie Perine, "Any calls?"

"One." She cast a look at Dundy, then spoke in a malice-laden voice as she consulted her notebook, though it was obvious she didn't need to. "Sid said he went to see Mr.—see our client about that problem he'd been having, that the client finds the result satisfactory, and that he's holding a check for you."

"That's my girl." To Polhaus, he said, "Let's go get that police launch to Sausalito, Tom. Bring your boyfriend with you. And tell him he never, not ever, threatens my secretary again. Not about anything. Ever. He got that?"

Sergeant Dundy was silent, pinch faced, simmering.

Tom Polhaus mumbled, "Yeah, he's got it, Sam."

The police launch was a white quick narrow cutter that sliced through the bay's Friday clutter of pleasure boats like a surgeon's scalpel through flesh. It threw spume out on either side of its bow and left a spreading wake.

Sam Spade, standing in the narrow prow, gazed out through the Golden Gate at a cargo ship waddling its way out, hull down on the horizon. Another was lumbering in from the open Pacific between Land's End and the Marin headlands. Also on the horizon were the low, irregular shapes of the Farallons, visited by nesting seabirds and little else except, in season, pods of whales migrating south toward the warm Mexican waters. Of course any night of the year bootleggers might be found out there, transferring Canadian whiskey from ships to fishing boats.

The wind whipping Spade's coat about him made smoking impossible. The roar of the engines made conversation almost as difficult, but Tom Polhaus tried, coming up to stand beside Spade and grip the rail with both white-knuckled hands.

"The Marin County sheriff is holding a friend of yours, Sam!" he yelled in Spade's ear. "He said he was doing some work for you! That's why we came to get you!"

Seeing Polhaus there, Dundy came bustling importantly up on Spade's other side. He looked pleased.

"Legger named Benny Ruiz!" he shouted. "Got him dead to rights! And for a lot more than bringing in Canadian booze!"

"Fisherman, not a legger!" yelled Spade automatically.

"Wait till you see what they caught him with!"

Dundy made a futile grab for his black derby hat as the wind snatched it from his head and twirled it around twice before dropping it in the wake far behind the boat. Dundy cursed impotently. Spade, plaid cap pulled down hard over his eyes, laughed aloud.

The Marin County sheriff's deputy who met them at the dock was long and lank with an unexpected watermelon potbelly under a gaudy yellow-and-green checked woolen shirt. He wore a black wide-brimmed fedora and a heavy tan corduroy jacket and black denim jeans over muddy boots, one of which was partially unlaced.

"Glad to see you fellers," he said, shaking hands all around. He had a two-day stubble and his left eye was slightly cocked. "The boss's at the site of the crime, waitin' for us." His voice got excited. "Caught Benny Ruiz right there, didn't we? Still had the shovel in his hand, didn't he? We've had our eye on him for months, haven't we? A criminal type for sure."

He led them to a long black touring car with the sheriff's decal on the door and a red light mounted on top.

Spade asked indifferently, "What does Benny say?"

"Officially, he ain't talkin'. But hell, everybody in town knows he was lookin' fer Fingers Lisboa."

"And found him," said Dundy with great delight.

They drove south along the waterfront until the road made an abrupt ninety-degree turn to the right, where Richardson Street slanted up the hillside behind the bay. The deputy pulled off on the sandy shoulder beside another sheriff's car and killed the engine.

The four men got out, the slam of the doors loud above

the slosh of waves. They were beside a large pale-lemon frame house set on the high ground back from the shore, its front room extending out from the land on creosoted posts sunk into concrete bases. Its windows faced Richardson Bay above a strip of sandy beach, with the water washing in beneath it.

When Spade saw where they had stopped, he shook his head and gave an ironic chuckle.

"What's so funny?" demanded Dundy suspiciously.

"The Stevenson house," said Spade.

As he spoke a substantial man, who, unlike his deputy, was in uniform, got out of the other car. He had a meaty face with a heavy sandy mustache and bristling brows above muddy eyes. His hat was like those worn by Canadian Mounties in dress uniform. He nodded ponderously to each of them in turn, but thrust his hand out to shake only with Spade.

"Sorry to drag you over here, Sam, but we have questions that need answers."

"Sure you do."

The sheriff led them, slipping and sliding, down over the rocks to the sandy beach. Spade went slowly, favoring his cracked ribs while trying not to show it. He drew a breath between clenched teeth when he jumped down to the beach. The floor of the Stevenson house was fifteen feet above their heads.

"Seems mighty strange the bootleggers know it's safe to land their booze right here in town," said Dundy accusingly.

"Just some of 'em some of the time," said the sheriff. "I

ain't got but two deputies and me to cover the whole damn county, and the feds ain't much help. Sometimes things slip through."

Spade walked in and up under the house to a large rectangle of dug-up sand. Beside it four loglike objects had been laid out in a neat row under heavy tarpaulins.

"Dead men tell no tales," said Spade.

The sheriff had come up beside him. "These sure ain't talkin'. We're relyin' on you to shed some light on events."

"This is where you grabbed Benny Ruiz?"

"We got a tip and snuck down here, an' didn't we find him right here with a shovel in his hand?" said the deputy eagerly.

"Benny was digging them up," said Spade, "not burying them. I asked him to look for Fingers Lisboa and asked him to think about where the *San Anselmo*'s missing gold might be. He must have seen this dug-up sand and thought he'd found it."

"What'd you want with Lisboa?" demanded Dundy.

Spade said to the sheriff, "How long have they been dead?"

"Coroner says different times most like. I wanted you to see 'em here in situ, like the feller says, fore he moved 'em."

Spade went down the row of corpses, stooping to flip the tarps down to expose each of the faces. He showed no reaction. Then he came back, indicating each man in turn.

"This one is Quartermaster Kest from the *San Anselmo,* as Dundy knows full well. This one is Fingers Lisboa. The next one is his cousin Figueiro Mondego. This fourth one is a shiv artist name of Villalba Berlingas."

"We know who they are," barked Dundy. "How come you do?"

Spade looked across the bodies to address Tom Polhaus. "Lisboa, Mondego, and Berlingas are the three thugs I asked you about, Tom, the ones who tried to mug me on the Embarcadero."

Dundy had been standing stiffly, bent at the waist, tensely expectant. Now he almost sprang forward, exclaiming, "Samuel Spade, I arrest you for the murders of—"

"Better ask the sheriff about that," said Spade, stepping neatly out of his grasp. "On this side of the bay you don't have the authority to arrest a dog for lifting its leg."

"That's right, Sergeant," said the sheriff quickly. "In fifteen, when Sam was with Continental, he done a couple of nifty jobs he wouldn't take no credit for. Didn't hurt me none with the voters come election time. So we're gonna let the coroner get at these bodies an' all of us is gonna go up to my office at the San Rafael Courthouse an' we're gonna put our bottoms on our chairs and put our heads together and figger out where we stand 'fore anybody starts arrestin' anybody."

13

Roll Your Dice

"And that was that," said Sam Spade. "I told them what had happened the night the gold was stolen, and who killed those four men, and why, so now Benny Ruiz is out of jail and Dundy'll have to wait for another day to put the cuffs on me."

"That's an explanation that doesn't explain anything."

"Explanations usually don't, Sid."

They were eating lamb chops and roasted potatoes and lettuce and tomatoes in one of the dark-wood back booths at John's Grill on Ellis Street, just a block from Spade's room.

"Who did kill them?" asked Effie Perine.

Spade pointed a carrot stick at her. "I told you all along that your missing passenger who didn't have any luggage—St. Clair McPhee—was the mastermind behind all this."

"Will they get him?"

"He's too slick. But I'm not going to forget him, and someday . . ." He began counting off on his fingers. "Fingers Lisboa dead with the back of his head stove in with a shovel. Kest dead with his throat—"

Wise said in a warning tone, "Sam."

Effie Perine's hand had gone to her throat and her face had turned pale at his offhand descriptions.

"Sorry, sweetheart," said Spade.

"That—that's all right. I need to hear it."

Spade returned to his count. "Kest with his throat cut from ear to ear. The coroner couldn't find a mark on either of the other two thuggers, Mondego and Berlingas, but I'm betting on poison in their whiskey. They knew his face and hadn't enough brains to stay out of trouble. That'd be enough for McPhee."

"How do you connect all four dead men to him?" asked Wise.

Spade leaned back to roll a cigarette, wincing slightly.

"Start at Sydney. That's where the heist was put into play. Previously McPhee had told Kest to switch the strong room locks. McPhee would come aboard at Honolulu. Geaque found that the record shows he'd made that round-trip twice before and could have known that fresh green bananas were stowed on wooden latticework racks on the poop deck with enough room left to work the mooring lines. Until the ship docked at San Francisco, a perfect place for Kest and the two graveyard-watch hands, Grost and Grafton, to hide the five chests of gold they'd stolen."

Wise put a forkful of pink lamb in his mouth and chewed. "Where was McPhee while they looted the strong room?"

"In his stateroom. He didn't want anyone except Kest to know who he was. I think even then he planned to kill Kest."

Effie Perine said, "I can't believe that none of the pursers or cabin boys or crewmen could describe him."

Spade shook his head in disgust. "Oh, they described him. Late twenties, heavy beard, dark-haired, sort of a dandy. But when he boarded at Honolulu he was bundled up despite the climate. Looked frail, claimed to be recuperating from a long illness, so he took his meals in his cabin and never ventured out on deck. Not when anyone could get a look at him, anyway."

"So the chests were hidden on deck under the bananas."

"Sure. McPhee was counting on the ship to arrive here too late for quarantine. It almost always did."

The waiter brought coffee and honey-soaked Greek baklava. Spade ground out his cigarette and was silent until after Effie Perine had poured coffee and passed the sweets.

"That meant the *San Anselmo* would have had to anchor off until dawn. By ten thirty the ship was a seagoing morgue. At, say, one a.m. McPhee got busy. A one-man job aboard, another man with a small boat waiting in under the stern of the ship."

"Fingers Lisboa from Sausalito?" asked Effie Perine.

Spade nodded appreciatively. "You've got it, Effie. McPhee started lowering the chests down to him, one at a time. But the tug showed up early. He only got three chests off-loaded before Lisboa had to leave so he wouldn't get spotted. Predawn, McPhee told Kest to have Grost and Grafton hustle around hiding the rest of the gold aboard ship and dumping the empty chests off the stern, open, so they would sink."

"Tom Polhaus sent divers down to find them like you told him, and found them," said Effie Perine. "It was in the papers."

Sid Wise said, "How do you know all this, Sam?"

"Because it's the only way the facts we have can be fit together to make sense."

"Dundy would think prior knowledge."

"Dundy never thinks. Anyway, our boy disembarked with the rest of the passengers, that night caught the car ferry at the Hyde Street pier to pick up Lisboa in Sausalito. Together they buried the gold under the house in Sausalito." He shook his head. "It's ironic in a way."

"What is, Sam?"

"That's the house where Robert Louis Stevenson lived before he sailed for the South Seas. One of the main reasons Henny Barber wanted to stow away was to see Stevenson's grave up on Mount Vaea in Western Samoa. His romantic dream brought us into the case to mess up McPhee's plans. Once I was in, I wanted to break the robbery and get the guy behind it. From the start something about him—"

"How about Kest?" asked Effie Perine.

"He was always a dead man, he just didn't know it. Getting in a panic and demanding his cut right away got his throat cut sooner. They found his motorcycle below Yellow Bluff."

Wise finished his baklava. "And the three Portagees?"

"I'm just guessing here, but I think that on the day I went to see Benny Ruiz in Larkspur, McPhee was a busy little man. He separated Lisboa from the other two, took him to the Stevenson house. Lisboa would be thinking they were going to dig up the gold where they had buried it. Instead, they dug up the gold and he got his head bashed in. McPhee then lured Mondego and Berlingas to the Stevenson house, fed them whiskey with poison in it to celebrate their success. He was always too smart for the cops." Anger darkened Spade's eyes. "Too smart for me, too. He almost got me on the ferry back from Marin. And still nobody living knows what he really looks like."

"Why *exactly* did McPhee set those men on you and then try to kill you?" asked Effie Perine.

"At first he was worried I might grab Kest, who'd dealt with him face-to-face and could finger him. Then I recovered fifty thousand dollars in specie before he could get it. That frustrated him and he doesn't take frustration easily. And, he likes to kill."

"You're drawing quite a profile of a man you've never met."

The muscles bulged along Spade's jaws. "But I know him just the same, Sid. And one of these days I'll find him."

"Meanwhile, you're looking at trouble from the authorities. Dundy wants the D.A.'s office to go after your license."

"Yeah. I've been summoned to appear in"—Spade checked his watch—"thirty-five minutes."

The interrogation room in the Hall of Justice had a single window so dirty the sunshine-flooded rise of Washington Square below Chinatown was just discernible through it.

Assistant District Attorney Matthew Bryan stood when Sam Spade entered. With Bryan were two men. One had a jovial red Irish drinker's face and red hair. His pulled-down tie had cigarette ash on it. The other man was thin, colorless, with round eyeglasses and a bland face and a mole on his upper lip. He remained seated with a steno pad resting on one knee.

"Samuel Spade?" asked Bryan in a formal, resonant voice.

"Guilty," admitted Spade.

"No attorney with you?"

"I won't need one."

Only then did Bryan, with a gleam of satisfaction in his eye, shake Spade's hand and sit down again. He was just past forty, of medium stature, with a tennis player's fitness. His eyes were blue and aggressive; his black-ribboned nose glasses were for the moment hanging below a wide determined cleft chin. His almost-patrician face had a too-mobile orator's mouth.

"We are here today for a formal exploration of certain charges that have been leveled against you by the San Francisco Police Department, Mr. Spade. Mr. Riley will observe, Mr. Levinger will take shorthand notes. I was not with the district attorney's office when you were a Continental agent in this city, but I have heard that you often acted with little regard for the dignity and solemnity of the law."

"You shouldn't listen to Dundy," said Spade.

"This is not an adversarial procedure, Mr. Spade. We are only interested in the truth here today."

Spade dug in his vest pocket for papers and tobacco. "My truth or your truth?"

"There is only one truth." Bryan raised his glasses and hooked them over his nose, tried to drill Spade with aggressive eyes. "The truth is that you have been operating in a very high-handed manner for the past week."

"And have recovered fifty thousand bucks worth of stolen gold for the International Banking Corporation."

"And let seventy-five thousand slip through your fingers."

"Without me there would have been no recovery at all. I was working a case and ran across the theft by accident."

"Aha! What case? For whom?"

Spade shook his head almost sorrowfully as he rolled and licked his cigarette, lit it. "Sorry, I can't tell you that. A grand jury can maybe make me cough up his name or spend some time in the can, but you—"

The phone on the table rang. The redheaded assistant D.A. stubbed out his own cigarette and picked it up. He listened, hung up, walked quickly out, leaving behind only the whisper of the stenographer's pencil recording his departure. Bryan frowned. The pencil stopped moving. Bryan cleared his throat.

"According to our information, Spade, you knew a great deal about those dead men over in Sausalito."

"One slipped through the cops' fingers after I told them repeatedly to grab him. The other three attacked me a few nights ago on the Embarcadero at midnight."

"You do not strike me as the sort of man to take such assault without seeking redress."

"Maybe I am and maybe I'm not, but I would have to know where they were before I could act, right? I didn't see them again until I was shown their bodies over in Sausalito. And how did they die? One had his throat slit. According to the Marin County coroner, the other two were poisoned. A knife? Poison? Me?" Spade smiled sardonically. "Your truth or mine, Bryan?"

Bryan cleared his throat, perhaps angrily. "Then there's the matter of your impersonating an officer."

"*If* I did, a minor port official." Spade blew smoke from one corner of his mouth. "Nobody who was there has pointed a finger at me."

Bryan began slapping the back of one hand into the palm of the other in time with his words.

"You do not have the power of the Continental Detective Agency behind you now, Spade. You are a lone-wolf operator on the fringes of the law. Your answers to my next two questions will determine whether you retain your license or not."

"Fire away."

"Who was the client you were working for when you ran across the gold theft? And what did your investigation entail?"

"It was a domestic inquiry for a private individual."

"I demand to know his name and the nature of the case!"

"I've said it before, you birds on the city payroll all think the law ought to be what you say it is."

The blood rushed to Bryan's face. "The law is the same for every man or woman, rich or poor, educated or—"

"The law is what I can get away with and stay out of jail."

Bryan pointed an accusing finger across the table. His voice filled the room.

"You've had your chance, Spade! I will move against you with the full power and majesty of this office. You will receive your summons to appear before the grand jury tomorrow." His blue eyes gleamed triumphantly. "I will have your license in my hand by the end of the week."

The door opened and the redheaded Irishman hurried in. He stopped close to Bryan and talked urgently, glancing obliquely at Spade, gesturing with a raised shoulder and movements of his hands and head to indicate something or someone outside the room.

"I see," Bryan said finally in a strangled voice.

Spade stubbed out his cigarette, stood without haste, pulled the points of his vest down, and pointed a finger at Bryan as Bryan had pointed a finger at him.

"You'll be having ambitions to be district attorney—all assistant D.A.'s do. So roll your dice, Bryan. And that's all right, I can find my own way out."

"Something took the wind out of his sails, Sid."

Spade was sitting across from the diminutive attorney, his hat balanced on the near corner of Wise's desk.

"Charles Hendrickson Barber," said Wise.

Spade got a startled look on his face. "I just got raked over the coals for refusing to divulge his name to Bryan."

"Oh, Barber wouldn't do anything as compromising as appear in this thing personally." Wise began playing with the pencil on his desk. "But apart from being president of Golden Gate Trust, he's also president of Golden Gate Saving Trust. He has a hand in the commission house of Kittle and Company. He's a director of the Shipowners' and Merchants' Tugboat Company and was vice president of the nineteen fifteen Panama Pacific International Exposition. He's a real power in this city, Sam, and—"

"And that's why he came to you to hire someone to find his son when the kid ran off. He didn't want his power-structure cronies to know there was trouble in the Barber family."

"That's also why I called him and told him Bryan was going to try and get his name out of you. I said he had nothing to worry about, you were a boulder without a fissure, but . . ."

Spade pulled his brows down in a black frown. "I can rake my own chestnuts out of the fire, Sid." His face brightened, he stood, picked up his hat. "Still, it's not so bad to declare our weight and come out punching. Because Barber made a phone call and someone dropped by the hall, I won't have to be dodging a summons and complaint from Bryan any time soon."

"I'm glad you're pleased," said Wise drily.

"When I'm not, Sid, you'll be the first to know."

He found Effie Perine making diagonal cuts across the long stems of a dozen red roses.

"Secret admirer?" he asked.

"Of you," she said ruefully. "Mrs. Barber sent them."

His eyes gleamed theatrically. "Mrs. Barber, huh? Any calls? Any clients waiting in my office?"

"Nothing. I think the whole town knows that the district attorney's office had you on the carpet all morning." Her face turned serious. "How do we stand, Sam?"

"On our own two feet." He sat down across from her. "Here's how it works, sweetheart. The cops don't like us. The D.A. doesn't like us. City Hall doesn't like us. But even though they're going to welsh on the reward money, the International Banking Corporation does like us. Because Charles Barber's son is back in the fold unharmed, Barber likes us."

"What good does all of that do us, Sam?"

"Just this: this city's big-money circles will know that and take it into account when they need an investigator who isn't with one of the big agencies and can keep his trap shut." He took the cigarette she had rolled him, lit it, blew smoke luxuriously at the ceiling. "Which will translate into a better class of client who will pay bigger fees for our services."

"Does it translate into a better office in a better part of town?" she asked.

"Not yet. I need a lot of people to talk to me because they feel they can trust me. Too much flash makes 'em nervous." He ground his fag out in her ashtray, stood. "But as of now you're on the payroll full-time at twenty-five bucks a week. Tell that to your mother."

She was on her feet also, eyes alight. But all she said was "She likes you, you know. She trusts you won't get her little girl into any trouble you can't get her out of."

"Does that mean I can use your mother as an informant in the Greek community?"

"You're an impossible man, Samuel Spade!" she exclaimed.

He started toward his private office, then paused and turned back. "When you finish with those roses, you'd better make a file headed 'St. Clair McPhee.' We don't have anything to put in it—yet. But I'm betting we will."

He went on and shut the door. Effie Perine began arranging the roses in a vase. She began softly singing the refrain from "Ain't We Got Fun?" to herself as she worked.

In the morning,
In the evening,
Ain't we got fun?

The phone rang. She stopped singing to pick up.

"Samuel Spade Investigations."

She grabbed her steno pad and started making notes.

1925

Three Women

The chief business of the American people is business.

—Calvin Coolidge

14

The Eberhard Death

Apparently aimless, Samuel Spade wandered through the throng lying or sitting or picnicking on the grassy slope above the Fleishhacker Pool. Crowds of people in bathing costumes, summer frocks, and shirtsleeves were enjoying the warm, sunny day, rare out near the beach at the foot of Sloat Boulevard.

Spade was tieless, collarless, in rolled-up shirtsleeves, his suit coat slung over one shoulder with his forefinger hooked through the loop inside the back of the collar. The *Chronicle* for Saturday, September 12, 1925, was folded in a coat pocket.

He worked his way through the border of low pine trees and bushes to come up behind a mid-forties sandy-haired man standing at the edge of the vast outdoor plunge. The bright horizontal pattern of the man's V-neck cricket sweater emphasized his thickening waist. A light breeze mingled the sharp salt tang of the ocean with the clean fragrance of the evergreens.

"What brings us out here on a sunny Saturday, Ray?"

Ray Kentzler turned to look at Spade. He had a square Germanic head and a pleasant broad-mouthed face with pale, smart, watchful eyes under blond brows.

"I'm working this one outside the system, Sam."

"Fair enough. But who's paying me, if it comes to that?"

"Oh, Bankers' Life—if it comes to that." He moved his head slightly. "C'mon, let's walk; I've been wanting to get a gander at this place since it opened."

"Largest outdoor pool in the country," said Spade solemnly.

But Kentzler took his gibe at face value.

"Open maybe four months. Three city blocks long, nearly half a football field wide, six and a half million gallons of warmed circulating seawater. Twenty lifeguards on duty—"

"Who need rowboats to go out and get anyone who's in trouble, the pool's so big. If your wife was at one end, Ray, she wouldn't be able to identify your kid at the other end."

"Probably wouldn't want to," said Kentzler.

"They built it in the wrong place. It should be down the peninsula near Stanford, where they get hot weather."

"I notice you have your coat off, Sam."

"And in another hour, when that fog rolls in from the ocean, you'll notice I have it back on again."

They strolled through drifting adults and running kids, past tulip-shaped light fixtures on tall metal poles.

"Let me buy you a late lunch, Sam."

At the bathhouse, 450 feet long, done in Italian Renaissance style, with a glazed tile roof and dining rooms on the second floor, they chose the room looking out toward the ocean rather than the one facing east over the pool toward Lake Merced. Their salads arrived, along with Boston clam chowder for Spade and oysters for Kentzler. The insurance man leaned across the table, his voice low and confidential.

"There's a big life insurance policy at Bankers' Life I can't talk to anyone at the office about because we've privately agreed to settle even though we aren't admitting it yet. But . . . I'm bothered. What do you know about the Collin Eberhard death?"

"What's been in the papers. He was swimming in the bay out in front of the Neptune Bath House when he got into difficulty. Some witnesses say he was struggling against the current, others say he was just floating facedown. They rowed out in a small boat to rescue him, but he was already dead. The tabloids started hinting that there were rumors of irregularities at California-Citizens Bank, where he was founder and president."

"Are you sure you didn't *memorize* the papers?"

"Then they decided that he was financially ruined and because of that had taken out a very large life insurance policy in favor of his wife and then ingested a vial of poison. I don't know what made them come up with that, but it sold a lot of newspapers." Spade pulled the folded *Chronicle* from his suit coat pocket and slapped it on the table. "It still does. Today's big question seems to be whether he died of suicide, accident, or natural causes."

"Yeah. The autopsy was held seventeen hours after his death and the coroner held the inquest two weeks ago—"

"With you guys pushing for suicide. Because the policy hadn't been in effect long enough for you to have to pay off if he killed himself, suicide would let you off the hook."

"Can you blame us? This is a lot of money that would go to the widow, Sam—I mean a *lot* of money. Bankers' Life's money."

Spade stopped spooning soup with an abrupt growl.

"I don't blame anybody for anything. But I don't work domestic cases, I don't take pennies off dead men's eyes, and I don't pick the pockets of new widows."

"What do you know about this one?"

"Nothing, Ray. Not a thing."

"She's nine years younger than Eberhard was. Married him seven—no, eight years ago, just about when he founded his little private bank. They were struggling. Just scraping by. Then four years ago the bank started growing, getting prosperous. He started getting rich. She was suddenly sitting pretty. A lot of money and no children. She didn't want any."

"Did he?"

Kentzler looked surprised. "I don't know. But I do know that once you know rich, you don't want to know poor again. I think she could be the sort of widow who'd fill up those pockets you talk about by defrauding the insurance company."

"Dear, you're in trouble at the bank and you've got this huge life insurance policy, so let me help you poison yourself?"

"You can laugh, but even so—"

"You're saying there was?"

"What?"

"Collusion on her part?"

"How the hell do I know? I just want to find out one way or the other. If everything's jake, then OK, the wife honestly should get her big payoff. If it's suicide I want to keep her from getting one thin dime."

"What do the forensics say?"

"Unclear. Natural causes, suicide, even murder—it could have been any of them. But who except the wife would benefit if it was murder, and how would she have rigged it? That's why I dragged you down here today. You did such a good recovery job for us on that Pasadena bearer-bond theft—"

Spade grinned sardonically and returned to his chowder. Kentzler finished his oysters and began slathering butter on a warm, light-as-air popover.

"OK, I'll skip the soft soap, Sam. I came to you because you're tough, nasty, smart, and bullheaded. I'll be sending a copy of the autopsy report over to your office on Monday."

"It's a man. He's dead. That's all I need to know unless something in the report shows that someone else made him dead."

"There's something screwy about the Eberhard death," said Kentzler gloomily. "I just can't put my finger on it. At the coroner's inquest it was suggested that maybe he died of asphyxia with cerebral congestion. Or maybe he died of shock. Or maybe he died of a stroke."

"Or maybe he died of old age at age forty-nine."

"The only really sure thing about it is that Collin Eberhard did not die by drowning. No water in the lungs."

"So he didn't die by drowning." Spade began rolling a cigarette while Kentzler called for the dessert menu. "But how do we get from there to suicide—or murder? I take it there was indeed cerebral congestion but no fracture of the cranial bones. Anything in the stomach to suggest that he was poisoned?"

"Nothing. But during the inquest the coroner said that a preparation of opium could produce cerebral congestion, kill you quickly, sometimes without leaving any mark on the stomach wall."

"If he wanted to kill himself and hide the fact, why not just accidentally fall off a ferryboat some foggy night? If he *was* poisoned—and you say there's no physical indication of that—I'd as lief say it was murder as suicide. But murder wouldn't get Bankers' Life off the hook, would it?"

"No," mumbled Kentzler around a big mouthful of chocolate cake. "But the coroner's jury was composed entirely of Eberhard's friends, who ignored the puzzling details and said it was a stroke as a result of cerebral congestion that killed him. We have privately *almost* decided on a settlement with the wife, even though the possibility of poison has not been ruled out."

"All I know about poisons is what I read in *The Count of Monte Cristo* when I was a kid. Take a small but increasingly larger dose of arsenic every day and you build up an immunity to it. I don't even know if that's true of arsenic, let alone opium."

"Sausalito, four years ago," said Kentzler. "You were involved in a case where two men were poisoned in connection with the gold theft off the *San Anselmo*."

Spade's face changed, darkened. "St. Clair McPhee," he said. "Disappeared without a trace."

"And that bothers you? After all this time?"

"I keep an almost-empty file on him," Spade admitted almost ruefully. "I hate being made a sucker of. Someday I'll figure out where he went, and how, and I'll find him . . ." He shrugged. "It was the Marin coroner who said the two Portagees were poisoned, not me. I never even read his autopsy report."

"Well, you're going to read this one," said Kentzler.

15

The Man with No Name

At 8:30 Monday morning Sam Spade bounded up the stairs to his office above Remedial Loans on Mission Street whistling "Gut Bucket Blues" slightly off-key. He found Effie Perine staring with uncomprehending eyes at an oblong of colored paper.

"What's this, Sam?"

He went around behind her desk to look at it over her shoulder as if he had not stuck it between the pages of her shorthand pad after she had gone home on Friday night.

"A check for fifty bucks. Last week's wages."

"I don't make fifty dollars a—"

"It's nineteen twenty-five. Yesterday was your twenty-first birthday. Today you can vote. Today you can make fifty bucks a week. How was the surprise party your Greek friends threw for you Saturday?"

"How did you know about that?"

"Your mother called on Friday to make sure I wouldn't

have you working over the weekend." He paused in the doorway of his office. "You'll earn it, sister, and then some. Any calls?"

She slowly settled back in her chair. "No. But a document was delivered by messenger from Ray Kentzler."

"It's an autopsy report. Open a file on Eberhard, Collin. Leave the 'Client' space blank, but it's Bankers' Life."

Her face lit up. "They're saying he poisoned himself."

"They're probably wrong. But see can you round up the newspaper coverage on Eberhard since his death."

Spade went down a long brown linoleum hallway on the ground floor of the Hall of Justice in Kearny Street, his footsteps echoing hollowly. Motes of suspended dust moved with him as he went in the door marked CORONER'S OFFICE.

Behind the anteroom desk was a middle-aged woman with gray hair pulled into a bun held in place by a tortoise-shell comb. She wore a shapeless gingham apron frock with a square-cut collar. Flowers doing poorly on the left front corner of the desk did little to brighten the room.

She looked up from typing a form to ask sharply, "Yes?"

"Dr. Leland, please. About the Collin Eberhard autopsy."

"The coroner is in conference. The chief deputy is in conference. The assistant deputies are in conference."

"This is a public office. I'm a citizen. I'll wait."

He took a chair against the wall, leaned back, stuck his legs out straight in front of him, crossed them at the ankles, and tipped his hat down over his eyes. He began to hum, very softly, "Sweet Georgia Brown."

She said almost shrilly, "If you don't stop that I'm going to call upstairs for a police officer to escort you—"

Spade lifted his hat to say, "Try Tom Polhaus in Homicide."

He lowered the hat again. He resumed his humming. After long moments her chair creaked. He raised his hat brim enough to see her disappearing through the door behind her desk. Her dress was taut across an ample backside. He grinned, took off his hat.

Ten minutes later she reappeared, followed by a square, chunky man with a wide face and dark hair low on his forehead. He jerked a thumb at Spade. "You. In here."

Spade sauntered across the room, bowing slightly to the woman as he passed. He followed the man through a suite of offices to a cubicle with no windows and a lot of paperwork on a battered blond-wood desk. The room smelled of cigar smoke and, very faintly, disinfectant. The square man sat down behind the desk. He did not offer to shake hands, instead tented his fingers, half-sneered as Spade sat down across from him.

"Assistant Deputy Coroner Adolf Klinger. We're sick of you newshounds coming around with your lies and innuendos. The coroner's jury has rendered its verdict upon the Eberhard matter. Natural causes. We have released the body for burial. Period."

"Not a newshawk." Spade laid a business card on the desk. "The autopsy report showed blood, not water, in Eberhard's lungs, and serum blood in the right ventricle of his heart. So it was not a drowning. And there also was bleeding through the scalp."

"And no lacerations," snapped Klinger. "The blood was from the cerebral congestion that brought on the fatal stroke."

"Did anyone ever follow up on the statement at the inquest that a lethal concoction of opium sometimes leaves no discernible trace in the stomach lining?"

Klinger sneered again. "No discernible trace. You said it yourself. No evidence of anything." He stood up, jerked a thumb again, this time at the door. "Private op, huh? Take the air."

In the drab, crowded detectives' assembly room on the hall's third floor Spade found Tom Polhaus and Dundy, both newly promoted to the San Francisco Homicide Detail.

"Congratulations, Sergeant Polhaus," Spade said to Tom; then, to Dundy, with no trace of irony in his voice, "And congratulations on your promotion too, Lieutenant Dundy."

Dundy looked at him suspiciously, said gruffly, "Thanks, Spade," then couldn't refrain from "What brings you here?"

"Collin Eberhard."

"Oh. That." Dundy gave a contemptuous bark of laughter. "That one's dead and buried."

"Just trying to drum up a little business. His widow's going to be mighty well off if they can't prove suicide." Spade hooked a hip over the corner of a desk. "You boys got anything to add to what's in Eberhard's autopsy report?"

Dundy uttered something that sounded like "pfaw,"

waved a dismissive hand, said, "I'm sure you'll come up with some angle to make money off it, Spade. You always do."

Spade nodded, said to Polhaus, "Let's take a walk."

They crossed Kearny Street to the gentle green slope of Portsmouth Square. It was another sunny September day, so they sat on the grass below the Stevenson monument.

"OK," said Polhaus, "what's this really about, Sam?"

"What I said. The Eberhard death. I've got a client."

"The widow?"

"I couldn't tell you even if she was."

"If not her, then the insurance company," said Polhaus with smug finality. "There's no one else got enough money to pay you except the tabloids, and I don't figure you'd work for them."

"What do you have on Eberhard?"

Polhaus tipped his hat down over his eyes against the sun, gave a disgusted grunt. "Not a damned thing. Oh, I know the newspapers are still screaming about suicide because of something wrong at the bank or in his personal finances. Course we'd love to pin a murder rap on the widow, but I figure the coroner's jury got it right. Cerebral congestion and a stroke."

"Did you read the autopsy report?"

"Like the lieutenant said, that one's dead and buried. Literally. They released the body for burial. Why don't you go talk to the coroner's office if you're so all-fired interested?"

"I just came from there. All I got was a stiff-arm from an assistant coroner named Klinger."

"Him. Their troubleshooter." Tom chuckled; then unease entered his face. "*Should* we have an open file on Eberhard?"

Spade idly watched the hips of a stylishly dressed young matron pushing a pram up the walk that flanked the square.

"Even back in sixteen, when I went up to Seattle for Continental, people were bellyaching that San Francisco coroner's inquests had the weight of a legal proceeding even though coroners weren't trained in the law. That's a perfect setup for a packed jury. This one was made up of pals of Eberhard."

"I ain't gonna cry over big insurance takin' a K.O."

"It came out at the inquest that a lethal dose of opium can be hard to detect in the stomach lining."

"You're grabbin' at straws, Sam. Opium's easy to get, right enough, but the wife wasn't at the Neptune Bath House."

"Maybe he did it himself. Maybe the newspapers are right."

"In that case it was suicide and the Homicide Detail don't care anyway 'cause the guy made himself dead." With a grunt Polhaus heaved himself to his feet and brushed off the seat of his pants with both hands. He looked down at Spade. "You get something, Sam, you come to us with it first."

"You're starting to sound like Dundy. The case is dead and buried, but if it isn't we want you to solve it for us."

Polhaus started off down the slope. "Aw, go to hell."

Spade chuckled and stubbed out his cigarette on Stevenson's left foot.

. . . .

The Neptune Bath House, for men only, was built back from the curved sandy beach just west of the Hyde Street Pier. It had a thirty-yard pool and shower, steam, massage, and locker rooms.

Spade paid his two bits for a swimsuit, towel, and locker he had no intention of using. He sat down on a bench. A half dozen affluent-looking men were changing in the locker room, several with setups of ice and ginger ale for the bottles of whiskey they had taken out of their lockers. The damp air was heavy with the smell of salt water and liniment.

Spade gestured the towel boy over. He was a kid of maybe fourteen, towheaded and skinny, with knobby knees and, like a Labrador puppy, feet too big for the rest of him.

"Whaddaya need, mister?"

"I hear some rich guy drowned out in the bay just off the bathhouse three weeks ago. Were you here that day?"

"Yeah." The boy's round blue eyes tried to look crafty. "What's in it for me?"

Spade flipped him a quarter. He palmed it expertly, looked around, sat down on the bench.

Spade started rolling a cigarette, asked without looking up, "What's your name, son?"

"Jerry." He added in a wise guy voice, "What's yours?"

"Sam. Tell me about it. Kids always know everything."

Jerry's face got excited. He darted his eyes around. "You think he didn't drown? You think he was murdered?"

"Sure. Why not?"

"Who do you suspect?"

"You."

Jerry got a startled look on his face, then started to giggle and was no longer a wise guy, just a towheaded kid.

"I can't see nobody putting poison in his own booze and then just goin' out swimmin'. Wasn't nobody done it to him neither. There was five or six of 'em smokin' cigars an' havin' their drinks outta the bottle from Mr. Eberhard's locker. They all would of died!"

"His locker always locked when he wasn't around?"

"Sure. They all are. All these guys, they're bankers an' big industrialists an' shipowners or somethin'."

"All regulars? Any you didn't know?"

Jerry didn't have to think. "Only one guy. I saw him talkin' with Mr. Eberhard over near the shower room where nobody could hear 'em like. Mr. Eberhard started out kinda red in the face. Then the other guy sorta sighed and shrugged an' looked sheepish, and Mr. Eberhard looked pleased an' took him over to have a drink with the others. None of them know him neither."

"What'd he look like?"

"Dark hair, eyes that could sorta look right through you."

"Big man? Little man? Fat? Thin? Young? Old?"

"Wouldn't of weighed a whole lot, but sorta strong an' quick lookin' even so. Like maybe he played tennis or somethin'." Disdain entered Jerry's voice. "He had little hands and feet, made him look like a dancer sort of. A—whadda they call them guys what live off of women?"

"A gigolo?"

"A gigolo! Yeah! That's it! But he was sorta old for that. Not like them bankers, not old like that. Maybe old like you an' my old man. They had their drinks; he went back out to the street while Mr. Eberhard was goin' down to the beach."

Spade stubbed out his cigarette and tossed the butt into a trash bucket. As he spun Jerry a silver dollar, a man across the room yelled, "Boy, bring me a couple of fresh towels chop-chop!"

Spade stopped at the Neptune Bath House office, but nobody admitted knowing anything about the stranger who had been there on the day of Eberhard's death. Eberhard had not formally signed him in as a guest so there was no record of him. They refused to name the other men in the group that day.

16

The Grieving Widow

It was a four-story Pacific Heights brownstone, not quite a mansion, perched above the 2400 block of Broadway. Spade mounted a steep flight of stairs between trimmed boxwood hedges to a gleaming marble landing. The brass door knocker was polished to a high gloss. He used it.

After thirty seconds the ornate hardwood door was opened by a German woman in a maid's uniform, unsmiling, eyes watchful, mouth determined. Spade removed his hat and proffered a card stating that he represented the Bankers' Life Insurance Company.

He said pleasantly, "I have come concerning the policy we carried on the late Mr. Eberhard."

"God rest his soul. I will see if Madame is at home."

The door shut. Spade turned to look over Cow Hollow to the low whaleback hump of Alcatraz Island out in the bay. Below him a brown and white gaff-rigged ketch, made a toy by distance, was just entering the harbor between the long finger of jetty and the Marina Green. A dozen sailboats were in their berths at the San Francisco Yacht Club. The sun was still warm, but tendrils of fog were ghosting their way through the Golden Gate between Fort Point and the Marin headlands. A Matson steamship was heading out toward the open Pacific.

"Madame will see you now."

On either side of the foyer, deeply carpeted, exquisitely appointed rooms fronting Broadway were illuminated by sunlight coming through open-curtained windows. Kitty-corner before one window was a Steinway baby grand with sheet music on its rack. Spade followed the German woman's stout figure down a maroon hallway runner of intricate design. She knocked on the frame of an open doorway, stepped aside.

"You may go in."

It was a library given over to dark leather-bound volumes. A woman sat in a leather armchair with an open book in her lap. A reading lamp was directed over her left shoulder, leaving her features in relative obscurity. On the reading table was a half-full cut glass cognac decanter and an empty snifter. Also a humidor and a crystal ashtray with a fresh, unlit corona del Ritz laid at an angle across it.

"Tea, Hilda," the woman said. As the maid wordlessly withdrew, the woman held out a hand palm down, fingers bent: royalty bestowing a favor. Spade bowed over the hand, released it. He chose a French Chippendale chair with elaborate Louis XV decorations on arms and back.

"This was my husband's hideaway from his responsibilities, mainly me. He would sit in here for hours on end, smoking costly cigars and sipping costly cognac and reading the Victorians with their insufferable sentimentality." She shifted the volume in her lap. "The last book he was reading. Fitting. *Bleak House.*"

Evelyn Eberhard was a handsome woman except for faint bitter crow's-feet at the corners of dark eyes deep set under exquisitely arched brows. She was pale of visage, her mouth was generous but thin lipped without discernible lip rouge, her hair youthfully cut, with pin curls at the temples.

"On those evenings I was barred from this room. I did not mind. I never liked it. But since Collin's death I have often found myself in here. I wonder why?"

"Looking for a connection to whatever it was he withheld from you when he was alive."

She looked surprised, even startled. "Freudian analysis from a"—she paused, then continued with subtle, not easily explained irony—"an insurance adjuster?"

Hilda silently wheeled in a tea wagon with a cozy-covered teapot on it, two Meissen china cups, silverware, milk and sugar in matching pitcher and bowl, lemon slices, small plates, and an assortment of tea cookies. She hovered as if about to pour.

"That will be all, Hilda." Evelyn Eberhard added, an oddly sharp note in her voice, "And shut the door behind you."

The maid departed, irritation in her movements.

The widow leaned forward to pour two cups of steaming Darjeeling. Her hands were long fingered, shapely. Her high-necked pale blue dress had ruffles at throat and wrists, a cinched waist that emphasized a shapely bosom. Crossed legs under the floor-length skirt suggested well-rounded thighs.

She chose milk and sugar; Spade, nothing. They sipped.

"Hilda was with Collin before our marriage. After the bank prospered, Collin became distant, he and I drifted apart. Hilda decided that I had become indifferent to his needs and wants, and would love to have Bankers' Life refuse payment on the policy."

"Were you indifferent?"

"In those later years, yes. We were in love at the outset. Ironically, when we became prosperous intimacy left our marriage. But Collin was an upright man. Which makes it unfair, you people trying to renege on your legal commitment to me."

"There have been suggestions of irregularities at your husband's bank and in his personal finances."

"I know nothing of his financial activities except what is hinted at in the tabloids. Collin did not keep an office in our home." She looked directly at him. "And should we stop sparring, you and me, Mr. Spade? You're no insurance agent. You're a private investigator with a shady reputation and a grubby little office on Mission Street above a loan company."

Spade ignored this. "There have been hints of murder."

"Murder, natural causes—they'd still have to pay off on anything except suicide." Her low laugh had intimacy in it. "Unless you could convince the authorities that I poisoned him."

"Did you?"

She leaned forward with a furious intensity that slopped tea into the saucer, which she held beneath her cup with her left hand, saying, "I won't dignify that with a reply," then immediately did so. "Women are barred from the Neptune Bath House."

"Maybe you snuck in when no one was looking and gave him a good dose of asphyxia with cerebral congestion."

Her laugh was full-bodied, not in keeping with her status as a widow. "I should be furious that you can make light of my husband's death. But—the image . . ." She nodded as if to herself. "I think you'll do." She opened the humidor, held it out to Spade. "Would you like a cigar?"

He selected one; she picked up the corona del Ritz from the ashtray. Spade trimmed the ends with his penknife and lit both cigars with his lighter, hers first.

He said, "You're unconventional. You work very hard to avoid the usual grieving-widow platitudes." He gestured toward her left hand. "Only three weeks dead and no wedding band."

"I was a woman trapped in a decaying marriage."

"You think I'll do for what?"

"My husband was a great friend of Charles Hendrickson Barber. Barber's wife, Rose, has been a good friend since my marriage. She told me about your finding Henny before he could stow away on some ocean liner and said you kept it out of the papers. She recommended you. She said you were trustworthy."

"Recommended me for what?"

"Collin was always a womanizer. Six months ago I became obsessed with identifying his then-current mistress because I believed the affair had become much deeper than a momentary infatuation, like the others. I believed he was finding with her, whoever she was, the—the comfort, the security, he once found with me."

"I don't do domestic," said Spade almost automatically.

A dismissive gesture with her cigar. "I was not seeking grounds for divorce. I was defending my position as wife. I abandoned the idea for two reasons. First, I had a very good life even if there was no love left in it. Second, I came to realize that whatever decision Collin had been struggling with during the past year was related to business, not to his private affairs. Then, in quick order, he took out a huge insurance policy with me as beneficiary. Then he died. Then he was suddenly reputed to have been ruined financially."

"Was he?"

"I have no idea. When the innuendo began about poison and suicide or, worse, murder, I realized that if he indeed had been ruined financially, suicide was possible and I might be denied the insurance money. Without that money I will lose everything I value. A life of ease. This house. My social position. Everything."

"No idea who the mistress was?"

"None. She was surely not of our circle." The thin lips twisted in a sudden, almost startling sneer. "I need you to find her. If he was in love with her, wouldn't that make suicide much less likely? I will pay you of course."

Spade stood, stubbed out his cigar in the ashtray. "Get me access to your husband's records at the bank and I'll find your mistress for you. She'll be somewhere in his papers. Canceled checks paid to her, department store bills, a love nest somewhere, weekends at a Sonoma resort."

"Impossible." For the first time she rose. In the two-inch

heels on her chic black patent leather shoes she was only some two inches shorter than Spade's six-foot-and-a-fraction-inch height. "Not because I refuse. Because the bank insists his financial records cannot be viewed."

"Not even by his widow?"

"Sometimes I think especially not by his widow."

"Well, there are ways." As if it were an afterthought he asked, "Did your husband have a friend, business aquaintance, what have you, who was about my age, dark hair, piercing eyes, built like a tennis player but with small, almost delicate hands and feet, maybe something of the dancer about him?"

She stood frowning, head cocked slightly in thought.

"Such a man was here one evening with Collin, in this room, for an hour or more. Just the one time, maybe a week before my husband's death. There were raised voices, but that was all."

"You couldn't hear anything that was said?"

"I do not snoop at doors, Mr. Spade. Is he important?"

"Darned if I know. Probably not. But he was in the group at the Neptune Bath House that day. If your husband was trying to make some financial decision, this man might play into it." He made an irritated gesture. "I need to get into those bank files, Mrs. Eberhard. I know a good attorney."

"It's in my interest that you see them, but the bank says no. In the face of that refusal I'm afraid to do anything that might hinder my getting the insurance money."

"If you change your mind . . ."

She gave him her hand. A firm grip, warm fingers. "I will surely let you know," she said.

17

Veiled Threats?

It was 2:55, five minutes before the official end of banking hours, when Spade went between flanking Doric pillars and through the inset decorative doorway of California-Citizens Bank at 832 California. Below the bank, at Grant, was Old St. Mary's Church; above it, on Powell Street at the crest of the hill, the Fairmont Hotel. A streetcar slowly climbed past, its wheels clacking on the tracks.

Inside to the left, behind a cast-iron divider decorated with the figure of a miner panning for gold, was a desk with no one behind it and no papers upon it. Its brass plaque read:

VICTOR SPAULDING
Vice President

Spade stood in line at the only teller's window that was still open. By the time Spade's turn had come an elderly uniformed bank guard had locked the front door and was letting out the last few patrons.

Spade told the teller, "I would like to speak with Vice President Spaulding concerning the bank's late president."

He was a slender youth with sandy hair that obviously resisted all efforts to tame it. He let his eyes slide sideways.

"Mr. Spaulding doesn't seem to be at his desk. He may be gone for the night."

"I have an appointment."

Spade sat down in the armchair facing Spaulding's desk. The youth fidgeted, closed his window, went through a door behind the cages, shutting it behind him. Spade heard the sound of an elevator. Five minutes later the teller returned, started closing out his cash drawer while managing not to look at Spade.

Two minutes after that a man in his forties came through the doorway behind the teller. He was of medium height, round faced, clean-shaven, nervous handed, slightly stoop shouldered, with receding black hair and a pince-nez on a cord fastened to his lapel buttonhole.

Spade stood, hand out. "Samuel Spade."

Spaulding took his hand very briefly, gave it a single shake, released it. His hand was soft, moist, short fingered. He sat down behind his desk as if it were a bastion.

"I do not recall any appointment with anyone named Spade."

Spade laid one of his business cards on the desk.

Spaulding read it, began shaking his head slowly. Perspiration shone on his forehead. His narrow mouth had gotten more and more pursed, as if he were tasting a lemon.

Spade said, "I have been hired to arrange a time when Mr. Eberhard's personal and business records may be examined. She—ah, my client has a legitimate interest in these affairs."

"She does not! No one outside this bank does. Bank records are always kept confidential. Always."

"Not from Eberhard's heir," said Spade coldly.

Spaulding's face cleared. He said in an almost smug voice, "The police have instructed us to open Mr. Eberhard's records to no one until their investigation is complete."

"This morning Lieutenant Dundy of the Homicide Detail told me the Eberhard matter was 'dead and buried.' His words." Spade was genial. "So the bank has no legitimate reason to sequester the records from"—a pause for emphasis—"my client."

Spaulding was shaking his head again, this time stubbornly.

"Let her take it up with our attorneys."

Spade stood, nodded pleasantly, put on his hat. "If I have to take more direct steps you will find them very distressing."

Spaulding was on his feet also, face flushed. "Are you making veiled threats against me? Against this financial institution? I'll have you know that . . ."

But Spade had walked away, leaving the banker rigid behind his desk, haranguing thin air. The old guard opened the door, said out of the side of his mouth, "Nasty sort, ain't he?"

Spade grinned. "So am I, my friend."

As he started up California Street, a swaggering Italian youth hopped off a streetcar while it was still moving. Spade hunched as if lighting a cigarette so he could watch the youth trot slantwise across California to the bank.

"Lemme in, you old goat," he yelled at the guard.

"Gino Mechetti," muttered Spade. "After hours at that."

It was after 6 when he got back to his office. There was an orderly sheaf of folded newspaper pages on the front corner of his desk, with a note: "Collin Eberhard coverage to date." Beside it were four memo slips with messages and phone numbers on them. Standing beside the desk he flicked through them, apparently found nothing of importance, tossed them aside.

Spade left the office with the newspapers folded under one arm. On Market he caught an F car up Stockton, got off at Broadway. At O Sole Mio at 506 Broadway, a small Italian restaurant redolent with garlic and spices, he checked his hat and bundle of newspapers with the coat-check girl. A wide, curly-haired man named Romeo Mechetti came trotting up to shake Spade's hand, then took him by the elbow to lead him to a table.

"Mama, she ask, 'Why Sam never come see us no more since we open up our new place here?' "

"Got a living to make, Romeo," said Spade. "It looks like you're doing well up here above Chinatown."

"Wait till you taste the food," boasted Romeo.

Dinner was forty-five cents. It was good and there was plenty of it. Spade made up for his missed lunch with a salad; an antipasto platter of salami, celery, olives, carrots, and peppers; ravioli; tripe with sausage and beans. He drank red wine served in a coffee cup, as was usual at the North Beach family-owned Italian cafés, to disguise that the cup held vino, not coffee.

People ate, laughed, talked loudly, smoked until the air was heavy with fumes. Spade contributed his share, finished with genuine coffee and homemade cookies. Twice Romeo came by to chat; the second time he sat down.

"I never got no chance to thank you, Mr. Spade."

"Thank me for what?"

"For what you done for my oldest boy, Gino. Since he got out he's going straight." Romeo clapped Spade on the back. "Best thing ever happened to him, you sending him away for those two years on that warehouse break-in. Now he's got a real job, night-time security at a bank."

"That's good news, Romeo." Spade seemed struck by a sudden thought. "You know, if you tell Gino to come by my office, I might have a little day work for him as well. He can make a buck or two." He winked. "An *honest* buck or two."

"*Ei,* Sam, *gli piacerebbe!*" Romeo gave a great laugh. "*Scusi,* sometimes I forgetta you no Italian. Gino, I tell him to come by your office."

Soon after, Spade retrieved hat and newspapers. He got off the Stockton car at Sutter, rode the trolley out to Hyde, walked down the steep incline to 891 Post. The clanking, groaning elevator deposited him at the fourth floor. Spade went around the corner and down the hall.

In the corner apartment he had rented the year before, Spade hung his hat and topcoat on hooks behind the door, went down a short hall that right-angled into the living room, switched on the white bowl light hanging from three gilded chains in the center of the ceiling. He tossed his newspapers on the sofa under the Post Street window.

From the kitchen he got a wine glass and a bottle of Bacardi. He set them on the floor beside a padded rocker angled in the corner, sat down, poured, sipped, rolled a cigarette. Only then did he start going through his sheaf of newspapers.

The battered alarm clock on the table in the far corner of the room read 1:22 when Spade tossed the last of the papers aside. The clock rested on *Criminal Investigation: A Practical Handbook* by the Austrian criminal investigator Hans Gross, published in English in London the year before.

Spade stood up, stretched, yawned, and groaned.

"Waste of time," he muttered to himself.

He got green-and-white pajamas from the closet, went into the bathroom for his ablutions, came out wearing the pajamas, and lowered the wall bed. He turned out the overhead light, wound the alarm clock, and threw open both windows. Shocking gusts of cold fog-laden air swept in, bringing with it the mournful bellow of the Alcatraz foghorn. He was soon asleep.

18

Drawing Blood

When Spade came into his office the next morning Miles Archer had a hip hooked over the corner of Effie Perine's desk, was leaning his jovial red face down close to hers, chuckling at something he was telling her.

"So the girl says to him, 'I don't drink anything but champagne, and he says—' "

" 'Lo, Miles," said Spade. "When did you hit town?"

Archer quickly straightened up like an errant schoolboy, paused, extended his hand. Behind his back Effie Perine was making exaggerated faces of relief. Spade and Archer shook.

"Two days ago. Iva's with me. We came down to see my brother Phil over in the East Bay."

"I see you've met my secretary, Effie Perine."

Archer looked over appreciatively at her. "Sure did." He invested his comment with more meaning than his words carried. He turned back. "Ah . . . Iva asked could we buy you dinner tonight?"

Spade shrugged. "Sure. I'll pick the spot."

They talked for another minute as Spade walked him to the door. They shook hands again, then he was gone.

"How do you know him?" Effie Perine asked in a neutral voice.

"He's with Burns up in Seattle. He's good at taking down Commies on the docks. You want to come with us tonight—"

"I've got a date to go dancing," she said too quickly.

Spade chuckled and went into his private office.

Gino Mechetti was in his mid-twenties, olive skinned with high cheekbones, black snapping eyes, and a mop of raven-black curls. He wore a cheap, flashy tie and a bright polo sweater under his suit coat. He turned to appreciate Effie Perine leaving Spade's office, then turned back to the desk.

"My old man tells me you might have daytime work for me."

"Nights at California-Citizens Bank, did your father say?"

"That's it." He waggled black level eyebrows, showed gleaming teeth in a broad grin. "Lotsa pretty Italian girls working there at the bank, you get my drift?" A hard light entered his eyes. "Mr. Spade, you wouldn't never of tagged me with that right hand two years ago if my foot hadn't of slipped."

Spade nodded in solemn agreement. "Dark in that warehouse, that's for sure. And like you said, your foot slipped."

Seeing Spade roll a cigarette, Gino lit a cheap cigar with the desk lighter. Spade nodded as if to himself.

"Anyway, Gino, I got a tip that a mob of bank busters might hit Cal-Cit because security is lax since Eberhard drowned."

Gino tipped back his head and blew out a plume of smoke.

"That's a load of bunk! Me an' another guy was hired right after he died. We trade off, night for night. They didn't have no nighttime security before then."

"Nothing to it, then," said Spade. "But even so, for my report, I need your take on the bank's security setup."

Gino chuckled. "The bank itself is tough, but it shares a side wall with a Chinese social club that closes up around ten at night. In the alley next to it, Pratt Place, there's a fire escape goes to the roof. It's a three-foot drop from there to the bank's roof and the service shed for the elevator shaft."

Spade stubbed out his cigarette, grinned.

"I knew I was asking the right man."

The handsome Italian youth chuckled. "I figure it's part of my job to look around just so I know what's what. That way, anyone tryin' to crush into the bank, I'd pop 'em for sure."

"Isn't the elevator shed always locked?"

"Sure, but there's locks and there's locks." Gino leaned forward to stub out his smelly cigar. "Nobody's bustin' in there, not after hours. Not with me on the job."

Spade came around the desk to shake Gino's hand warmly. Gino looked at the bill Spade had palmed off with the handshake.

"Hey, thanks, Mr. Spade!"

From his office door Spade watched Mechetti exit, went

back inside. Effie Perine followed with her notebook and sat down in the armchair across from his swivel chair. He gave her the fixings to roll him a cigarette.

"He's certainly a good-looking man," she said primly.

"Yeah. I put him away for a couple of years on a warehouse job. He's got the worm for sure."

"The worm?"

"Wormy. Like a bad apple. Most ex-cons are. He's got a larcenous mind, that boy, but now he's night watchman at Eberhard's bank. The bank's being very snotty about anyone getting a look at Eberhard's records, and I need to see them."

"Don't take chances, Sam. District Attorney Bryan would just love to put you into prison yourself."

"He's not liable to get the chance."

Spade recounted his previous day's work. It took longer to finish with the widow than with anything else because Effie Perine wanted to know all about what Evelyn Eberhard looked like and what she was wearing and what she said.

"A mistress? A man with no name?"

"The mistress and Mr. Nameless are two things that keep me from accepting natural causes for the death and closing out the case. A third is that the bank hired Gino after Eberhard died. The kid's carrying a two-year felony rap. No legitimate banker should let him within a mile of the place. Fourth, the bank's refusing to let *anyone* see Eberhard's financial stuff."

"Not even the widow?"

"Well, she's very far from the traditional grieving widow. Six months ago she wanted to hire me to find the mistress.

She gave that up, but then Eberhard went broke maybe, and then he died, maybe natural, maybe on purpose, maybe helped along. Now she wants me to find the mistress to help negate the suicide theory. Or maybe to hang any funny business about Eberhard's death on her. I offered the widow a deal. Get me into the bank's records, I'll find you your mistress. But she's too afraid of losing the insurance money to back me up."

"Nothing about this case makes a whole lot of sense."

"Yeah. Call Sid Wise's office, see if he's in."

As she waited for central to pick up she said, "I liked it a lot better when Sid was just next door."

Spade entered the pinkish office building on Sutter and Kearny just shy of 2 o'clock. He took the elevator up, went to suite 827, entered without knocking. In passing, he bent down to kiss Wise's receptionist on the top of her head.

She giggled. "Mr. Wise said to go right on in, Mr. Spade."

Sid Wise's big desk was loaded with papers and files, but he had his swivel chair turned so he could look out at the Sutter Hotel across the street. There were the usual flecks of dandruff on the shoulders of his suit coat. He was biting a fingernail.

"One of these days you'll draw blood," said Spade.

Wise spun his chair around. He started a hand gesture toward the chair across from him, but Spade had already dragged it to the side of the desk. Wise frowned. He fidgeted.

"Everyone in town says you're asking questions about the Eberhard death. That one's zipped up and folded away, Sam."

"Let me guess. The Neptune Bath House—"

"Doesn't want any more bad publicity. Cal-Cit's attorney says that you threatened a V.P. with—"

"I wanted a reaction, Sid. I got one."

"You sure did. You also said the widow was your client."

"Implied."

"Then Assistant Deputy Coroner Klinger is saying—"

"They're on record that Eberhard died of natural causes."

"Jovanen over at Bankers' Life wants you to stop snooping around while they decide whether to pay off the widow."

"Doesn't all of this make you just a little bit curious?"

"Lawyers are never paid just to get curious."

"I am."

"You have a client? This isn't just Sam Spade trying to drum up business?"

"I haven't had to do that for three years." Spade's smile was sardonic. "Not since you moved away from Mission Street and I started upgrading my client list. Ray Kentzler at Bankers' Life hired me. Under the table. That's why Jovanen doesn't know anything about it."

A speculative look came into the attorney's eyes.

"So Eberhard's death isn't cut-and-dried after all."

"Don't tell anybody," said Spade. "It's supposed to be a secret, but the fact is they won't open those files to *anyone.* Not even the widow. Questions of confidentiality, propriety, that sort of thing." He leaned toward Wise and lowered his voice too dramatically for it to be genuine. "Want to represent her in this matter, Sid?"

Wise leaned back and looked up at the ceiling and got his faraway look in his eyes. "Yes and no. I'd love to have a widow who's probably going to be rich for a client. But what if Evelyn Eberhard did have a hand in her husband's death? And I get a lot of work from the Bankers Association through Charles Barber at Golden Gate Trust and I'm just waiting for *that* shoe to drop." He shrugged regretfully. "So I have to pass."

"Same thing Evelyn said when I offered her your services," said Spade cheerily. "You two were made for each other. A pair of old maids." His brows drew down. "I'll get into those files my own way."

"That's what I'm afraid of," said Sid Wise gloomily.

19

The Chest of Bergina

Spade and the Archers were at a front corner table for four in Julius Castle on Telegraph Hill. Far below, the ferryboats were toys moving between the Ferry Building and the Oakland and Sausalito ferry terminals. Lights glittered over the water from Berkeley and Emeryville. Above rose the round turretlike wooden structure that gave the restaurant its name. Iva Archer sighed.

"It's very beautiful, Sam," she said in a wistful voice.

"No prettier than Elliott Bay up at Seattle," boomed Archer.

"Oh, Miles, hush," she said.

"I wouldn't argue with you," said Spade.

They were each having the two-dollar dinner, Iva the fillet of sole with sauce Julius, Spade the tenderloin steak with zucchini Florentine, Archer the lamb chops.

Archer poured more Riesling into each of their glasses, leaned back, and patted his belly.

"You can sure pick the good places to eat, Sam."

Spade leaned forward to light Iva's cigarette, leaned back and drifted smoke into the air. "How's your brother Phil?"

"Got all the work he can handle," said Archer.

"Lawyer, isn't he?" asked Spade.

"He wants Miles to come down here and go in with him," said Iva. "Do all of his investigative work."

"Or I might transfer down with Burns. Like you transferred up to Seattle with Continental before the war, Sam."

"Well, good luck with whatever you decide," said Spade.

"You know, seeing your office today, Sam, maybe I ought to go out on my own like you did." He winked. "Get a pretty little girl to do all my—ah, paperwork . . ." He leaned forward, suddenly serious. "You ever think of taking in a partner, Sam?"

Spade shook his head. "Nope," he said.

It was midafternoon when Spade stopped at Effie Perine's desk to ask his standard, "Any calls?" She looked up and shook her head, then raised a detaining hand when he started toward the closed door of his inner office. He stopped abruptly, scowling.

"It's not Miles Archer, is it? You know better than to put anyone in there when I'm not around."

"Not Archer. A—a friend. Of mine."

Spade dragged the other chair over to sit down.

"OK, sweetheart, out with it."

Fingering the little jeweled gold locket she always wore, Effie Perine looked up at him, looked away almost shyly.

"Remember the day you found me mooning over this locket and I showed you how it folded open into a sort of cloverleaf—"

"With pictures of your mother and your father and their wedding day. Sure, I remember."

"And a picture of my best friend . . ."

"Penny . . . Penny Chiotras. Penelope. She's six years older than you, right? Like a big sister to you." Off her surprised look, he added with a grin, "I never forget a pretty face."

"She's not just pretty. She's beautiful. You'll see."

He frowned, gestured at the closed door to his office. "So she's the one who—"

"Yes. She showed up at my birthday party on Saturday. She looked terrible, haunted, like she wanted to look over her shoulder all the time. I got her alone and finally got her to admit that a sinister Turk has been following her."

"A Turk." Spade said it flatly.

"In Greece, Dad and Penny's father had opposed the Turks, like everyone else. But her father was a true revolutionary; he fought as an *andarte.* They're sort of bandits. After the war ended he went back to fight them again, and regularly sent money to her mother until he was killed, at Smyrna in nineteen twenty-two. I think it was stolen Turkish money, so it stopped and she had to take in boarders to make ends meet. That's when Penny moved out so there'd be another room to rent, and found a job. Something secretarial, she said. We always knew she was all right because she makes those regular deposits into her mother's account. But nobody knows where she lives or works, and I hadn't seen her since—until the party on Saturday."

"She told you about this Turk and you believe her."

Effie Perine raised a defiant chin. "Of course I believe her. She doesn't so much see him as *feel* him behind her in the street. And she can't tell me where she's working or living, not now. It wouldn't be safe for her or for me if I knew."

"Everybody lies, darling. You just have to keep chipping away at them until they wear down and finally get so tired that they end up telling you the truth."

"She's *not* lying. She's truly frightened."

"How do we get from there to her hiding in my office?"

She met his yellowish eyes with her clear brown ones and said in a sudden defiant rush of words, "Not hiding. I told her you could help her, and she showed up after you went out and I was afraid she might not come back later, so I told her to wait in there, out of sight." Effie Perine impulsively reached a hand toward his arm, withdrew it. "Just help her, Sam. Please."

"If she'll tell me enough of the truth so I know what's going on." He checked his watch. "Go on home, sweetheart. I'll talk to your Penny. Just don't come around bellyaching if things go bad later on."

Penny Chiotras started up from the client's chair beside Spade's desk, embarrassment giving added color to her cheeks. She was quick of movement, with huge brown eyes and long, utterly black hair. Her face was strong boned yet softly feminine. She wore a stylish brown and tan satin frock with embroidery and an antique-looking Greek coin as a buckle ornament.

"Effie told me it was all right to wait in here for you." Her voice was low, throaty, well modulated. "But I'm afraid that I'm imposing dreadfully on you, Mr. Spade."

Spade, at his most bland, bowed slightly to her as he took the hand she held out to him. Her palm was dry, her grip strong. The little finger of her left hand had been broken and set badly. He went around his desk to his swivel chair, waved her back into the oaken armchair from which she had risen.

"No imposition, Miss Chiotras, you being Effie's best friend and all." His words seemed utterly sincere, but his eyes were assessing. "She said you were being followed by a sinister man."

Even white teeth glinted between full parted lips.

"Hearing you say it makes it sound very melodramatic."

Spade smiled pleasantly, making all of the V's in his long face longer. He put his elbows on the desk blotter, tented his fingers in front of his chin, and was silent. The silence became demanding.

"I—I think I am being followed after work by a man who looks . . . foreign to me. I almost see him out of the corner of my eye just disappearing around a corner, if that makes any sense."

"Sure it does. Effie said you think he's a Turk."

"He's not wearing a red fez and slippers with curled-up toes and a scimitar in a sash at his waist, if that's what you mean. But, yes, a man with black hair and a swarthy face and glittery eyes."

"Why a Turk? Why not a Russian or Syrian or Montenegrin?"

"You're laughing at me," she said.

Spade's smile again lengthened the V's in his face. "Not even if I felt like it." Then he repeated, "Why a Turk?"

"Because of the chest of Bergina. It's spelled B-e-r-g-i-n-a, but *b* in Greek is spoken as *v*, so it's pronounced *Vergina.* It's supposed to be a gold-bound metal box."

Spade picked up a pencil, drew a pad toward himself. "The chest of Bergina." His eyes had gotten very attentive, but his voice was flat, without nuance. "What's supposed to be in it?"

"No one knows. It was made by Greek artisans as a gift for Bergina, the sister of Alexander the Great." She said almost defensively, "Everyone thought the sacking of Troy by the Greeks was just a legend until Heinrich Schliemann excavated the ruins. I have a letter from my father."

She delved into a black French-tailored calfskin handbag, removed a letter that was written in Greek.

"It is dated 1920, but a man came to my mother's house and gave it to her only a month ago."

"This man with the letter was a Turk?"

"A Greek. He told my mother that he was a brigand in my father's band of *andartes* and was with him at the end. He said he didn't know what was in the letter, but it had been steamed open and clumsily glued shut again. He said he needed money."

"Your mother give him any?"

"A little. She didn't believe his story, but the letter is in my father's handwriting. She gave me the letter on Saturday. On Monday the man started following me." She opened the letter. "My father writes that he is in a little nameless town in the Balkans somewhere north of Greece. He says he knows where the chest of Bergina is hidden and that no one else does. He says it is his legacy to my mother and me." She looked up. "If it's real, wouldn't the chest have immense monetary and historic value?"

"Maybe, but it doesn't explain why a Turk would be tailing you around San Francisco five years later."

"He writes that he is enclosing detailed directions to its hiding place. But there is nothing else, no directions, just the letter. But if the man following me thinks there were and finds out where I live, mightn't he . . ." Her hands crumpled the letter. "I need to *know* I'm safe."

Spade stood. "Where are you working?"

"I'm a secretary for Hartford and Cole. They're in—"

"The Russ Building. Stocks and bonds. Go back to work, Miss Chiotras, leave at the usual time, go someplace you might go after work. You won't see me, but I'll be there."

"I sometimes eat at the Gypsy Tea Shop in Grant Avenue."

"Good. Afterward, walk up to Sutter. Window-shop. Go along Powell, walk through Union Square to Stockton. Take at least a half hour, then go to a movie at the Cameo, on Market between Fifth and Sixth. Then go home. If anyone's following you he'll have to show himself during that time."

Spade frankly appraised her, her face, her body. A possessive gleam came into his eyes.

"But *I'll* have to know where you live."

"No!" She cried. She looked very young, very vulnerable. "You have to promise that you won't try to follow me home."

Spade shrugged, said blandly, "OK. No reason to do so."

"I—I trust you, but if he should follow *you* and . . ."

Spade tossed his pencil into the air, let it fall on the desk. "*Nobody* can follow me without me seeing him. Come to the office tomorrow morning on your way to work. I'll know more then."

20

Shadow Man

The Gypsy Tea Shop in Grant, half a block above O'Farrell, was tricked out to look like a fortune-teller's *duikerrin* room, where palms are read and psychic readings given. The crystal shades of the hanging lamps tinkled whenever the door was opened. On the side walls were framed Greek icons of the Virgin Mary, Saint Nicholas, and Saint Constantine. Pinned to the back wall was a diaphanous red, yellow, and purple skirt spread wide to add color to the room. On a corner table was a crystal ball made pastel by the votive candles glowing behind it.

Penny Chiotras sat at a window table alone. In profile her face looked tranquil, untroubled, but the tendons of the hand raising her teacup were taut with tension. She left money on the table, issued into busy Grant Avenue. Without looking around, she walked up toward Sutter two blocks above, following instructions.

"Good girl," muttered Sam Spade approvingly.

He waited until she was lost from view in the evening

press of strollers, then left his recessed entryway across from the tearoom. For the next thirty minutes she followed instructions, but then instead of going down toward Market and the Cameo Theater, she went into the front entrance of the St. Mark Hotel across Powell from Union Square.

"Not so good," Spade muttered.

He got into the front cab in the taxi line, reached over the back of the seat to give the goateed driver a silver dollar.

"Go around the block, cap, and pull up just beyond Mason."

The driver checked his rearview, grinned as he drifted his cab away from the curb.

"I don't suppose you remember me, Mr. Spade, but I drove you all over hell and gone last year behind a Flip doorman who was shakin' down guests stayin' at the Baltimore Hotel with ladies not their wives."

"Sure. Erle, isn't it? I recognize the goatee."

As they rounded the corner into Post, Penny Chiotras issued from the side entrance of the St. Mark. She checked the street, then walked to Powell and caught a down cable car to Market. But not to the Cameo Theater. Instead, she went down a block to Mission, boarded a number 11 streetcar, rode it all the way to the end of the line at Twenty-fourth and Hoffman in the Outer Mission, nestled below Diamond Heights in usually fog-free Noe Valley.

She waited outside the car until it started its return trip, jumped aboard when it was already moving, got off at Dolores and Twenty-third. Spade told the cabbie to wait, then followed her.

Penny ducked into Severn, one of three narrow half-block alleys that run off Twenty-third between Dolores and Church. By the dim streetlight he watched her go up the stairs of a narrow wooden row house of uncertain color. He waited until a roller shade was pulled down in the third-floor front window on the left. Pale light went on behind it. When the light went out Spade returned to his waiting cab, went home and to bed and to sleep.

At 8 a.m. he was explaining to Effie Perine, "I told her I would tail her last night, see if anyone was behind her. I waited outside the Russ Building, where she says she's a stockbroker's secretary, picked her up, shadowed her. No one. Nothing." Spade spread his hands wide to show how devoid of shadowers the back trail had been. "She ditched me at the St. Mark instead of going to the Cameo Theater. And what she told me doesn't hold up. No sinister men ducking around corners." His smile was without humor. "Except me."

"Ditched you?" asked Effie Perine in an unbelieving voice.

She handed him the cigarette she had rolled for him; he lit it with a match from the desktop dispenser. She was frowning.

"So you don't believe her," she said.

"That she's scared, yeah. That a Turk is shadowing her, no—at least not last night. She told me a wild tale about a gold-bound chest that's supposed to be from the time of Alexander the Great, but—"

"The chest of Bergina!" exclaimed Effie Perine.

"Not you too," Spade growled in mock disgust.

"It's true Greek legend. Alexander was one of the greatest Greeks, a real hero to our people. Bergina was his sister. But how does that tie in with Penny's father?"

"She showed me a letter written in Greek, said it was her father's handwriting, said it was dated nineteen twenty. She said it was delivered to her mother last month by a man who said he had been a brigand in her father's revolutionary band. Said he got some money from her ma and disappeared."

Effie Perine's mouth drew up almost primly. "Delivered? By hand? Five years late?"

"You don't like it either, huh? The letter supposedly says her father found the chest and that it would be his legacy to his family. All I know, darling, is that her story about the Turk is hooey. I think the chest is hooey. She made me promise I wouldn't follow her home because he only knows where she works. That's hooey too. If he can pick her up at the one place he can follow her to the other." An unholy glow came into his eyes. "I'd better follow her home tonight after all, see what's so—"

"Don't you dare!" Her eyes were flashing. "It would be a—a betrayal of trust."

"Like all the trust she's giving me? Nu-uh, sister."

"So that's it? That's all you're going to do for her?"

"Are all Greeks as hard to get along with as you are?" asked Spade. "I'll follow her again tonight, just to make sure."

The phone rang. Effie Perine reached across the desk,

picked up the receiver, said, "Samuel Spade Investigations." She listened for a moment, said, "I'll see if he's come in yet," put her hand over the mouthpiece, said, "Ray Kentzler."

Spade took the phone. "Jovanen finally figure out that I'm on the payroll?"

"He did indeed, and hit the roof. Even wanted me to pay you out of my own pocket! I talked him out of that, but you're off the case."

"You're the one wanted me on it."

"I was tilting at windmills."

"Well, I've got a couple of feelers out, but since I don't work for you anymore, Ray, I'll just have to let 'em drop."

He hung up. Effie Perine was wide-eyed.

"You quit?"

"Was fired." Without a pause he said, "Those Cal-Cit bank records are the key, darling. They'd tell us what we really have to know: did Eberhard suddenly go broke, and if he did, why?"

"What difference does it make? We don't have a client."

"Give the merry widow a call, tell her I need her backing to get into those bank records if I'm going to find out the truth about how and why her husband died and be able to prove he didn't commit suicide. Tell her I'll find the mistress at the same time."

The phone rang again. Effie Perine went through her standard formula, again covered the mouthpiece, said, "Charles Hendrickson Barber this time, sounding angry."

He took the phone from her, said into it, "It's Spade."

The banker's voice was cold and tight.

"I'm calling you on behalf of the Banking Commission, Spade. We want to know what the devil you're playing at."

"Yes, nice to hear from you too, Mr. Barber. I'll be at your office in half an hour." He hung up without waiting for a reply. "Progress," he told Effie Perine. "I'll get more out of Barber than he'll get out of me." He was on his feet. "Your Penny's coming in this morning to find out if I saw anyone shadowing her last night. Tell her no, but that I'll try again tonight. Tell her no more silly little tricks like ditching me. See can you get her to open up about a few things. Maybe take her to lunch for a nice girl-to-girl chat."

21

That Fire's Out

Tobias Krieger led Spade through the labyrinth of bank offices to the door bearing the legend:

CHARLES HENDRICKSON BARBER
President

In four years the minor bank official's pencil mustache had flourished and thickened over his pink upper lip. He knocked on Barber's door. A voice rumbled from within. Krieger opened it. Barber, now sixty-four, was still walrus mustached, distinguished, tall, thick. He stood up behind his ten-foot-long teak desk and bellowed.

"Get out!"

Krieger evaporated. Spade crossed to the padded hardwood chair in front of the desk, sat down.

"It's been what, Charles? A bit over four years?"

"Goddamn your insolence, Spade!"

Spade leaned forward, took a cigar from the box on Barber's desk, sniffed it, took out his penknife, cut off the end, and lit it with the fancy lighter on the desk.

"Insolence? I don't work for you. I don't work for your bank. I don't work for the Banking Commission."

Barber slowly sat back down, still outraged. "One phone call to City Hall and you don't work for anybody, Spade."

"If it comforts you to think so." Spade leaned back, blew luxurious smoke into the air. "But I'm the boy who kept your son out of trouble and your family name out of the newspapers."

"That was four years ago. I don't owe you a thing now."

"Tell your wife that."

"Leave Rose out of this! She has nothing to do with it."

"If it comforts you to think so." Spade made as if to rise. "Just leave me out of it too, Barber."

"Sit down, damn it, man." The banker's voice had taken on a querulous note. "I'm under a lot of pressure on this. You running all over town asking questions, alienating people, upsetting people—"

"Somebody has to."

"What's that supposed to mean?"

"Eberhard's death. Who else is doing anything about it?"

Barber was getting hot again.

"I resent your implication, sir! Collin Eberhard was a great good friend of mine, and poor Evelyn is a dear friend of my Rose. If there was something irregular about his death I would be the first one urging a full investigation. The very first. But that is not the case. The coroner's jury returned a verdict of death by strictly natural causes."

Spade puffed his cigar. "You mean that a roomful of

Eberhard's cronies returned a finding of death by natural causes so his widow would get that big insurance payout."

"Collin had an eye for the ladies and led Evelyn a pretty dance over the years with his string of mistresses. It's only right she should be . . . comfortable now."

"Who was the most recent one?" Spade asked it idly.

"A gentleman doesn't inquire into such things."

"Was Eberhard ruined financially?"

"Not Collin! He was addicted to gold speculation, but—"

"Gold specie, like the *San Anselmo*'s missing gold coins?"

"Of course not. And don't tell me you're still looking for the *San Anselmo* gold four years later."

"I'm still looking for the man who stole it."

Barber chuckled. "Well, it wasn't Collin. He speculated in gold-mining *stocks,* and he was shrewd, no man shrewder."

"If he was ruined, *somebody* was shrewder."

"Damnable lies by the tabloids." Barber made a sweeping gesture. "You aren't stirring up this mud for the newspapers, are you, Spade? No one else could have any reason to hire you."

"So all of this bellowing and blustering is to find out who I'm working for? You should have just asked." Spade knocked ash off his cigar. "Until two hours ago, Ray Kentzler at Bankers' Life. Now, nobody. Jovanen canned me."

"But—but—" Barber was almost stuttering. "Jovanen was asking the commission if *we* had hired you."

"Jovanen didn't know. Kentzler hired me under the table

to find out if there was something fishy about Eberhard's death."

Barber leaned back, hands laced across his middle, and said in a relieved voice, "Then that's the end of it."

"Nope. The cops have closed the file on Eberhard's death and someone with a lot of influence is trying to keep it closed. When I started asking questions everyone was suddenly shy, or had amnesia, or was hostile. The coroner says natural causes, hands me off to his troubleshooter. The insurance company finds out I'm working for them and fires me. California-Citizens throws me out on my ear. Now you tell me the Banking Commission wants me to desist. And the Neptune Bath House won't even tell me which of Eberhard's pals were with him on the day he died."

"I was, for one," said Barber unexpectedly. "Collin looked glum when he arrived, but not suicidal. And after he talked with some chap off in the corner he looked like his horse had come in at Tanforan. Got out his bottle, insisted we all have a drink with him." He shook his head. "No. No suicide there."

"Poison in his drink?"

"Hell, man, we all drank from the same bottle. We'd have all gone down. Do you have a single fact that says it was *not* from natural causes?"

"Yeah, two. First, the man who was huddled off in the corner with Eberhard. He drank with you, easy to drop something into Eberhard's glass. I bet you don't even know his name."

Barber was frowning, enmity forgotten.

"Now I think of it, it's strange Collin didn't introduce him."

"A week before Eberhard died this guy was at the house. In the study. Evelyn Eberhard heard raised voices but no words. I think he was in business with Eberhard."

Barber shook his head contemptuously. "That gigolo?"

"Second, Cal-Cit won't open Eberhard's financial records."

"Damn it, man, the tabloids—"

"—will be yelling about some other crisis in the body politic in another week."

Barber shook his head. "Bankers are notoriously conservative, Spade, and adverse publicity is bad for business."

"Why not at least open the books for the cops? They're good at keeping secrets for the power people in this town."

"Since there is no active investigation of Collin's death, the police couldn't get a judge to issue a warrant."

"What about your precious Banking Commission?"

"Like the D.A., we have no probable cause for such a demand. California-Citizens Bank is solvent. And powerful."

"Why refuse his widow access to her husband's accounts? She's his heir after all." Spade paused, a suddenly speculative look on his face. "She is his heir, isn't she?"

"Of course she's his heir. Who else could it be? The will hasn't been made public, but I'm sure Evelyn . . . Hmph. Damned odd Evelyn *hasn't* mentioned it to Rose, now you say it. She could initiate legal action to become administratrix of Collin's affairs, but it would be messy . . . damned messy."

"I spoke with her about that. She doesn't want to do it."

Barber looked relieved again.

"Tell you what, Spade. I'll drop by California-Citizens informally, have a chat with Vice President Spaulding. Banker to banker, learn what I can. He's acting president for the moment. Evelyn at least should be able to see those records."

As Spade emerged into Montgomery Street, a low voice called urgently behind him.

"Mr. Spade."

It was Henny Barber, no longer the gangly kid Spade had hauled out of the *San Anselmo*'s lifeboat four years before. Now a sturdy youth of twenty-one, conservatively dressed. He grabbed Spade's hand and wrung it with a ferocious fervor.

"I heard you'd been summoned by Pater for a dressing-down." He drew Spade almost furtively up the street. "I'm dying of boredom and I'm hoping there is something, anything, I can do to help you in your investigation of Mr. Eberhard's death."

"Aren't you already working at Golden Gate Trust?"

"Not a real position. Just looking over shoulders."

"You knew the Eberhards, didn't you?"

"He was an unofficial uncle when I was growing up. I liked him." Henny grinned. "I like Aunt Ev a lot better."

"OK," said Spade. "You want to help, go get a teller-trainee job at California-Citizens Bank. Tell your old man you want to try it there—but don't tell him it came from me."

His face lit up. "Undercover? At Uncle Collin's bank?"

"Just for a few days. When can you be in place?"

"Tomorrow. Banks always need tellers."

"Don't be disappointed if nothing happens," said Spade.

Effie Perine, watering the vase of African violets she kept on her desk, answered Spade's inevitable "Any calls?" with "Three, nothing important. But a beautiful Chinese girl was in."

His eyes quickened. "Chinese? They usually go to their own people for help. She want an appointment? Leave a name?"

"No appointment. She said her name was Mai-lin Choi and that she is here on a student permit that's running out. She has to go back—to China, I guess—but said she'd return."

"That sounds straight enough. The Chinese Exclusion Act bars all Chinese except teachers and students and diplomats and the clergy from entering the country from China. I doubt we'll hear from her again."

He made a beckoning gesture, went into his private office.

"How was your lunch with Penny?"

Effie Perine didn't meet his eyes. "I had a sandwich at my desk. She had to get to work."

"That's it? Open up. It's like pulling teeth."

"She *is* playing some game, isn't she?" Her face was

troubled. “She told me the same things she told you and said she’ll come in tomorrow morning again to find out if you learn anything tonight. She promised no more games.”

“Still a believer?”

“She’s honestly scared, Sam.” She made a visible effort to change topics. “How did it go with Barber?”

“That fire’s out.” He smiled without mirth. “He’s going to talk to Cal-Cit Bank tomorrow. Did you get the merry widow?”

“The housekeeper said she was out.”

“Keep trying.”

Effie Perine returned to the outer office. Spade smoked cigarettes, various expressions passing across his face. He finally left, stopping at Effie Perine’s desk to tell her he’d make sure that no terrible Turks were following Penny that night.

22

Everybody Lies

Spade was in a coffee shop across Montgomery when Penny Chiotras emerged from the Russ Building's ornate front entrance at 5:07 p.m. She went down to Bush, turned toward Grant Avenue and the Gypsy Tea Shop. No one followed her, not even Spade. He left a dime on the counter, dodged quitting-time traffic to the Russ Building to consult the directory beside the elevator bank.

"Six, please."

Spade left the elevator, went down the sixth-floor hall to a lighted pebbled-glass door that read HARTFORD & COLE in blocky capitals, with STOCKS AND BONDS below in smaller cursive writing.

A tall sharp-featured dark-haired man already wearing his hat was coming from an inner office, pulling on a tweed topcoat.

"I was hoping to catch one of your employees before she left," said Spade. "Penny Chiotras."

"Sorry, chap, you're a month too late." He belatedly stuck out his hand. "Desmond Cole, junior partner of the firm."

Spade shook. "Eric Gough."

"Like the street?"

"He was a great-uncle."

"Native son? A rarity. Anyway, Penny's mother died, she had to relocate to Brentwood over in the East Bay to look after her aging father. We hated to lose her. Penny was a whiz."

"My secretary quit, and I remembered Collin Eberhard some time ago was raving about how competent Miss Chiotras was." Spade smiled ruefully. "I was hoping to steal her from you."

"Penny started out as a secretary right enough, but she soon became a de facto broker, near as damn to swearing. We were urging her to get her own license when she had to leave. We specialize in timber and mineral stocks—copper, tin, silver, and gold, and she had the touch. She handled some of Collin's speculative gold-mining stocks and his bank prospered mightily because of her during the past four years—" He broke off, looking guilty. "I shouldn't be telling you all of this, but I guess it doesn't matter now that Eberhard is dead and Penny has moved on."

Spade walked brisky over to Grant Avenue to take up his position in the same convenient doorway across from the Gypsy Tea Shop. Penny was there, went through the same routine, except this time she actually went to the movies. Spade followed her to Noe Valley, saw her safely into her apartment, went home himself. He set his alarm for 6 a.m.

. . .

When Penny emerged from Severn Place at 8:30 the next morning Spade was loitering in a little market in Twenty-third Street. Against the morning chill Penny wore a woolen cloche hat and a worn calf-length coat over a cheap working-girl's frock. Spade laid a nickel on the counter by the cash register.

"Use your phone?"

The gray-haired heavy-faced German shopkeeper waved a hand. "You wouldn't believe the people use that phone, and without offering me no nickel either."

Spade gave central his number. While he waited he picked out an apple, laid down another nickel.

Effie Perine's voice said, "Samuel Spade Investigations."

"Me. When Penny gets there, tell her nobody was behind her last night and that I feel she has nothing to worry about. But give her my apartment address and the phone number. If she sees anyone, she should get somewhere safe and let me know right away. Day or night."

Her voice was low, relieved. "Thanks, Sam." Then she added, "When I came in the phone was ringing. Charles Barber. He wants you to meet him for lunch at the Bohemian Club. I think he wants to apologize for yesterday." Excitement entered her voice. "They say you have to spend years on the waiting list just to become a member."

"And no women allowed, ever."

"Not even as waitresses?" Then her voice changed, got catty. "They have women at the Bohemian Grove up on the Russian River during their two-week summer camp up there. At least lots of girls stay in Guerneville cabins that are close by."

"What would your mother say if she heard you talking that way, sweetheart? Tell Barber I'll be there at noon."

Spade went down Severn Place eating his apple, turned in at the narrow row house that in the morning light proved to be a paint-peeling gray. He climbed five worn wooden steps.

There were six name tags to the right of the front door, two per floor. Apartment 3A was Drosos. Apartment 3B was Donant. No Chiotras. The front door was unlocked. He went in.

Backed up against the wall inside the door was a battered Queen Anne–style library table with mail strewn across it. Nothing for Chiotras. Nothing for Drosos. Spade dropped his apple core on top of discarded mail in a wastebasket beside the table, without stealth climbed to the third floor.

The hallway ran straight back to a communal bathroom at the far end, where the toilet, tub, and sink would be. Halfway down were facing doors, 3A to the left, 3B to the right. It was in the window of 3A that lights had gone on and the roller shade had been lowered after Penny had entered the building.

Spade laid an ear to the door of 3B, heard a radio playing "Sleepy Time Gal." He stepped quickly across the hall, tapped on the panel of 3A while fingering his keys. No response. The third key worked. He glanced over his shoulder, slid through the half-opened door, closed it without sound.

He was in a small, narrow apartment. An easy chair with

frayed arms and the fiber-and-hardwood magazine stand beside it were the only furniture in the front room. Behind it was a chest-high wooden counter topped with oilcloth enclosing a minuscule kitchen with a stained porcelain sink, a two-burner stove, and two chairs shoved under a two-by-three kitchen table.

Behind that a closed three-wing hardwood screen with a floral-patterned cretonne panel and two-way hinges partitioned off the final bit of space. Spade folded back one of the end wings. Hooks on the inside of it held a bath towel, a hand towel, a woolly robe. Inside on the floor were fuzzy slippers.

It took Spade only twenty minutes to methodically search the entire place, inch by inch, using quick eyes that missed nothing and surprisingly delicate fingers that probed everything. In the kitchen, no icebox, no dishes in the sink. A slightly warm coffeepot on the stove. A bread box with half a loaf in it, butter and jam and three eggs on the shelf over the drainboard, a can of Lipton's coffee. Plate, cup, saucer, one set of cutlery.

The space created by the hardwood screen was just large enough to hold a single bed, a chest of drawers, and a battered wardrobe. Between the bed and the wall was a cheap suitcase, empty. On top of the chest of drawers were a few cosmetics and a bar of bath soap wrapped in a washcloth. The chest held a meager array of neatly folded blouses and underclothes.

The wardrobe held one hat, two scarves, and three skirts on hangers, all the same size. There was only one dress, the expensive brown and tan silk frock with the Greek gold coin as a buckle ornament Penny had worn to his office on her first visit.

Spade found no papers, no checkbook, no money or jewelry, no rent or utility receipts. No phone, no books, no magazines, no radio. No crumpled letter written in Greek. No chest of Bergina. Apart from the silk frock, nothing to suggest that anyone named Chiotras lived there. Nor anyone named Drosos. But on the shelf of the magazine stand beside the easy chair were two dozen newspaper clippings about the Eberhard death.

Just as Spade slipped out of 3A the radio in 3B went silent. He palmed the knob, began knocking on the door he had just closed as a thin, slightly haggard blond woman in a cloth coat emerged from 3B. She held the hand of a girl of four or five, who was carrying a doll. The girl wore a woolen coat, a two-color hockey cap with a pom-pom and a matching scarf with a knit fringe. Blond curls peeped out from beneath the cap.

Spade had turned with an ingratiating smile. "I wonder if you might know where I could reach Mrs. Drosos."

"Miss Drosos," the blond woman corrected automatically. The little girl was examining Spade with gravity, clutching her doll to her chest. The woman absently patted her head. "Julia Drosos." Her voice bore traces of erstwhile refinement.

"Yes, ma'am. We got her letter, you see."

"About a job?" she asked quickly.

"Her professional qualifications sound fine, but we need a little more personal information."

"I'm Beverly Donant. I—we, my husband and I—we don't know Julia well, she's lived here only a month. She's all alone in this world. She was caring for her aged mother down in Santa Barbara, and after the poor woman died she found herself bursting into tears all the time. She wants work taking care of children. Some youth and gaiety in her life after all that heartbreak."

"This would be a nanny situation for a well-to-do family down the peninsula."

Beverly Donant's smile illuminated her long, narrow face, made her suddenly pretty. The daughter smiled with her. She had her mother's same radiant smile.

"I'm sure Julia would be just right for the job," Beverly Donant said enthusiastically. "She's stayed with my little Jenny twice when Tom and I went to the movies."

"She sings me songs and tells me stories," said Jenny.

"Stories about ancient Greece?" asked Spade.

"Greece!" exclaimed Beverly Donant. "I should have known! All that life and vitality, all that long black hair and those dark eyes and that lovely complexion. I thought maybe Irish, but Greek fits even better."

"She sounds like just the person we're looking for."

23

At the Bohemian Club

Spade went up slanting Taylor Street to the unmarked entryway of a red brick building half covered with ivy. At the top of eight wide marble steps was a foyer with, to the right, a four-foot cast-bronze owl standing on a bronze life-size human skull.

Charles Hendrickson Barber's heavy but mellifluous orator's voice said, "The owl was done in nineteen thirteen by Jo Mora."

The difference in Barber's attitude from the day before was marked. The banker shook Spade's hand warmly, then led him past an unattended reception desk and down a long hall lined with framed photographs of the Bohemian Club's earlier days.

"It started out in eighteen seventy-two with rooms on Pine Street above the old California Market. In the eighteen nineties they expanded to a better suite of rooms, at one hundred thirty Post, between Kearny and Dupont Alley. But that burned down in the fire after the nineteen oh six quake.

In oh seven the club started over again, like everyone else in the San Francisco of that day. Then we moved into this building, and I believe here we'll stay."

They came to a bank of three elevators, whose brass doors were decorated with ornate scrollwork. A craggy-faced man, beautifully dressed, came out of one of the elevators with a marked, crabwise limp. He greeted Barber effusively, shook Spade's hand as if truly delighted to meet him, and went his way.

"We keep rooms on the upper floors for the use of club members from out of town," explained Barber.

He led Spade through the lounge, a sprawling room with a carpeted floor and twenty-foot-tall windows facing Taylor Street. Drawn back from them were heavy wine drapes; closed over them were gossamer white net curtains. Four men were seated in leather armchairs dotted around the room, reading newspapers with cups of coffee on round end tables beside them.

"The founding members were journalists and artists and musicians and writers who lamented the lack of culture in post–gold rush San Francisco. They wanted something like the Century Club in New York, the *vie bohème.* But pretty soon, for financial reasons, they had to start admitting prominent businessmen."

"Writers and artists and musicians never make any money."

Barber ignored Spade's words to walk almost majestically down the room. He paused in the wide entrance to a modest dining room.

A serious-faced white-aproned man dressed otherwise in

black came up to greet them. Barber addressed him as Reginald and asked for a table away from the others.

"Certainly, Mr. Barber," said Reginald gravely.

The surprisingly plain dining room was three quarters full of San Francisco movers and shakers, a few of whom Spade knew by sight. Barber was greeted by most of them. They were seated.

"Yep," Spade said, "no women. Effie'll be delighted."

"My wife isn't. She's never been inside the place."

He broke and buttered a sourdough roll; Spade sipped ice water. A waiter appeared, hovered. Barber said the minute steak was edible. Spade said that was fine; Barber ordered for both.

"How's Henny doing these days? He must be out of the university by now," said Spade, bland faced.

Barber banged the linen tablecloth in delight.

"He graduated with honors from Berkeley in June. Between the social whirl and tennis, I've had him coming down to the bank and observing, part-time of course—have to avoid the nepotism issue. I've wanted him to start out as a teller and learn the ropes. It's paying off. Yesterday he came to me and said he'd like to apply for a teller's position at somebody else's bank besides mine, so he could advance on his own merits."

"So he's gotten the urge for adventure out of his blood."

"Has he? He took his degree in literature. His mother and I offered him a year in Europe to soak up some culture, but he said if he went to Europe it would be to climb the Matterhorn. He's been trying his hand on Half Dome in

Yosemite, scaring his mother half to death. I think he enjoys doing it."

"And how is the good Mrs. Barber?"

"More involved in her charity work than ever."

Barber leaned in, lowered his voice.

"I had a long discussion with Spaulding yesterday about Cal-Cit's refusal of access to Collin's financial papers. He says it's because of embarrassment, plain and simple. They were sloppy in their controls on certain accounts that—that Collin was intimately involved in."

"Those accounts have to do with mining stocks?"

"How did you know that?"

The waiter appeared with their meals. Spade cut into his steak, gestured across the table at Barber with the knife.

"I talked with Eberhard's broker. He said Eberhard—and his bank—got wealthy on speculative gold-mining-stock investments during the past four years. Before that—"

"Before that both Collin and his bank were struggling." Barber grimaced. "Spaulding says they're embarrassed because the bank stopped monitoring their dealings with the mining syndicate on Collin's word that he was monitoring both his investments and the bank's very closely."

"It was unwise banking procedures, nothing more?"

"So Spaulding says. I have no, er, solid reason to disbelieve him."

"Then why the stonewall with Eberhard's widow?"

"They're waiting for the insurance situation to resolve itself." He met Spade's eyes. "I'm waffling, aren't I?"

"Yeah."

Barber glanced around, leaned closer again.

"There are some things that continue to bother me. But . . . we can't discuss them here."

He gestured to the waiter, signed the chit. Their exit from the dining room was again a progression, with nods and waves and handshakes and polite comments from the wealthy and powerful in the room. In the doorway Reginald materialized.

"Brandy and cigars in the library, Reginald."

"Very good, Mr. Barber."

After leaving the elevator at the second-floor foyer, Barber and Spade turned left through a wide doorway into the library. All four walls, between windows and doors, were lined with bookshelves from floor to ceiling. Around three sides of the room was a balcony with a waist-high railing.

There was a single window in the right-hand wall that looked down on Taylor Street. In front of the window was a bookcase topped by an ancient-looking three-foot-high brass statue of some fierce-eyed predatory bird with its beak broken off or worn away by time.

"A falcon?" Spade asked.

"An owl. It is a replica of an ancient Athenian owl acquired for the club by Henry Norse Stephens during a trip to Greece in nineteen eleven. The owl is the symbol of the Bohemian Club."

"Why?" asked Spade bluntly.

"Um—the—er—the owl sees through darkness to—to . . ."

"To truth?"

"Yes. To truth. And from truth comes knowledge."

"And from knowledge comes wisdom?"

"That's it. Wisdom. That's why the club slogan is 'Weaving Spiders Come Not Here.' "

Spade moved farther into the library. "I don't see the connection with the weaving spiders," he said.

"Wisdom only comes from contemplation and discussion of philosophical views, not from business. So, no business here."

"I read somewhere that during medieval times, even the Renaissance, the owl was the symbol of evil because it was the bird of darkness."

Down the center of the room, on a pinkish Turkish rug laid over a green carpet, were several hardwood tables on which lay several open reference volumes. There were three more windows in the long Post Street wall, with gauzy lace curtains to cut the glare. Below the high ceiling were three ornate chandeliers, each with twenty electric candles in brass candelabras.

In front of the center window were pairs of leather armchairs faced at comfortable angles to each other. Beside each chair was a brass floor lamp and a smoking table.

Reginald appeared with a tray bearing brandy snifters, a cut glass decanter of cognac, and a silver humidor. He set the tray down on a large table in the front corner of the room, bowed, departed. They selected cigars, poured cognac, moved to two of the padded leather armchairs, sat down. They toasted each other, sipped, drifted fragrant smoke into the air.

"OK," said Spade, "nothing illegal about Cal-Cit's banking practices. But if everything is on the up-and-up, why deny the widow access? Why not make the will public?"

"Spaulding tried to reiterate that it was confidential bank business. I said I was the president of a bank myself, and knew better. Plus I was a member of the Banking Commission. Then he tried to say the police had told them not to release any information. Then he tried to refer me to counsel. I said I was talking with him, right then and there, face-to-face. He finally opened up about the mining stocks. Under Collin's direction the bank had lent money to a Sacramento-based Blue Sky Mining and Development Syndicate, run by a speculator named Devlin St. James, so they could develop mines in the Sierra."

"What does St. James look like?" demanded Spade quickly.

"Apart from Collin, nobody ever met him. Communication was by telephone or letter. For each new mine the syndicate borrowed ten thousand dollars on a note from Cal-Cit co-signed by St. James and endorsed by the syndicate. After a mine was developed the bank loan was repaid with interest and a fifteen-percent commission override. In return the syndicate kept very heavy deposits in the bank, which were vital to Cal-Cit's financial health."

Spade swirled his snifter. "Ring around the rosy."

"But then Eberhard died and the syndicate, and St. James, drew out all of the money they had on deposit. The bank panicked. Spaulding, as acting president, tried to call in the syndicate's notes. The syndicate said all of the money had been spent in developing new mines."

"So of course the bank tried to seize the syndicate's assets," said Spade, "and there weren't any."

"Just a storefront office on a Sacramento side street with a filing cabinet and a chair and a desk and a typewriter and a telephone. A dollar-a-day clerk to answer the phone and type the letters he was told to type. If anyone came around asking, St. James was in the High Sierra searching out new mines to lease."

"They get a description of St. James from the clerk?"

"He was hired by an employment agency."

"And the agency was hired by letter?"

"By phone, actually. How do you know all of this, Spade?"

"You know banking. I know con games and frauds. Your Devlin St. James is the mystery man you saw at the Neptune Bath House, and was the man arguing with Eberhard at his home. He somehow got Eberhard to help him run a shell game with the bank's money and Eberhard's money and his own money from *some* source—I'm pretty sure not from gold mines."

"I refuse to believe that Collin Eberhard was a crook!"

"He's dead, so we can't ask him."

Barber mopped his face, gulped the last of his cognac.

"Yes, Collin is dead. And St. James is gone, the syndicate is gone, the syndicate's records—including the names and locations of the mines—are gone. The bank's money is gone. If that gets out there will be a panic among their depositors. So I feel their actions reflect incompetence, not anything illegal."

Spade drained his own snifter, shook his head.

"I could almost buy that everyone was conned. Almost. But it doesn't work. Spaulding has to be in on the fraud now, or Eberhard was before his death, or both. Otherwise Cal-Cit would be seeking criminal indictments from the state attorney general and opening up their books. And then there's Evelyn Eberhard."

"Surely *Evelyn* wasn't involved."

"Not involved. Defrauded. As Eberhard's heir, she would step into his controlling interest in the bank and could demand to see the books. If they showed Eberhard was ruined, she would get the insurance money and nothing more. And be glad to get it. If he wasn't ruined, then somebody's been cooking the books."

"Well, there's nothing I can do about it."

"There's something I can do about it," said Spade.

24

Seven Lies

When the key turned in the lock, Spade was sitting in Penny's easy chair reading the clippings about Eberhard's death. His empty coffee mug was perched on one frayed arm of the chair.

Penny came through the door, turned and closed and locked it before she registered that the lights were on. She whirled, her face going deathly pale and her mouth becoming a round O of terror when she saw someone sitting in the armchair.

"Don't yell. You'll wake little Jenny across the hall."

She recognized him. Fire replaced fear in her eyes.

"I thought I could trust you! Instead you followed me here after you promised you wouldn't. You lied to me."

"As you lied to me." Spade tossed the clippings back onto the magazine stand, stood up, and carried his empty mug around the linoleum-topped counter to the tiny kitchen. He refilled his mug from the pot on the stove, raised it. "Coffee?"

Penny shook her head. Her eyes were hostile. He poured a second mug anyway, set his on the counter, hers on the chair arm.

She burst out, "What do you mean I lied to you? I didn't want you to know where I lived, but I told you where I worked."

"You haven't worked there for a month," said Spade.

Her magnificent dark eyes dulled. Moving like a suddenly old woman, she groped her way to the armchair, sat, and then, despite her refusal, began greedily drinking thick, hot coffee.

"Let's stop playing games," said Spade in a softer voice. "Let's stop accusing each other of things. Just tell me the truth, Penny, so I'll know what I'm dealing with."

"I have been telling you the truth!"

Spade snatched up the sheaf of clippings on the Eberhard death from the magazine table beside her chair. "These say you're lying." He slammed them down again. "To your mother. To Effie. To me. To everyone. Want me to list all the lies?"

"They weren't lies. They were—"

"One"—Spade folded in his left thumb—"the Turk that's supposed to be following you. There is no Turk." He folded down his forefinger. "Two. The chest of Bergina. Maybe there is a chest. Maybe your father even wrote to you about it. But it has nothing to do with you either way." He folded down his index finger. "Three. You told me you were a secretary at Hartford and Cole. You started out that way right enough, but by the time you quit you were a de facto broker." He folded down the ring finger. "Four. You told Cole you had to care for your aged father. Your father is dead." The little finger. "Five—"

"Stop it!" she cried.

"Five," he repeated inexorably, his left hand now a closed fist. "You moved in here under a false name—Julia Drosos."

He opened his left hand, then folded in his right thumb.

"Six. You told Beverly Donant across the hall that your mother had died down in Santa Barbara and you had come up here because being there made you sad." Folded the right forefinger. "Seven. You told her you were looking for work as a nanny for little children like her Jenny." Right index finger. "Eight."

Her mouth twisted with some deep emotion, perhaps anger.

"What about your lies to Beverly? That you were looking for someone to take care of the small children of a wealthy family outside the city? I should have known better, but I so much wanted to get away from here and be safe and—"

She stopped, on the edge of tears. The harsh lines drawn in Spade's face eased. His voice was once again soft.

"You're right. Seven lies are plenty." He took a turn around the room, stopped in front of her again. "But don't you see? Now that we've cut through all the evasions, you have to tell me the truth."

"I—I have nothing to tell you."

Spade rolled and lit his first cigarette since she had entered the room. He looked at her through the drifting smoke.

"OK, I'll tell you."

He swept the clippings off the magazine stand and sat down on the edge of it so he could loom over her.

"Three years ago your father was killed in Anatolia—unless that's a lie too. Anyway, the money stopped. Your mother had to take in boarders. You moved out, found a room somewhere, and became a secretary for Hartford and Cole, who specialized in timber and mineral stocks—copper, tin, silver, gold."

Animation lit her face. "I told Effie I was working—"

"Yeah. But not where. And not where you were living. You had a head for the business, so pretty soon you were handling bits and pieces of some of Hartford and Cole's accounts like a bona fide broker. 'Near as damn to swearing' is the way Cole put it to me. One of the accounts was Eberhard's."

"Even if that were so, it doesn't mean that I—"

"Of course it does." He dropped the butt of his cigarette hissing into her half-empty mug. "Eberhard started an affair with you, God knows it would be easy enough to want to, and then told them he wanted you handling more of his work."

Penny put her hands over her ears, as if she didn't want to hear him. Spade gave a jeering laugh and leaned closer still and put even more steel into his voice.

"He came to trust you. To tell you things he couldn't—or wouldn't—tell his wife. She knew he had a mistress. A few months ago she wanted to hire me to find out who you were, to save her marriage. Now she wants me to find you and throw you to the wolves. I think you knew that the money Devlin St. James was investing wasn't coming from any gold mines. I think you know, or at least suspect, maybe from things Eberhard had told you, that Eberhard was murdered."

She squeezed her eyes shut, shaking her head.

"Hear no evil? See no evil? Speak no evil?" He gave his jeering laugh again. "Not this time, sister. You came to me in the first place because Effie had told you I was looking into the Eberhard death, and you either wanted to sidetrack me or use me as protection against whoever's out there looking for you."

She raised her eyes to his. "I don't know anything."

He stared at her for long moments, then frustration and anger faded to resignation. He put a thick, wedge-shaped hand under her chin and raised her face so she had to look up at him from clear dark eyes. He bent and gently kissed her on the lips.

"Good-bye, Penny," he said.

When Effie Perine entered Sam Spade's inner office the next morning at 8 o'clock, he was slouched behind his desk, dull eyed, smoking a cigarette. The bottle of Manhattan cocktail that was usually in the lower drawer stood empty on the desk. A dozen paper cups were crumpled in the wastebasket beside it. Butts overflowed the ashtray onto the blotter. The open window behind Spade's head swirled and eddied ash like wind from the bay eddied the summer fog on Mission Street below the window.

Spade raised bloodshot eyes at her entrance. His face

was lined. The hand holding his smoked-down cigarette shook slightly when he smeared it out among the other butts in the ashtray.

" 'Lo, snip," he said in a slightly hoarse voice. "I got hootched up like a bat last night."

"I never would have known." Then her sprightly voice changed to gravity. "Any reason?"

He didn't speak. She dropped the bottle into the half-full wastebasket, followed it with the butts from the ashtray. She took a cloth draped over the S-shaped pipe under the sink and wiped the ash off the desk. Spade's bloodshot eyes followed her as she started for the door with the wastebasket.

He said to her back, "I'm dropping the Eberhard case."

She turned back in the doorway, shocked.

"But Sam, didn't you read the memo? Mrs. Eberhard has accepted your offer—to trade the name of her husband's mistress for her cooperation in trying to get into the Cal-Cit bank records."

"I saw it." He gestured at the wastebasket she was holding. "I filed it."

She took a step closer, then stopped.

He said, "I'm dropping Penny's case too."

She responded instantly, putting her knuckles on the desktop so she could lean across it toward him.

"That's rotten, Sam!" Her eyes were flashing. "She's in danger, you said so yourself. You can't just—"

"Can and am." His voice was sullen. "Too many lies. She made her bed with them, let her lie in it. Or die in it."

She began, "You're despic—" then caught herself. Her eyes widened. She began, "What? Are you—"

"I don't know, angel," he said with an almost shocking frankness. "I just can't . . ." He said again, "Too many lies."

After a long moment she picked up the wastebasket and left quietly, as from a sickroom, shutting the door behind her.

For half an hour Spade rolled and smoked one cigarette after another while the chill wind through the window whipped the curtains and mussed his pale brown hair. Stubborn thoughts and emotions played across his face as they only did when he was alone. Anger gave way to mulish determination, replaced by irritation, by resignation, finally by a sort of acceptance.

He stood, crossed the office in long strides, threw open the door, crossed to Effie Perine's desk, said in a rush of words, "You're right, damn you. I can't walk away from her. I'm—I can't let anything happen to her."

He took hat and topcoat from the rack beside the office door on which appeared SAMUEL SPADE backward on the glass and left.

Three hours later Spade, clear-eyed and quick of step, emerged from the Turkish bath above the billiards hall at 47 Golden Gate Avenue. He walked down to catch a streetcar at Taylor and Market, where the Golden Gate Theatre advertised its current variety acts. It was fifteen minutes shy of noon.

At fifteen minutes past noon, Henny Barber, dressed in a banker's conservative suit and dull tie, turned from the counter of Van's Grill on California and Grant with his corned-beef sandwich, apple pie, and coffee. He stopped dead when he saw Spade drinking coffee at his table.

"Eat," said Spade. "You're the one with the half-hour lunch break. Is anybody using Eberhard's office these days?"

"Spaulding. He's declared himself acting president of the bank, and he's in Uncle Collin's office all day every day."

"Like he's making sure nobody else gets in there? Maybe like there's paperwork in there he can't let anyone else see?"

"Just like that," agreed Henny in a surprised voice.

"Can you arrange to stay late tonight?" Spade leaned forward. "After hours?"

Henny said around a big bite of corned-beef sandwich, "Sure, easy. I'll just make sure that my cash fails to balance. Old man Spaulding is death on balancing to the penny. Two nights ago he made Renata Ferrano so nervous that she kept making simple arithmetic errors and had to stay until eleven o'clock to balance out. She told me the night security guy kept bothering her."

"Gino Mechetti," said Spade.

Henny was again surprised. "How did you know that?"

Spade grinned and pulled down a lower eyelid with a finger. "She say how many security rounds Gino made while she was there?"

"None. All he did was hang around and bother her."

"Mmm-hmm, but we can't count on that. Tonight you have to keep him on the main floor from ten p.m. until one a.m."

"That might be hard. He knows I want to punch him one on the beezer."

"You'll ply him with dago red and make him think he's the cat's meow." Seeing Henny's puzzlement, Spade added, "Pretend you're acting in one of those Bohemian Club plays. Outwitting the villain who's going to tie Pearl White to the railroad tracks."

Henny started on his pie, laughing as he did. "OK."

"Do you know exactly where Eberhard's office is?"

"It takes up the back half of the second floor. Big inner office, with Spaulding in it all day, smaller outer office with one of the tellers sitting there during banking hours even though Uncle Collin is dead."

"The elevator is where?"

"Fifteen feet away."

"At night, is it left on the first floor, locked down with the door open? Stairs beside it?"

"Yes on both counts. Gino uses the stairs for his rounds."

"Tonight make sure he doesn't get off the ground floor."

Henny nodded and wiped his mouth with his napkin. "If I have to bonk him on the head to keep him there."

"Good man. I'll tell you all about it when it's over." Spade grinned. "Unless my foot slips and you end up reading about it in tomorrow morning's *Chronicle.*"

25

Dago Red

At 9:32 p.m. hulking Mickey Linehan slammed down five cards faceup on a conference table cleared of everything except chips, cards, whiskey, money, and the players' elbows.

"Boat!" he chortled with his idiot's grin. "Jacks over nines. Read 'em and weep, gentlemen."

Tall lean Woody Robinson shook the big head on his thin stalk of a neck and tossed in his hand. Phil Haultain followed suit. Spade was already turning his pant pockets inside out.

"I'm on the hog, but don't let me bust up your little game, boys. Just so long as I went broke three hours from now."

Mickey Linehan, making his half-wit's face, said, "We done plucked you clean at . . . twelve forty-three a.m."

Spade walked down the echoing third-floor hallway to the back stairs, took them down to the street so no one could clock him leaving the Flood Building.

. . .

In Pratt Place beside the Chinese social club Sam Spade crouched, leaped up. His gloved hands caught the bottom of the folded-up metal stairs. His weight dragged them down, unfolding them with a shriek of rusted iron. He climbed the three flights of fire escape to the waist-high parapet. On the far side of the flat black tarred roof he dropped lightly down three feet onto the similarly flat roof of California-Citizens Bank.

Shielding his flashlight so only a small circle of light showed, Spade illuminated the lock and hasp on the door of the weathered wooden shed that gave access to the bank's elevator shaft. It was a solid brass Corbin padlock that weighed a pound.

"Not good," Spade muttered to himself.

But his light picked out raw wood under the hasp, paint peeled and dried out despite San Francisco's persistent fog.

"Better," muttered Spade.

He took a short pry bar from under his mackinaw and inserted it behind the hasp, pulled down. The lock-and-hasp assembly fell onto the roof. Spade opened the shed door, shone his light inside.

There was an eighteen-inch-wide maintenance walkway around the two big wheels that filled the top of the shaft, over which the elevator cables passed. The air was heavy with the smell of lubricating grease.

Spade stepped in and shone his light down. The elevator's roof was some twenty feet below Spade's narrow walkway. He pulled up his shirt to unwind a length of rope from around his waist, tied one end around the bottom of one cable wheel, pulled hard to test the knot, grabbed the rope with both gloved hands, and stepped off the walkway. He lowered himself by arm strength alone.

When his booted feet touched the elevator roof his chest was level with the bottom of the second-floor elevator doors. He jammed his pry bar into the intersection, heaved sideways. The doors separated a few inches. He shoved the bar in farther, heaved again. The aperture widened. A third heave gave him an opening he could wriggle through. He listened at the top of the stairs to the muffled sound of male voices, a low burst of laughter. He grinned.

"Dago red," he said to himself.

The door to Eberhard's outer office was not locked. Spade went past the deserted secretary's desk to the private office. He used his light on the door, his penknife on the lock, and was in. His light swept the room. There was a conference table of modest proportions with six chairs arranged around it. The light stopped on Eberhard's executive-style rolltop desk.

"That'll do it," said Spade softly.

The roll curtain was down and locked. His penknife easily jimmied the lock. He slid up the curtain, heard the locking device on the pedestal drawers down each side of the desk click open. Rifled the pigeonholes. Flicked open the private locker pigeonhole with his penknife, stuffed the contents into one pocket of his mackinaw without looking at them.

From the double-depth pedestal drawer on the right-hand side of the desk he extracted three files, folded them, and stuffed them into his other coat pocket. He shut the drawers, returned everything to its original position, closed down the roll curtain to lock the drawers.

Spade paused again at the head of the stairs and was rewarded with faint male voices singing "Ukulele Lady" quite badly.

"Dago red indeed," he muttered again, grinning.

He slid through the narrowly opened shaft doors to the roof of the elevator, grunted his way up his rope to the cable wheels, muscled himself up to crouch on the narrow catwalk, and used his knife to worry open the knot on his rope and haul it up.

On the roof he broke a wooden match into four short pieces and shoved one piece into each of the hasp's screw holes, used a coin to tighten down the screws in their holes. He reversed his way back over two roofs and away.

It was just after midnight when Spade left the Sutter car to walk down Hyde Street. As he angled across the intersection a big black Buick sedan roared up Post toward him. He threw himself headlong into the gutter in front of his apartment house as the driver's heavy revolver spat fire four times. The third of the shots neatly plucked Spade's hat off his head and sent it rolling across the sidewalk. The sedan squealed downhill into Hyde and was gone.

Spade was on his feet and snatching up his hat before the

car had disappeared. He twisted his key in the vestibule door lock, jerked it out, sprinted up the stairs before any window could be raised, any head thrust out in response to the shots.

The phone was ringing when he came into his apartment. He ignored it to cross the front room in the dark, part the curtains enough to peer down at the people in the street. They were pointing in various directions, none of them toward his darkened windows. The phone stopped ringing, started again. A uniformed policeman was using his key on the police call box on the corner.

Spade let the window curtain fall back into place. He put the papers purloined from Eberhard's desk under the pillows of the sofa, removed his hat and mackinaw, and hung them on the hooks inside the front door. Ignoring the police sirens, the squeal of police car wheels, Spade poured himself a shot of Bacardi. He sat in his easy chair in the dark and smoked cigarettes and drank.

When he returned to the window a half hour later, only a few citizens now stood around in the street below, talking and gesturing. The police had departed without ringing his doorbell.

Spade had just lowered the wall bed when the phone rang for the sixth time. He picked it up from its place on the bedside table, atop Duke's *Celebrated Criminal Cases of America.*

"Spade," he said.

Effie Perine's voice said, "Penny is here. She's been here for hours. She's terrified. She needs you, Sam."

Spade sat down on the edge of the bed. "Put her on."

After long moments Penny's voice came, small and hesitant.

"I saw him. On Market Street." Her voice steadied, strengthened as she talked. "And he saw me."

"When?"

"Around nine o'clock. I was just crossing Market when I saw him walking toward me, very fast. I—I jumped on a passing car. He tried to get on, but it was moving too fast and the doors were shut. I rode it to Sixth Avenue in the Richmond, got off, and ran out here to Effie's place. I—I've been here ever since. If he should think to come here—"

"Put Effie back on," said Spade soothingly.

"I'm here," said Effie Perine.

"How's your mother with all these shenanigans?"

She got closer to the phone. "She's worried, maybe a little scared, but she's always been strong for Penny."

"OK, make sure all the doors and windows are locked till I get there. Call the Monroe Hotel out on Sacramento Street and reserve a room for a Mary Kutina, that's K-u-t-i-n-a. I don't think he'd try to crush his way in there, but if you see anyone hanging around call the cops and report a Peeping Tom."

Spade hung up, got central, gave the operator Davenport 1000. A man's gruff voice answered. "Bluebird Cabs."

"Eight nine one Post Street, ten minutes," said Spade.

He started out of the apartment, grabbing his hat and the mackinaw. He stopped, wiggled his fingers through the entry and exit holes in his hat, tossed it aside, and got another. It was tan and did not go with the rest of his clothes.

26

Penny

The Monroe Hotel was between Van Ness and Franklin at the lower edge of Pacific Heights. Spade had money in hand for the cabdriver. He hurried into the hotel so fast, with Penny in tow, that she was on the sidewalk a bare five seconds.

The clerk was a slightly bug-eyed man with an old-fashioned monocle on a velvet cord that passed through the lapel buttonhole of his three-piece suit. He had a judging face, a tightly trimmed sandy mustache, slim fingers that drummed nervously on the desktop.

"May we help you, sir?" His voice was supercilious.

Spade spun the hotel register around, wrote "Mary Kutina, City," in a bold slashing hand, saying without looking up, "My secretary phoned ahead for a reservation for Miss Kutina."

The clerk's eyes took in Spade's disreputable appearance, Penny's frightened eyes and cloche hanging precariously to the side of her head, the cheap frock under a calf-length coat that had seen better days. The eyes slid to the lobby clock.

"I think not, sir." His voice just avoided having a sneer in it. "We are not that kind of hotel."

"You are now," said Spade. "Tell your house dick, Skip LeGrande, that Sam is stashing a witness for a day or two." He tossed money on the counter, reached across to the keyboard and snagged a key, held it up, said, "Three three three."

Spade put their hats on the shelf of the closet inside the door, hung up their coats. When he turned, Penny was standing in the middle of the room with a dazed look on her face, as if she couldn't remember where she was or how she had gotten there.

"Sit down, precious," Spade said.

She sat down obediently in the closest chair in that same all-at-once-boneless way with which she had sat when Spade had braced her the night before. Her face was pale, exhaustion rimmed her eyes with red and made their lids seem transparent.

Spade half-filled two glasses with water from the sink, set them down on the table beside Penny's chair, poured generous doses of dark liquid into each glass from a curved, leather-covered metal flask off his hip. He kept one glass for himself, put the other into her hand. He clinked his glass to hers.

"Success to crime," he said.

She shuddered. "Can't we drink to something else?"

"To truth," said Spade. This time she drank, greedily, as she had drunk the at-first-refused coffee at her apartment.

"I'm just so tired of running and hiding and lying all the time," she said. "Of being so scared for so long I can't remember what it's like to not be scared."

"The running and hiding and lying are all finished," said Spade. "You're going to tell me all about it—*all* about it—and then I'll fix whatever is broken."

"Is that a promise?" She had a sort of hope in her voice.

"Guaranteed."

She took another slug of her drink. He darkened it with more bourbon. She started talking, her voice getting stronger.

"You had almost all of it right last night, Sam. I was working at Hartford and Cole as a secretary and they let me start handling little jobs a broker would usually do. Collin was one of their main clients. Almost immediately he started taking me out on the sly and wining and dining me. He was twenty years older than I, I knew he was married, but he didn't seem to care about it so I didn't either. Pretty soon he took me to bed."

"And made sure you handled more of his business?"

"Yes. And set me up in an apartment at eleven fifty-five Leavenworth."

"Hmm. Three-story brownstone at the corner of Sacramento?"

"Yes. I—it meant I could send more money to my mother. Last night you made it sound like it was cold and calculating and commercial. It wasn't like that. Not for either one of us."

"I said that to try and shake the truth out of you."

"I guess you've succeeded," she said with a wan smile. "Collin took me places on the weekends. Sonoma. Carmel. I was handling most of his gold-mining stocks by then. A few months ago he changed. He was wrestling with a decision. At first I didn't know if it was about me or the bank, but then he started to talk about his worries and a man named Devlin St. James."

Spade hiked his chair a little closer. His eyes had taken on a yellow glow. "When was the first time you saw St. James?"

"I never did. Not while Collin was alive. At the time Collin told me that St. James had come to him four years ago with a lot of illegal money. He needed someone to front it for him, turn it legitimate. Collin was desperate, he and the bank were floundering, that cash would save them."

Spade made a cigarette, poured bourbon from his flask.

"Collin said yes to St. James. He even came up with a plan. He set up a gold-mining syndicate that existed only on paper so they could run the money through the syndicate's accounts at the bank."

"What did he mean by a lot of money?"

"Seventy-five thousand."

Spade's eyes narrowed. "Where did the money come from?"

"A bootlegging syndicate in Half Moon Bay. There were no mines, there never had been any mines. Collin said the bootleggers brought the liquor down from Canada and off-loaded it into small boats outside the eleven mile limit.

Some got caught, but nobody could betray the syndicate because none of the men knew who they really were working for."

"A sweet setup," mused Spade. "You run illicit profits from bootlegging through a tame bank as if they are legitimate profits from a gold-mining enterprise. Nothing can go wrong—unless your tame banker gets cold feet."

She made a small distressed sound in her throat.

"I hate to think of Collin that way but, yes, he was the tame banker, and I suppose you could say he got cold feet. He told me that St. James was also violent and unpredictable and liked to brag of killing people who got in his way."

Spade's frown put deep creases between his eyebrows, as if he were chasing elusive memories. "Bootlegging syndicate . . . seventy-five thousand." He stopped, shrugged, nodded. "Go on."

"Collin finally decided to have it out with St. James at home, with his wife in the next room. That way, he said, St. James couldn't do anything violent and unpredictable."

"But a week or so later Eberhard was dead."

"Collin was usually waiting for me at the apartment when I got home from work, but on that day this slender insignificant-looking man I had never seen before was sitting in the living room. He just said that Collin was dead, nothing more. I sort of collapsed into a chair, I was so shocked and so . . . devastated. It was only later that I realized this was less than an hour after Collin had died."

"St. James must have gone straight to your apartment from the Neptune Bath House." Spade's frown had deepened. "But Eberhard was alive when St. James left the bathhouse."

"He took my hand like he was going to—to comfort me and then . . ." She held out her left hand with its badly set little finger. "He twisted my finger and broke it. He laughed and said if I ever told anyone about him he would kill my mother, and then Effie, and then me."

She stopped there, drained her glass, set it aside.

"I panicked. I jerked free and ran down the stairs and jumped aboard an outbound streetcar. I got off in Jordan Heights and got my finger set at the Nurses' Training School there."

"Set badly."

"I didn't care. That night I got a room at the Y.W.C.A. boarding home in O'Farrell Street. At six the next morning I hid in the Russ Building ladies' room until Hartford and Cole opened. I went in, told them my lies, and got my last paycheck and left. I hated it, they had been so good to me, but I needed that money and I knew I had to get it right away. I knew St. James would come looking for me there."

"You're a survivor, sweetheart," said Spade admiringly.

"Barely." She tried another weak smile. "I chose the apartment on Severn Place because I thought he'd never find me out there in Noe Valley. Which meant more lies."

"Why didn't you go to the East Bay or down the peninsula?"

"I would have had to have gone to a stage terminal or a ferry terminal. I'd be in the open. Exposed. So I hid in my apartment. But a month went by and I was running out of money. So I went to Effie's on her birthday and she told me about working for you and that you were looking into Collin's death. So I—I told you that tale about my father finding the chest of Bergina and that a mysterious Turk was after me. The chest is real, I believe, but my father never wrote me about it. I just wanted you to keep me and my mother and Effie safe."

"Well, they're safe in their homes and you're safe here. Take all your meals in your room. Don't talk to anyone."

"Can't—can't you stay?" There was panic in her voice. "I—I *saw* him, Sam! He saw me! He chased me. With murder in his face . . ."

He put his arms around her to comfort her. "You poor kid."

She pressed herself tight against him, her arms went around the back of his neck. His arms came up, went around her body. She clung to him. What was simple comfort seemed suddenly to be something more for both of them, surprising both of them, but then seemed inevitable.

His hands moved over her like electricity. She kissed him, openmouthed. He lifted her effortlessly off her feet and carried her to the bed. His eyes burned. When he spoke his voice was thick with a passion that seemed to go beyond protecting her, beyond wanting her, to something deeper.

"I won't let him hurt you ever again, Penny," Sam Spade said. "Not now. Not ever."

27

Five Murders

Spade entered his office at 10 a.m. His eyes were clear; he was freshly bathed and shaved. His blue broadcloth dress shirt had a new soft white collar, his gray silk tie a conservative pattern. As usual, his gray woolen worsted suit, though expensive, fit him indifferently. He carried a briefcase.

Effie Perine was on her feet as he came through the door.

"How is she? Is she OK? Is she safe?"

"Yes on all counts. She's in room three three three at the Monroe Hotel as Mary Kutina." He set down his briefcase. "Roll me a cigarette, that's a darling."

As she did he prodded the briefcase with his shoe.

"I raided the bank last night, late. I haven't had a chance to look over my haul yet. With any luck they won't even know the stuff is gone. Not until it's too late."

She handed him his cigarette, lit it. He went on.

"And St. James tried an ambush last night outside my apartment." In response to her shocked look he added, "All he did was shoot a hole in my hat."

"But that's crazy! How did he even know who you were? Earlier Penny saw him and he chased her and—"

"Over three hours earlier. Plenty of time to try to gun me down when I got home." He waved a dismissive hand. "Anyway, sweetheart, Penny's been so elusive because she had become Eberhard's mistress and was ashamed to let you know about it."

"Penny? A kept woman? I—I can't believe it."

"Oh, it's true, right enough. It started out as a way to get money for her mother, but it turned into something else. Toward the end Eberhard was telling her everything."

Spade told Effie Perine about the money Devlin St. James had brought to the bank and the phony gold-mining scheme worked out by Eberhard to front for it.

"Just an hour after Eberhard died St. James was breaking Penny's little finger. He planned to kill her too."

"Too?" demanded Effie Perine. "But Eberhard was still alive when St. James left the Neptune Bath House."

"Yeah, so the only way he could have known it that soon was if he had set it up so he'd be gone when it happened." Spade scooped up his briefcase. "Dig out that four-year-old autopsy report from the Marin coroner's office, the one I never read. Those two Portagees were poisoned. I want to know if it was opium."

Her eyes went round. "You think Devlin St. James is the St. Clair McPhee who masterminded the *San Anselmo* robbery?"

"Yeah." His face tightened, became almost ferocious. "Four years off and on I've been looking for that bird. Now here he is, back again. The money he corrupted Eberhard with is the seventy-five thousand bucks from the *San Anselmo.* I should have caught it sooner, but I never saw McPhee and I haven't seen St. James even now. He tried to kill me back then because I cost him fifty thousand in gold bullion. He tried to kill me last night 'cause I'm taking apart his gold-mining scam."

She looked at him with worried eyes. "What are you going to do, Sam? To protect yourself?"

"Stop him before he stops me."

Five minutes later Effie Perine entered Spade's inner office with the Marin County autopsy report. Spade had papers spread across his desk, cigarette ash already drifting across them.

"Thanks, darling. Call Evelyn Eberhard and tell her to be at Sid's office at one thirty, then call Sid and tell him he has to cancel whatever else he might have on. Then go out to the Monroe Hotel. Change cabs two or three times, have the last one drop you a block from the hotel. You know the drill. Collect Penny, take her home with you, and feed her."

"What do I tell her?"

"That by tonight she'll be safe."

Both Wise and Spade stood when Evelyn Eberhard was ushered into Wise's office. She was dressed in black, as befit a widow. But her silk sheath had a collarless neckline, and the bands and sash bows at the waist were a shocking flesh-pink color. The briefcase was beside Spade's chair.

"Mrs. Eberhard, meet Sid Wise, your new attorney."

They both looked surprised, but Wise extended his hand.

"Delighted, Mrs. Eberhard," he said.

She was looking at Spade with fire in her eyes.

"I did not come here to hire an attorney, Mr. Spade."

"You can expect client-attorney confidentiality even if you later decide to seek other counsel," said Wise.

She sat down, removed her stylish clipped velour hat. It also was black, but without the widow's veil that was de rigueur for mourning. She crossed her legs, showing knee.

"Isn't anyone going to offer me a cigar?"

Spade gravely brought a corona del Ritz from his inner suit-coat pocket. He offered it to her with a flourish.

"George Sand to the very end," he observed.

She took the cigar with a low laugh.

"How sweet. You remembered." Spade gave a slight bow. He was holding his lighter to the tip of the corona when she said, "All right, who was his mistress and where can I find her?"

"Forget the mistress. She's irrelevant."

Abruptly, any playfulness Evelyn had shown was gone. She started to rise, said angrily, "This meeting is over."

"Sit down," snapped Spade, sudden iron in his voice.

She looked astounded. Sid Wise looked astounded. But she sat back down. Spade stood, started to lift his briefcase.

"Since I don't represent Mrs. Eberhard," Wise said quickly, "I have to see these papers before you show them to her."

"You're now my attorney," she said just as quickly.

"I withdraw my offer of representation," said Wise.

"Jesus God!" Spade burst out. He leaned his hips against the windowsill so he could take in the lawyer and the widow.

Then he pointed at Evelyn. "All you want to do is get back at the girl who stole your favorite toy." He pointed at Wise. "You, you're afraid of losing your license. Neither one of you seems to give a damn about what the mistress has to say about Eberhard's death."

Evelyn began, "My husband was not a toy. That woman—"

"—can give testimony proving he was murdered. Not by you."

The words hung in the air for long moments before Wise demanded, "How?" at the same time Evelyn demanded, "Who?"

"How? Poison. Opium in his drink at the Neptune Bath House. Who? Devlin St. James."

They looked at each other blankly. Wise said, "Who's he?"

The widow said, "Why did he do it?"

"Why do they always do it? For the money."

"Wait a minute, Sam." Sid's lawyer's mind seemed to be getting belatedly back in gear. "Why do you posit murder, and why opium? There was no indication of poison in the autopsy."

"Four years ago the Marin County coroner found opium in two dead men. He did a good job; it can't always be found."

"Ah." Wise eased back in his swivel chair. "The *San Anselmo* heist. I see. Devlin St. James is St. Clair McPhee."

"Yeah. I finally have a chance of sticking him with those four murders from back then with this murder now."

"I don't understand any of this," said Evelyn weakly.

Spade got his briefcase. "You don't have to. Let's go."

. . .

As the trio went past him, the young man who had been a teller the last time Spade had officially been in California-Citizens Bank started up from his chair.

"Wait! You aren't allowed in there."

But Spade had flung open the door to Eberhard's office and the others had crowded in behind. Spaulding stood up from behind Eberhard's desk. His face was red with anger. He barked at the bewildered young man behind them, "Call the guards!" To Spade he blustered, "We'll see what the bank's attorneys have to say about this outrage." He reached for the phone.

"Why don't you stamp your foot?" said Evelyn Eberhard.

"As her husband's heir," said Spade, "and thus majority stockholder in this bank, Mrs. Eberhard is replacing you and all of the other officials, effective immediately."

"But she isn't the bank's majority stockholder," said Spaulding with a suddenly smug look on his face. He turned to Evelyn, who was still gaping at Spade. "I'm sorry, Mrs. Eberhard, but the bank felt that the terms of your husband's last will and testament made it too delicate for disclosure at this time. Since you're here, however, I can tell you that the will leaves you the house, but his holdings in the bank go to—"

"To his widow, like the will says," said Spade.

"I don't know how you learned of the first will, but that will was superseded by one dated just a week before Mr. Eberhard's death."

From his briefcase Spade brought out a sheaf of papers

like a magician bringing a rabbit out of a top hat and tossed them on the table. Wise sat down, looking numb. Spaulding was still standing, looking indignant.

"Here's the original," Spade said. "*And* the forged one you've been planning to palm off on everyone as genuine."

"That's impossible!" Spaulding was feverishly unlocking desk drawers. "You—you *burgled* this office! The police—"

"Mrs. Eberhard, was I acting with your permission when I secured these documents for safekeeping?"

"Certainly," said Evelyn Eberhard.

"How big a piece of the pie did St. James offer you to help steal the bank away from her, Spaulding?" asked Spade.

"That is a libelous canard that—"

"Not that it matters. Within the hour St. James will be arrested for committing five murders, and you will be arrested as accessory before and after the fact of one of them."

"Fi—five *murders*?" Spaulding's face had turned ashen. He sank back down in the swivel chair.

"Get out from behind my desk!" snapped Evelyn Eberhard.

Spade laughed aloud. "Never get between a widow and her husband's money."

She shot Spade an angry look, then had to chuckle herself. Numbly, Spaulding obeyed her. Evelyn sat down in his place. There was ownership in her movements.

"Five murders," repeated Spade. "Eberhard and four men in Sausalito four years ago. There's no statute of limitations on homicide." He cocked a heel on the desktop, looked at Spaulding. "You might have a chance to get out from under the murder-accessory rap for a lesser charge of embezzlement if you turn up St. James for us—right now. Otherwise Mrs. Eberhard will bring civil suit against you for . . . what, Sid?"

"Fiduciary mismanagement for a start." Wise warmed to his task. "There are some interesting statutes that—"

"Eleven fifty-five Leavenworth," said Spaulding very quickly. "Third floor, rear corner apartment. He . . . he's waiting for my call about finalizing the money transfers."

"Damn!" Spade was at the desk, snatching up the phone. To central he snapped, "Connect me to the Homicide Detail in the Hall of Justice. Quick." His hand over the receiver, he said to Evelyn, "Your husband's love nest . . ."

He removed his hand.

"Tom? Get over to eleven fifty-five Leavenworth, right now . . . Yeah, that's right, up behind Grace Cathedral. Go in quiet but go in quick. The murderer of Collin Eberhard is in the third-floor rear corner apartment, waiting for a telephone call . . . Yeah, I'm sure. Bird calling himself Devlin St. James . . . That's right . . . St. James. Also, under the name St. Clair McPhee he's good for that slaughter over in Sausalito four years ago. Surround the place before you go in or he'll give you the slip. Don't let Dundy hog all the glory."

His left thumb depressed the receiver hook for a long moment, released it. He gave central a number. When he heard Effie Perine's voice, he brought the phone closer to his mouth. There was elation in his voice.

"You have Penny with you there at your mother's?" He nodded. "Good. It's all over, sweetheart. I'll get out there eventually."

28

Effie

Tom Polhaus was leaning against a side wall with his arms folded on his chest and an embarrassed look on his face. Dundy was holding a lace window curtain aside to contemplate the looming bulk of Grace Cathedral in the next block. Phels, heavy bodied with a deeply lined grayish face, was sitting in a velour-upholstered davenport chair, hands hanging down between spread thighs, staring at the floor.

Sam Spade was striding up and down the room. His face was red and the veins at the sides of his thick throat were swelling dangerously as he raged at the three Homicide detectives.

"What do you mean you missed him?"

"He wasn't here, Sam," said Tom with chagrin in his voice. "His clothes and everything was still here, but he wasn't."

"Did you come in like I said? Quick but quiet?"

Dundy said, "How we come in don't matter. He was tipped."

"Who was going to tip him, Dundy?"

"Spaulding."

"Spaulding didn't tip anyone. Sid Wise is sitting on his chest right now waiting for someone to come take him away."

A detective with his hat on, known to Spade only as Mack, burst open the splintered front door.

"Lieutenant, the fire escape is right beside the bathroom window of the first-floor rear apartment, and it rattles like crazy, anybody uses it. Before the tenant went out for lunch, he heard us runnin' up the stairs yellin' we was the police, then heard someone comin' down the fire escape, fast. Uh . . . it was him, Lieutenant. St. James. He took off down the alley afoot."

"How you went in don't matter?" demanded Spade bitterly.

"How was we to know it wasn't you sendin' us on another of your wild-goose chases, Spade? You should of come to us sooner."

Spade's grimace deepened the V's of his face.

"I hope to God you've got men in the bus and train and ferry terminals, got 'em checking hired cars, got 'em—"

"Yeah, yeah, we'll get to all that. But—"

"*Get* to all that?"

Dundy's voice was defensive. "All I've got even now is your phone call to Tom. I ain't talked to Spaulding yet. I ain't seen nothing like proof of anything. I ain't seen the two wills. I don't even know why this St. James was livin' here."

Spade took another frustrated turn around the room.

"Eberhard was keeping his mistress in this apartment. With the lease paid up, what safer place for St. James to hole up? With her story and Spaulding's story you'll have enough to—"

"How much can we trust some cheap tart who was just in it for the money? Maybe she was even in cahoots with St. James."

Spade started across the room toward him, white-faced. Big Tom Polhaus got in his way, arms wide. He spoke in a low voice.

"Where's the girl, Sam?"

The tension went out of Spade. "I've got her stashed."

"Gimme her name so we can check her out," said Dundy.

"I keep telling you, this St. James is deadly. Go out and find her yourself. I'm not stopping you."

Spade parked his hire car at the curb in front of a two-story brick building in the 300 block of the Richmond District's Ninth Avenue. On the small square stoop a glazed Greek pot held a wide-spreading ficus plant. A riot of daisies crowded the living room windowsill planter. He rang the doorbell.

The door was opened by a dark-haired handsome woman in her early forties. Her face broke into a smile when she saw Spade. He bowed slightly to her. "Mrs. Perine."

"I'm so glad this terrible thing is finally over," she said. "Effie's in the front room. I'll get you a cup of coffee."

As she went down the hall to the kitchen Spade entered the living room. Effie Perine stood up from a low-slung Coxwell chair in one corner. She echoed what her mother had said.

"I'm so glad it's all over, Sam. So is Penny."

Spade stopped in the middle of the bright, cheery room. An Oriental carpet was on the gleaming hardwood floor. Framed photos crowded the foot-square taboret under the front window; its lower shelf was crammed with books. Gold-threaded tassels hung from the armrests of the upholstered Chesterfield.

"It isn't quite over," said Spade uneasily. "Not yet. But Penny's safe enough here."

"But she isn't here!"

In two quick strides he had Effie Perine by her upper arms, was almost shaking her. "Not here?"

"After we ate she decided to go get her things from her apartment out in Noe Valley. She said she wanted to close that chapter of her life for good." Effie Perine rubbed her arms through her sweater. "What—what's wrong, Sam?"

"St. James is still on the loose. The cops missed him. How long ago did she leave?"

"Two hours. Should I—"

"If she calls from the Donants' across the hall tell her to stay there with them with the door locked till I get there."

Spade ran up the five worn steps and through the unlatched front door, took the interior stairs two at a time. Thin glass sharded under his feet: the third-floor hallway light had been broken. He followed his torch: the Donants' door was locked. Penny's door drifted open to his touch. He turned off his torch.

Vague light from the street showed him the easy chair and the magazine stand beside it. Undisturbed, as was the kitchen behind its counter. The bedroom's three-wing screen was closed.

Spade folded back one wing to blackness, went in with no more noise than a cat crossing a carpet. Here was the coppery smell of blood. He lit his torch. Its light found the chest of drawers. The battered wardrobe. The cheap suitcase between the side wall and the narrow single bed.

Penny was on the bed, naked, violated. Her head was strained back into the blood-soaked pillow. Her throat was slit. Her face was distorted. Her lip rouge was smeared grotesquely around her mouth. Spade pulled the blanket up over her, stood beside her, head lowered, breathing hard.

The creak of the apartment door gave him animation once more. He killed the torch, in darkness and silence went past the screen, past the kitchen counter, death in his movements.

But it was Effie Perine who stood in the middle of the front room, hands clenched into fists on drawn-back wrists. She gave a little startled cry when she saw Spade, then started toward him.

"Sam! I got a cab, I had to come, I couldn't stand not knowing. Where is she? Is she . . ."

The muscles stood out like marbles along his jaw. His eyes glittered redly in the dim light. He jerked his head toward the bedroom.

"She's in there."

She tried to dart past him. He grabbed her by the upper arms, spun her around against the magazine stand.

"She's dead." He paused, said again, "She is dead." Effie Perine gave a little cry, again tried to get past him. He held her effortlessly, as if she were a rag doll. "You don't want to go in there. You don't want to see it. He forced her back on the bed. He put his hands on her. Then he slit her throat."

Spade flung himself away from her, stood in the middle of the room with his back to her, legs wide, head drawn down between thick shoulders, hands clenched at his sides.

"Don't trust me, Effie. I don't want anyone to trust me. Not now. Not ever."

Finally he turned to face her. She was standing beside the chair, hands hanging laxly at her sides, tears pouring down her cheeks. She made no attempt to stop them, as if she did not know that she was crying.

Spade said softly, "I'll take you home. Dundy would hound you forever if he knew you'd been here, so you never were."

She finally wiped away her tears with the back of her hand. "I was never here," she repeated in a soft, obedient voice.

29

The Third Woman

Spade was in his armchair, a glass of Bacardi on the floor beside him. He was freshly bathed, cleanly shaven, wearing slacks and a gray plaid flannel shirt open at the throat. His lion-yellow eyes were dead, without animation.

The street doorbell rang. His head came up. He stood, tossing *The Great Gatsby* that he wasn't reading onto the sofa. He crossed the room to the telephone box beside the bathroom door that connected to the downstairs door.

"Who is it?"

"Tom Polhaus."

"Is Dundy with you?"

"No."

Spade pressed the button that released the street-door lock, went into the kitchen, and poured a second glass of Bacardi. He set it on the table beside the lowered made-up wall bed.

When he heard the elevator door rattling open and closed down the hall, he stood framed in his open apartment doorway, almost at attention, as if to make sure that Dundy was not sneaking down the hall behind Polhaus.

"He ain't with me Sam," said Tom bluntly.

"He send you?"

"Yeah. You ain't been to your office for ten days."

Spade stood aside, let Tom enter past him. He gestured at the drink on the table beside the bed, returned to his easy chair. The bedsprings squeaked under Tom's weight. They faced each other across the breadth of the room like adversaries taking each other's measure.

Tom picked up his drink. They toasted silently, drank. Polhaus looked exhausted and bulky in his topcoat and the hat he had not yet removed. With an abrupt movement, he took it off and dropped it on the bed beside him.

"You're gonna have to talk to Dundy sometime, Sam. We need your statement signed."

"I'll talk to you. I won't talk to Dundy."

"You will if you expect to keep operating in this town."

"Not now. Not yet." Spade drank, added without emphasis or emotion, "If I saw him now I'd kill him."

Polhaus leaned back, opening his arms so abruptly some of his drink slopped over his knuckles.

"For hell's sake, Sam! It would of happened anyway. Spaulding says he didn't know nothing about the Eberhard murder, and I believe him. He went along with the forged will because St. James offered him a lot of money, pure and simple."

Spade sprang to his feet to point hotly at Polhaus across the room. "Penny'd still be alive if Dundy'd done his job!"

Tom was on his feet also. He drained his glass, set it on

the table. "There's no talking to you. If you'd of told us where she was we'd of had her safely in custody . . ."

The look on Spade's face, the tension in his body, stopped the policeman cold. But it was Spade who looked away.

"You know he wouldn't have moved on it. Not Dundy, not for me. And Penny wasn't at Effie's, where she was supposed to be."

"If you'd of called us when you knew she'd gone to the Severn Place apartment—"

"She was dead an hour before I knew where she was."

Polhaus started to speak, stopped. Spade sat, started rolling a cigarette. He said evenly, "Any word on St. James?"

Polhaus looked embarrassed. "When we, ah, finally got moving on it we found an eyewitness saw him on a ferry to Oakland. Dead end. But first thing Mrs. Eberhard did when she took over at the bank, she hired Continental to find the murderer of her husband. She's spending a lot of money on it."

"Is it doing any good?"

Polhaus leaned forward, suddenly intent, his coat opening so the gun holstered under his left arm could be seen. "St. James bought a train ticket to New York. By the time Continental got that the train was already past Salt Lake City. They had agents waiting in Denver. He wasn't on it. He could of got off anywhere, Sacramento, Reno, Salt Lake City—if he got on at Oakland in the first place. So they've lost him, for now."

"Good," said Spade.

"Good? I'd of thought you'd want to see him—"

"I want him for myself," said Spade gutturally.

Tom seemed to be waiting for him to say more. He didn't. Polhaus shrugged, stood, jammed his hat back on his head.

"I'll see you at the hall in the morning, right? We gotta get that statement signed." Spade was silent. "Right, Sam? I'll make sure Dundy ain't around."

After a long moment Spade said, "I'll be there."

For ten minutes after Polhaus left Spade walked around the apartment, his chin jutting, his eyes gleaming red. He stubbed out his cigarette, didn't roll another, didn't take any more Bacardi. Finally the muscles knotted along his jaw relaxed. The fire in his eyes was replaced by a leaden indifference.

The street doorbell rang again. The indifference left Spade's face. The gleam returned to his eyes.

"Dundy, for a dollar," he said aloud.

He crossed to the front door once again, pressed the button that released the street-door lock. When the rattle of the elevator could be heard he stood in the opened doorway as he had while waiting for Polhaus. But soft footfalls, those of a woman, came up the hall from the elevator. A frown gouged deep lines between his eyes.

Iva Archer swept around the corner. Her big blue eyes were round and guileless as ever. The smile on her generous red mouth was ripe with promise.

"Iva." He said it gravely, without moving aside. She tried to see around him into the apartment.

"Am I interrupting something?"

"Where's Miles?"

"You're no fun!" she exclaimed pettishly. "If you must know we've been here for a week, looking around again. You know, what we talked about over dinner that night. He went back up to Seattle this morning. Do we have to talk out here in the hall, Sam, with the neighbors listening?"

Spade stepped back. She went into the living room.

"I stayed over to do some shopping. Spokane has no fashion sense." She turned in a circle, displaying her coat. It had deep fur cuffs and a wide fur band around the lower back and sides. "Like it? Velana suede trimmed with Mendoza fur and lined with silk crepe."

"Yeah, stunning."

"It's a design by the famous Parisian couturier Paul Poiret." She buried her hands sensuously in the wide fur collar. "Aren't you going to buy a girl a drink?"

Spade went into the kitchen, got another glass, and poured rum into it. By the time he returned she had thrown her coat carelessly across the sofa and was standing by the bed. She was wearing a silk dress, navy blue with beige trimming, that had a softly bloused bodice giving a generous glimpse of her bosom.

"Another copy of a Poiret original."

Spade's face was cold, rock hard, but he let his eyes run deliberately up and down her finely honed body. She preened under that gaze. He gave her the Bacardi, got his own. Standing beside the bed, they clinked glasses.

"To us," said Iva.

"Sure, why the hell not?" said Spade. They drank.

"I have to go back up to Spokane in the morning." There was an open challenge in her voice, her eyes. "I checked my luggage at the train station and didn't keep the hotel room."

"Sure, why the hell not?" said Spade again.

He went to lock the apartment door. There was a tired finality in his movements. Before going back up the hall he rested his forehead against the doorframe for a moment.

When Sam Spade returned to the living room Iva Archer already was carefully removing her designer dress.

1928

Miles Archer

Hello, sucker!

—Texas Guinan

30

Miles Archer

Mabel—Wise, Merican & Wise's redheaded receptionist—opened the door of Sid Wise's private office. Wise was behind his desk with his usual cigar; Spade sat beside the desk, his back toward the windowed side wall, smoking a cigarette.

"Mr. Archer is here," Mabel said.

Miles Archer came in. She left, closing the door behind her. Archer removed his brown hat, ducked his head slightly in greeting. Spade, still seated, nodded. Wise stood up.

"Sid Wise. A pleasure, sir." He held out his hand. They shook. Wise gestured Archer toward the straight-backed chair across the desk from him. "I hear that you and Sam may be going into business together."

"No maybe about it," said Archer in his coarse, heavy, confident voice.

He wore a brown vested cashmere-blend suit; his brown hair was now shot with gray. Spade gestured with his cigarette.

"Sit down, Miles. We've got papers to sign."

The appraising look in Archer's small brown eyes did not match the habitual joviality in his red heavy-jawed face. He finally put his hat on the edge of the desk and sat down, took a cigarette from a flat nickel and silver cigarette case. He tapped it against the case, put it between thick lips pulled taut.

Sid Wise leaned forward to squirt flame against the cigarette tip from his desktop lighter. He sat back again, took three sheets of legal paper from a folder. He handed both Spade and Archer one of the carbons, kept the original himself. He went down the document line by line, looking up at them often to make sure they were getting it.

"What we have here is a simple partnership agreement. No corporation is being formed, so it is not a complicated document. At the top, today's date, October twelfth, nineteen twenty-eight. Below that—"

Spade gave a short laugh that again touched only his mouth, leaving the rest of his bony face nearly sullen. "Almost the anniversary of the arrival and docking of the *San Anselmo* seven years ago."

Sid Wise jerked his head up sharply to look at Spade with speculation in his eyes. Miles Archer just dragged on his cigarette with a look between puzzlement and impatience. Wise lowered his gaze, continued with the articles of agreement.

"Article one lays out the understanding between the two parties: no salaries, just a fifty-fifty split right down the line. All net income and all expenses are shared equally."

"We work our own cases, or we work together on cases as needed," Spade told Archer. "Ten bucks comes in, you get five, I get five no matter who does the work or whose client it comes from."

"Article two states that expenses consist of Effie Perine's salary and rent of the Samuel Spade office, hereinafter to be referred to as the Spade and Archer office, in the Hunter-Dulin Building at one hundred eleven Sutter Street. The rent covers utilities—water, heat, and electricity. Incidental expenses will be paid out of petty cash."

"What about field expenses?" Then Archer guffawed loudly, jarringly. "You know—booze, bribes, and biddies?"

"We get as much cash up front as we can, and treat taxis, ferries, rental cars, hotels, and informants as expenses coming on top of that. Booze and biddies, Miles—you're on your own."

"In the event of the death of one partner," said Sid Wise, "the partnership is automatically dissolved." He looked from one to the other. "Any other questions or comments?"

"Nope," said Spade. Archer was silent.

Spade and Archer signed and dated all three copies, with Wise signing as witness. They all stood, they all shook hands. Spade and Archer left Wise's office together. Spade's hat remained behind on the floor beside his chair.

As they waited for the elevator outside the Wise, Merican & Wise office Spade said, "Better celebrate tonight. Because tomorrow night—"

"Yeah. I'll be on the docks. Undercover." Archer added the last word with relish, as if looking forward to it.

The elevator arrived, Spade shook his head in apparent chagrin.

"Left my hat in Sid's office. Give Iva my regards, Miles."

Archer, grinning from ear to ear, said, "I'll give Iva my own regards, Sam. She won't know what fell on her tonight."

"Of course she won't." Spade grinned wolfishly.

When Sam Spade reentered Sid Wise's office, the diminutive attorney was abstractedly chewing on a fingernail while staring out the window at the Sutter Hotel across the street. Spade picked up his hat, put it on the corner of the desk.

Wise spoke tonelessly without turning. "The *San Anselmo.* Still chasing ghosts, Sam?"

"St. Clair McPhee, Devlin St. James. Whatever name he uses he's no ghost, Sid."

"After all this time he might as well be."

"We'll see about that." Then Spade drew a deep, dismissive breath, gestured at the office door through which Miles Archer had departed. "So what do you think of him, Sid?"

Only then did Wise swivel his chair around to face Spade.

"Same as you do, Sammy. He's dumb as a post and greedy as a lawyer."

"Here lies a lawyer, an honest man."

"Why'd they bury them in the same grave? I've heard that one." Wise retrieved his half-smoked cigar from the ashtray. He relit it, carefully turning it to get it burning evenly again. "I don't trust him, Sam."

"Nor do I, but he's damned good at what he does. He turned up a lot of Commies for the Burns Agency in Seattle."

"How many were Commies just because he said they were?"

Spade nodded to that thoughtfully. Wise blew out a cloud of fragrant cigar smoke.

"I hear he's got a blond wife that's a knockout." He added deadpan, "Originally from Spokane."

"Yeah, I knew her up there," Spade said shortly.

"You don't need him, Sam, but now you're stuck with him for a year. It doesn't make sense."

"I've got an expensive suite of offices in the heart of the financial district, Sid. Half the politicians and the big rich in this town would like to see me in jail, but every once in a while they need me because I'm the only one they can trust to sweep up the breakage and keep my mouth shut."

"If you'd had too much work for one man you could have just hired extra ops from Continental. You didn't have to take in Archer as a partner. Three years ago when he hinted around at it you turned him down flat. Now . . ."

Spade leaned back in his chair, feathered smoke through his nostrils, said, "The Blue Book union. The boys who got control of the docks and crushed the trade unions after the war."

"They hate your guts, you hate their guts. You're trying to tell me that *they* want to hire you?"

"Not directly. But last week I was summoned by Ralph Toomey at Matson Shipping. He was speaking for the Industrial Association, the bankers and industrialists and oil-company and shipping-company executives who really run this burg and who set up the Blue Book union in the first place."

"Nobody's going to be able to take them down, Sam. They belong to the exclusive clubs, they helped found the opera, the symphony, they fund the Community Chest and Stanford and the Boy Scouts and the Y.M.C.A. and the California Historical Society."

"All noble causes." Spade deepened his sardonic voice to proclaim in ringing orator's tones, " 'We have succeeded in making San Francisco a free city where capital can safely invest.' " In his own voice he added, "Toomey said that right now there's the most wide-scale pilfering and theft on the docks that the port's ever seen. They want it kept quiet but they want it stopped."

Wise was thoughtful. "Sounds like a perfectly legitimate investigation to me, Sam."

"Maybe. But since I'm too well known on the waterfront to go undercover myself on the docks these days, Toomey 'recommended' I take on Miles Archer as a partner. Burns used Miles undercover in Seattle to ferret around, glad-hand people, get them talking, then turned them in as Commies. Toomey said he's heard only good things about him."

"As blatant as that?"

"As blatant as that. Between the lines no Archer, no job. So Miles is going down on the docks undercover tomorrow night for Spade and Archer."

"And Iva Archer has nothing to do with this?"

"Nothing."

"What if she thinks she does?"

"I can't help what people think."

Wise held up wide-open defensive hands. "I wouldn't be doing my job as your lawyer if I didn't ask these things."

"Yeah." Spade retrieved his hat, stood up. "Remember from high school, Sid? Shakespeare? 'First, . . . let's kill all the lawyers'?"

He chuckled at his joke. Sid Wise didn't.

31

At the Warehouse

Effie Perine came around Spade's desk to fish the tobacco sack and cigarette papers out of his vest pocket. She made a paper trough, sprinkled flakes into it, expertly pulled the drawstring at the top of the sack with her teeth. As she did she glanced at the bare-topped desk across the room.

"We haven't seen much of the new partner around here since he started," she said.

"He's working down on the docks nights, sleeping days."

"Leaving poor little Iva all alone in that big apartment."

"Enough of that, snip. You sound like Sid Wise."

She licked the seam, smoothed the cigarette, twisted the ends, placed one of them between Spade's lips, went back around the desk, and sat down in the oaken armchair.

"I don't like that woman, Sam. She's too blonde and too good-looking and she's got too good a figure." She added snidely, "For her age. I hear she's been talking about divorce."

"You women," said Spade, shaking his head. He picked a flake of tobacco off his lower lip. "Leave me out of it."

"Will she?"

Spade's face got sullen. "She'll have to."

The door opened. Miles Archer came in. He was dressed for the docks: watch cap, heavy mackinaw, waterproof khaki pants over heavy work boots.

"Mr. Archer," said Effie with a smile, then added cheerily, "I'll get those papers typed up for you to sign, Mr. Spade."

"Thanks, sweetheart."

Archer turned to watch Effie go through the door. When he turned back to Spade his eyes gleamed wetly. But all he did was sit down in the client's chair Effie Perine had vacated and say, "I've got my foot in the door, Sam."

"In just four nights?" Spade spoke with what seemed like admiration. "Does that mean you know who's doing it? Where they're storing the stolen goods? Are they in it for the money? Or for something else?"

"Of course for the money. This ain't nickel-and-dime stuff, Sam. This is big-time, organized thievery."

Spade said thoughtfully, "Maybe someone in the labor movement wants to disrupt the status quo, like the Wobblies kept trying to do up in Seattle after the union movement got squashed by all those ex-servicemen coming home needing jobs."

"The Wobblies were just a Commie front anyway," said Archer darkly. "Things are different down here. But maybe you've got something at that, Sam. My first night, a Commie named Robbie Brix I got blackballed in Seattle shows up at the Blue Book shape-up." The small brown eyes again became almost beady. He hitched his chair closer. "And he gets hired. Night work under the lights on a freighter with a tight turnaround schedule. A known Commie. When his shift ends he leaves real quick, like he has a date. A date at four in the morning? So the next night I follow him. Just a couple blocks."

"He spot you?"

"You kidding?" Archer sat back in his chair, lit a cigarette, blew out smoke, preened. "I been doing this a long time. Next night I picked him up where I'd left him the first night, followed him another couple blocks, dropped him again. Last night I tracked him to a warehouse where Green dead-ends up against the side of Telegraph Hill."

"Small two-story red brick, pre-quake, loading dock and a big overhead door? In the one-hundred-block stub just off Sansome?"

"You got it. There were lights on inside."

"Right across the Embarcadero from the cotton warehouse on Piers fifteen and seventeen," mused Spade. "That's where a lot of the dry goods have been disappearing from."

"Anyway, I climbed up on the loading dock. I could hear voices, like maybe Brix was reporting to someone, but I couldn't make out any words for sure. Then four men came out so quick I just had time to jump off the side of the dock without them seeing me. One gave money to Brix before they all went off together. Too risky to tail 'em. So I snuck a gander in a window. Place was crammed to the rafters with goods—just the sort of stuff's been disappearing from the docks."

"Could you identify the men if you saw 'em again?"

"Sure, all of 'em."

"That's great work, Miles. Think you should drop Brix for now? He knows you. He sees you, your cover's gone. We'll know where to find him if we need him. Instead, try to spot any of the others tonight, especially the one who paid Brix the money."

"That works." Archer stood, stretched, yawned. "All I wanna do is go home and make the little lady glad to see me."

After Miles Archer had departed, Spade rolled and smoked three more cigarettes. The phone rang twice while he did. He ignored it. Finally, he took a clipboard from the deep drawer of his desk, carried it into the outer office.

Effie Perine was opening the morning's mail with an ornate bronze Greek dagger. The porcelain designs on the metal scabbard included a two-headed green eagle and a peacock of many colors, both outlined in thin curved metal strips.

"Be careful you don't stick yourself with that thing."

She showed him the blade. "It's dull as a spoon. But it makes a good letter opener."

"Easy enough to sharpen it up. From a secret admirer?"

"From Penny. Years ago. I found it in a drawer at home the other day and . . ." Her voice faltered. "I just . . ."

"Yeah." He laid a hand on her shoulder. His eyes were bleak. He gestured at the opened mail. "Anything interesting?"

"Not in the mail." She set aside the dagger, recovered. "But there were two calls. Richardson wanting a progress report and a woman who sounded Chinese wanting an appointment."

"She leave a name?"

"No. But her voice . . . Remember three years ago, the student who said her name was Mai-lin Choi?"

"I never laid eyes on her, but yeah, I remember. If she calls again let's have her in to take a look at her. And tell Richardson the thief is his stepson, and does he want us to pursue it any further. We can get the goods on the kid right enough, but it'll be hard to keep the law out of it."

Effie Perine made a note on her shorthand pad.

Spade said, "Miles makes it sound like he's close to breaking the theft ring."

"That was quick." She sounded slightly disbelieving.

"Yeah, too quick. Too easy." He took his hat and topcoat off the rack. "I'm going to go snoop around, see if what he told me makes sense. Oh, and call Ray Kentzler at Bankers' Life, ask can he get a line on who owns a two-story red brick warehouse on the Green Street stub between Sansome and Telegraph Hill."

The morning fog was still seething over the bay, kept in motion by a biting wind through the Gate. The warehouse, built against the vertical slate face of Telegraph Hill, was locked up tight. The side windows were ten feet off the ground and covered with butcher paper on the inside. The double overhead door on the concrete loading dock had a huge new padlock that nothing short of a hardened-steel long-handled chain cutter could touch. It had no window. The access door beside it had an inset Yale lock and its window was reinforced with crisscrossed wires.

Spade found multiple fresh truck-tire tracks in the dust-covered street in front of the building. He clambered up on the dock, cupped his hands on the window of the access door, but its glass also was covered with butcher paper on the inside.

"Hey, what d'ya think you're doing? Get away from there."

A beefy red-faced Irish cop was puffing up Green Street toward him, nightstick in hand. Spade waved his clipboard, dropped nimbly down off the chest-high loading dock. He put the clipboard under one arm to dust off his hands, offered one of them to the cop.

"Ray Kentzler, Bankers' Life. We carry the fire insurance on this building."

"Fire insurance? The place's been empty for months."

"Still an asset." Spade said nothing of the recent tire tracks in the dust. "We got a report of some kids trying to get inside. I had to make sure the building was secure."

The cop shook his head. "Kids," he said.

They walked side by side back toward the Embarcadero. Spade turned north, walking, pausing thoughtfully. He walked. Stopped, frowning. Caught a bus down the Embarcadero to the Ferry Building, where he had lunch, then went to his office. Effie Perine was out for her own lunch; as usual, she had left half a dozen message slips on his desk.

Three caught Spade's eye: Ray Kentzler had called back

to say that tracking the warehouse owner would take a day or two. Richardson said to suspend the investigation into the activities of his stepson. And the Chinese-sounding woman maybe named Mai-lin Choi had called back for an appointment with Spade at 9 the next morning.

32

Mai-lin Choi

Effie Perine came in and shut the door, leaned back against it. Spade looked up from the papers on his desk.

"Any word from Ray Kentzler on that warehouse ownership?"

"Nothing. But your nine o'clock appointment is here."

Interest sparked Spade's eyes. He stubbed out his latest cigarette. "By all means, sweetheart, send her in."

She went back out, there was a murmur of voices, then she opened the door again and stepped aside.

"Miss Mai-lin Choi."

She was perhaps twenty-two, tall and full-bosomed for a Chinese woman, Western in bearing. Her hair, of indeterminate length, was jet-black, worked into a large bun at the back of her head. She wore an untrimmed felt hat, a tan tailored frock with a contrasting pongee collar and a matching silk ribbon tie. Her shoes were the latest flat-heeled style.

Spade stood, gestured at the client chair.

"Please, Miss Choi, sit down."

Instead, she remained standing for several moments, frankly judging him with black barely slanted eyes. Only then did she sit, turning her legs to one side so her feet were not flat on the floor. It was a graceful pose.

"You were recommended to me three years ago," she said. Her voice was strong but smooth, her English impeccable, with only the slightest singsong rhythm to suggest her heritage. Her nose was quite aquiline, her cheekbones exquisite, her skin a pale gold. "Now you have been recommended again."

Spade moved his head in a small bow, smiling slightly.

"Three years ago it was my pastor in Hawaii. Here, now, it is the Reverend Sabbath Zhu Pomeroy of St. John's Methodist Church in Chinatown. He has become my spiritual adviser."

"I will look forward to meeting him. Now, my secretary said you have a problem I might be able to help you with."

"You are a strong man? A steadfast man?"

Spade came forward in his chair, put his elbows on the desk with his hard, bony chin between his fists. He looked at her keenly, appraising her as she had him moments previously.

"You mean as a detective?"

"And as a man. Reverend Zhu states that you have the reputation of being devious and often untruthful, but that you protect your clients' interests at all costs. He said he could not be sure if you are also honorable."

"*Honorable.* Not a word gets used very often in my profession." He sobered abruptly. "OK, I know what Reverend Zhu has to say. What do you have to say?"

"I was a student three years ago, now I am not. Because the Chinese Exclusion Act some forty-odd years ago barred all Chinese except teachers and students and diplomats and the clergy, this time I am in this country illegally. You have heard the term paper daughter?"

"Sure. If I got it right, a Chinese American citizen can visit a wife back in China for long periods, when he comes back declare the number and gender of the kids born to him in China. All would be eligible for American citizenship if they came to this country. But if he says he's got more than he does—"

"—then there are slots, which often are illegally sold later to young Chinese trying to get into this country. I have bought such an identity to seek two men. I cannot know how long it will take to find them, or what dangers might be involved."

"So you feel someone might try to stop you?"

Her black eyes bored into his. "One cannot be sure."

"Fair enough." Spade drew a pad and pencil toward himself. "Who are these men and what do they do? Last seen where and when? Do you have photographs of them?"

"Charles Boothe and Fritz Lea. I was four years old in nineteen ten, living in poverty in Japan. When I came here three years ago, before I had to leave I could only learn that Charles Boothe was a retired banker with strong ties to military circles in New York. In nineteen ten he was living here in California. I could learn very little more about him. I do not have his photograph."

Spade poised his pencil. "What about Fritz Lea?"

"I know even less about him, but I do have a photograph." She took an envelope from her Spanish-leather pouch bag and handed it to Spade. "This is how he looked in nineteen ten."

It was a faded posed head-and-torso photograph of a young-looking man with soft blond hair parted in the middle, clean features, a short nose, direct eyes with a hint of dreaminess in them, a wide, well-shaped but determined mouth. He looked cool and collected and barely into his thirties. Lea wore some sort of military uniform with gold leaf around the collar. An eight-pointed gold star depended from a gold chain around his throat.

Spade studied the photograph, chuckled. "Your Fritz Lea looks like quite a lad."

"He was an amateur strategist who dreamed of changing the world map by making China a land of economic expansion."

"In whose army was he commissioned?"

"I have no idea. Perhaps my father's. My real father, of whom I am the unacknowledged, illegitimate daughter." She gave a small fatalistic shrug. "In traditional China marriage is a social contract. My father's first wife was a peasant woman from his village. An arranged marriage. She gave him three children, one a son to carry on the line, as was her duty, then moved to Hawaii. He ensured her subsistence, as was his duty, while he traveled. I was born in Japan to a servant. Of course my father could not acknowledge me."

"And your father is . . ."

"Dead. Three years ago. In Peking. What is important is that he was with Charles Boothe and Fritz Lea here in San Francisco in nineteen ten. I must talk with these two men."

"If they're still around and still alive," said Spade. "A lot can happen in eighteen years. Why do you want to find them?"

"I will tell you everything if you are successful."

"I'm sure you will, but meanwhile let's be perfectly clear. First, without this information I might do more harm than good, a bull-in-a-china-shop sort of thing." Spade picked up his tobacco and papers from the blotter and began constructing a cigarette. "Second, I need to know this is a legitimate investigation. You're not hiring me to break any laws, anything like that."

"You have my assurances of that. And those of Reverend Zhu if needed." She drifted up from her chair. "I am staying in a house on Old Chinatown Lane. Miss Perine has the address and phone number. Now I must go. After we discuss your fee."

"So she really has a case."

"Yeah, if you could call it that." Spade hooked one hip over the front corner of Effie Perine's desk. "Our Mai-lin is a very cool article, or pretends to be. She said she'll tell me why she's looking for these two guys *after* I find them. When I threw in some nonsense about legality, she brought up the Reverend Sabbath Zhu Pomeroy. 'Spiritual adviser' suggests a spiritual con game to me. Not unknown even among the organized religions." He bowed slightly. "Except for the Greek Orthodox Church, of course. And she was very cagey about who her real father was."

"Is that important?"

"Yeah. She let slip he was trying to raise an army. Call Charles Barber at Golden Gate Trust, ask if he's ever heard of Boothe. Then leave a message for Mickey Linehan at Continental that I'll be attending the services at his place tonight."

Sam Spade was the only passenger left when the Stockton Street cable car reached the turnaround in the 500 block of Greenwich. Above the Greenwich Street stub the steep, brushy side of Telegraph Hill gleamed with moisture.

Spade went downhill off Grant on Edith Alley. In the middle of the block he went up the steps to a two-story frame building and rang the bell for the lower flat. The door was opened on a narrow hallway filled with the hulking, loose-faced Mickey Linehan. His right hand waved a half-empty glass.

"We started without you," he said.

"I'll catch up," said Spade.

Male voices, light, smoke, the clink of chips, the rasp of bottle on glass, the smell of cigarettes, came from an open doorway halfway down the short hall. In the middle of a front room that overlooked Edith Alley was an oaken table littered with ashtrays, chips, bottles. Around it were five hardwood chairs.

"See whut the cat drug in!" exclaimed Mickey jovially.

Three heads turned. Two of the men were Woody Robinson and Phil Haultain. The third was a thick-bodied square-faced man with reddish close-cropped curly hair, a strong chin, a determined mouth turned down at the corners, and hard, direct eyes under slightly beetling brows. Mickey swung an arm.

"These two bums you know." He gestured at the third man. "Rusty McCoy, our new Continental op."

"The last I heard you were on Jack Manion's Chinatown squad looking for pails with false bottoms full of opium."

"Now I'm cleaning these guys at poker," said McCoy.

"Easier than cleaning up Chinatown," agreed Spade. "How is Jack these days?"

"Tough as ever. Still goes to Mass every morning at Old St. Mary's Church. Still Uncle Jack to all the decent people of Chinatown. He always had good things to say about you, Sam."

"Let's quit jawing and play some poker," said Mickey.

It was five-card stud, nothing wild. An hour in, Spade asked Mickey, "You ever hear of a guy named Fritz Lea?"

"Should I of?"

"His name cropped up in a case I'm on. Can you take a look through the files and let me know if Continental has a line on him? Last seen in San Francisco around nineteen ten."

"Since you just let me bluff you out of a ten-buck pot with a measly pair of treys, sure," said Mickey, grinning.

Another hour later Spade and McCoy were in the kitchen chipping ice for their drinks from the block in the old-fashioned zinc-lined cooler. Spade spoke casually.

"Rusty, you ever run across a pastor down in Chinatown, Methodist I think, name of Reverend Sabbath Zhu Pomeroy?"

"Of mixed blood is he, then, with a name like that?"

"I think so, but I've never met him."

McCoy stood, glass in hand, looking thoughtful.

"A half-Chinese Methodist pastor . . ." He shook his head. "Nope. I never heard of him. Is he in trouble?"

"Not with me," said Spade. "Again, his name came up."

"Maybe he's come to the big city from the Chinese community in Sacramento, or Fresno, or Salinas, or maybe Watsonville."

"Maybe so," agreed Spade.

The game broke up about midnight.

33

Hunting Harry

Spade and Archer met outside Marquand's Restaurant below the Geary Theatre. Above them was a sign, CABARET AND DANCING, but at a little before noon patrons were going in only for food, not entertainment. The two detectives shook hands as if casual acquaintances, took a corner booth, where there was little chance of being overheard. Archer leaned in and talked quietly, intensely, while seeming to study his menu.

"I think I've got a line on the ringleader of the group, Sam. The one who paid Robbie Brix for information. They did it again last night. Again, inside. But I was at the window watching when he gave Brix some more cash. I keep snooping around, but he only ever shows up at the warehouse so I can't point him out to anybody."

"You try tailing him?"

"Too risky. He's a little guy, wary as a fox."

Their meat loaf came. They started eating.

"So he's probably blacklisted for union activity. You

think it's lefty union guys trying to bring down the system who're behind the pilfering, Miles?"

"It wouldn't surprise me," said Archer judiciously. "They don't seem in any hurry to move the stolen goods out of that warehouse, do they? The paymaster has an Aussie accent."

"Aussie accent? Little guy, you said? How old?"

"Twenty-nine, thirty. Wiry. Lean face. Bloodhound eyes."

"Good work, Miles." Spade smiled with the lower part of his face. "Keep it up."

"I just had lunch with Miles. Anything from anybody?"

Effie Perine followed him into his office, open notebook in hand. He sat down in his swivel chair and tossed tobacco sack and papers on his desk. She sat down, started making his cigarette, talking as she did.

"Charles Barber isn't having any luck at all in finding Boothe, the retired banker."

"I should have put young Henny on him. The beautiful Mai-lin Choi would appeal to his romantic nature."

"I'd think running California-Citizens Bank for the Widow Eberhard would leave him no time for romance or derring-do." She handed him the cigarette. "How did the services go?"

"Mickey Linehan will run Fritz Lea through the files at Continental. The game was to welcome Rusty McCoy, a new op who used to be with Jack Manion's Chinatown squad. I went to the game to ask him if he'd ever heard of Reverend

Sabbath Zhu. He hadn't." He paused, lighter in hand. "Rusty said maybe he's from Watsonville or Fresno or Sacramento, but . . ."

"You make him sound more mysterious than Mai-lin herself."

"Maybe he is. Manion's squad knows most things going on in Chinatown." He gestured with the lighter. "Anything else?"

"Ray Kentzler called to say that you owe him a lunch. The warehouse at the foot of Green Street is owned by the Shipowners' and Merchants' Tugboat Company."

Spade stopped, lighter halfway to his cigarette.

"Hmph. Charles Barber's on the board of directors at the Tugboat Company. Be an angel, call him back and ask him if they're leasing the warehouse out to anyone."

She wrote in her notebook. "Is something the matter, Sam?"

"Yeah, I think maybe there is, but let's find out for sure about that warehouse first." He stood, stubbing out his cigarette in the ashtray before realizing he hadn't lit it yet. "If I'm not back by closing time leave any messages on my desk."

He paused in the hallway outside the office for a moment, staring at the new gold leaf lettering that had just replaced *Samuel Spade* on the glass panel of the door:

Spade & Archer

Spade stood at his ease, watching and smoking a cigarette while a crane lifted a load of netted cargo from one of the holds of the Admiral Line's steamship *Admiral Peoples.* Stevedores were on the dock to transfer the goods to an airless-tire Kleiber truck, built locally in San Francisco.

The craggy-faced foreman, named Stan Delaney, came limping over. Sharp wind off the bay stirred Delaney's thick white hair. They shook hands.

Spade said, "I'm looking for Harry Brisbane. I owe him some money from a poker game, and I thought he said he was working here."

"Yeah, for California Stevedore and Ballast, but he hasn't been to work for a week, ten days." He yelled at a longshoreman steering a platform truck with a pallet of wooden crates to the waiting Kleiber. "*Johnny!* Where's Harry living these days?"

It was a narrow two-story building in the 500 block of Harrison. Apartment 1B had a penciled BRISBANE stuck in the name slot on a torn piece of paper. Spade's knuckles tattooed the door.

"Yeah, yeah, for Chrissake, gimme a chance, will ya?"

After a few moments the door was opened and Harry Brisbane peered out. He was standing on one foot. The other foot had a cast on it. His eyes lit up.

"Hey, Sam! C'mon in."

He backed awkwardly away so Spade could go in past him. Harry hopped around him one-footed to flop back into a broken-down easy chair in one corner of the living room. The flat smelled of cooked food and enforced confinement.

"I heard you were home, but I didn't know you were laid

up." Spade brought a hand holding a pint of liquor out of his topcoat pocket. "But I came prepared, just in case."

"Bless you, mate." Harry jerked a thumb over his shoulder. "There's ice and glasses, water in the tap, and ginger ale in the icebox if you're a sissy about your drinks."

Ten minutes later they were tinking glasses and tossing off bootleg whiskey.

"I haven't seen you since you were lookin' for that rich guy's kid. What's that been? Six years?"

"Seven," said Spade. "I'm working for the Industrial Association, and some thin, wiry guy named Harry with an Aussie accent came up during the investigation."

The pleasure went out of Harry's bloodhound eyes, replaced by something like disappointment. "You gunning for me, Sam?"

"If I was, I wouldn't have told you my client's name." He gestured at the cast. "What happened?"

"Broke my foot two weeks ago. I was working in the hold of an Admiral freighter, standing on a pile of cases while we sent a load out. Two cases slid, my foot got jammed between 'em. I couldn't afford to lay off so I stuck it out for two days, but I couldn't work in the hold no more. Stan Delaney put me up on deck, but I couldn't even stand that. So I finally went to the sawbones and filed a claim."

"I hear the company union doesn't like injury claims."

"Yeah, but my foot had gotten swollen up so bad I just couldn't limp around anymore." Harry spread his arms wide. "So now I'm getting twenty-five bucks a week under workmen's compensation. That's more than I can make most weeks working on the docks."

"What happens when the compensation runs out?"

"I'll probably go on the Blue Book's blacklist again."

Spade went out to the kitchen for ice. He made new drinks, said, "I thought you were already blacklisted."

"Not blacklisted. Just not ever able to get work. Closed shop, they called it. Couple a months after you was lookin' for that rich guy's kid they got bighearted and let me back in. But in nineteen twenty-four we tried to set up the I.L.A. union again. We had maybe four hundred members but no contracts."

Spade lit a cigarette. "Why did they care? Without contracts you weren't going to take any business away from them."

" 'Cause we marched in the Labor Day parade that year, I guess. The company and union officials was standing along the parade route on Market between the Ferry Building and City Hall writing down names. Anyway, they got mine. But the union reps was so busy playing cards and chasing women and making money they couldn't bother with small fry like me. So I finally got back in, started getting regular work with California Stevedore and Ballast." He gestured at the cast. "Then this." He brightened. "At least my rent here is only fifteen bucks a month."

Spade finished his drink, checked his watch.

"You know a Wobblie from Seattle named Robbie Brix?"

Harry shook his head. "And if he was down here on the docks, I'd know about him, Sam."

"What I thought. I've been investigating the dock pilfering, and that's where your description came up." He grinned crookedly. "I can believe a lot of things about you, Harry, but being a thief isn't one of them." He finally stood up. "But you can see why I had to talk to you."

"Wouldn't be doin' your job if you didn't. But I haven't been out and around for ten days, not with this cast."

It was after dark when Spade trudged up Hyde Street from a westbound Geary streetcar. Miles Archer's dark sedan was parked squarely in front of 891 Post. Iva Archer's head was silhouetted behind the wheel by the midblock streetlight. By the time he got to the auto and had opened her door, his lips had turned up into a smile.

"Hello, precious," he said.

"I've been waiting for over an hour for you to get home."

"I thought you'd be resting up." Spade smiled again, insincerely. "Miles always seems in a hurry to get home."

She swung her legs out and put both feet on the pavement. This maneuver rode her skirt up well above her silk-clad knees.

"That's one of the things I wanted to talk to you about. Since Miles became your partner, I haven't seen much of you."

"Because he's my partner."

"Men!" she snorted. "They have such silly ideas." There was lingering asperity in her voice, but her blue eyes had softened. "Can I come up?"

"Sure," he said, "you look like you could use a drink."

He escorted her across the sidewalk to the street door,

keys in hand. They rode the elevator in silence, went down the hall to his apartment without touching.

But inside the apartment, with the door closed,. Iva was suddenly in his arms, pressed against him, mouth open and hungry for his. When they finally parted, Spade turned on the lights.

"Now I think we both need that drink."

When they were seated on the sofa, drinks in hand, she complained, "Sam, he's doing just what he used to do to me up in Spokane. He's been out four nights in a row, this is the fifth. He doesn't come home until dawn, and he won't tell me what he's doing or where he is. When I ask he just laughs and says maybe he's partying with some new girlfriend. I know that isn't true, at least I think it isn't, but it just drives me crazy."

Spade put his arm across the back of the sofa behind her, squeezed her far shoulder. She leaned her head against him.

"We've got a big new client. Miles is working undercover, nights, trying to get a line on things."

She laughed and made a dismissive gesture. "That's all I wanted to know."

She slid out from under his arm, stood, put her drink on the arm of the sofa. Spade stood also.

"Leaving so soon, Iva?" he asked politely.

Instead of answering, she crossed the room, opened the closet door, and swung the wall bed out and down. She let herself fall back on it, chuckled deep in her strong, rounded throat.

"I just wanted to be sure Miles wouldn't be home tonight." She sat up. "Come and undress me, lover. I can't wait."

Spade moved toward her, turning off the white overhead bowl light as he did.

34

Just a Son of a Bitch

Henny Barber was out of the swivel chair in his modest office on the ground floor of California-Citizens Bank. He wrung Spade's hand with enthusiasm, hiked himself up to sit on the edge of his desk, careless of the crease in his conservative banker's dark blue woolen worsted suit.

"Your father tells me you're running the place these days."

"Don't you believe it, Mr. Spade! Pater likes to brag about me, but it's Aunt Ev's show. She's grabbed Uncle Collin's office and comes in once or twice a week for a couple of hours. I keep things going day to day, but she's in control."

"She always struck me as a woman who likes to make sure she knows what's going on with her money," said Spade.

"Is she!" exclaimed Henny. "Want a cigar?"

Spade shook his head, getting out tobacco and papers while Henny clipped and lit his cigar.

"Can you get me into the Bohemian Club library?" Spade asked. "I want to do a little reading up on Chinese history."

"Pater can."

"OK, set it up." Spade lit up. "The bank making money?"

"Tons of it. If you have the routine down and don't make any crazy investments or shaky loans, it's all so darned easy."

"Ever dream of the exotic South Seas anymore?"

"The South Seas!" Henny threw his arms wide. "All the time. Maybe I could open a Cal-Cit Bank branch in Tahiti!"

"Bored, huh?" Spade blew smoke toward the ceiling. "I'm going to change all that. I want you to find a retired New York banker named Charles Boothe, last seen in San Francisco in nineteen ten."

Henny's face fell. "A retired banker? That's no challenge. A couple of phone calls and—"

"Your old man couldn't find him."

Interest came back to Henny's face.

"Boothe was last seen in the company of a Fritz Lea and an unnamed Chinese gentleman. My client is named Mai-lin Choi, a couple of years younger than you are. She's the Chinese gent's beautiful, mysterious, unacknowledged illegitimate daughter. She's counting on me to find Boothe and Lea for her. I'm counting on you to find Boothe for me."

Henny was off the desk and on his feet, eyes alight.

"I'm your man, Mr. Spade!" Then he added craftily, "But only if I get an introduction to the mysterious Mai-lin Choi."

Spade leaned over the plump redheaded girl at the switchboard while he put his hand on her shoulder.

"Think you can get my office on that dingus, Mabel?"

"For you, anything, Mr. Spade."

"Better not let Sid hear you talking that way."

She giggled and flicked a toggle on the switchboard, got central. She pointed at one of the phones on her desk, said, "It's ringing, Mr. Spade."

Spade picked up the phone with his right hand, put the receiver to his ear with his left hand in time to hear Effie Perine's invariable "Spade and Archer Investigations."

"It's me, sweetheart," he told the mouthpiece. "I'm at Sid Wise's office now. Before I go in, have we heard anything more from Charles Barber on that warehouse?"

"Nobody is leasing it from the Tugboat Company. They've had it standing empty for months."

Spade nodded, hung up the receiver, and left Mabel giggling again as he went down the inner corridor to the frosted-glass door at the far end. Sid Wise was behind his immense paper-and-file covered desk, moodily smoking a cigar. He was in shirt and vest, his suit coat draped over the back of his swivel chair. He waved a hand at the files.

"I hope you won't be long, Sam," he said rudely. "I'm up to my ears in work."

Spade sat down. "I've got things to tell you."

Sid Wise groaned audibly, then tented his fingers in front of his chin. Spade outlined Miles Archer's reported work on their case for the Industrial Association, ending with the lunch at Marquand's. Wise looked puzzled.

"Where's the problem? I think we've misjudged our man."

"Except that most of it is a passel of lies," said Spade.

A sudden, attentive frown appeared on Wise's tired olive-hued face. He hitched his chair around to better face Spade. His high, sometimes almost shrill voice had dropped almost an octave.

"What's that supposed to mean?"

"Like I told you, Miles said he spotted a Commie from Seattle named Robbie Brix getting hired at a Blue Book shape-up. Night work under the lights. When his shift ended, Miles followed him for two blocks, dropped him so he wouldn't get wise. Two more blocks the second night. Third night he tracked Brix all the way to the warehouse at the foot of Green Street."

"Sounds like good investigative technique to me."

"And it gets better. Lights on inside the warehouse at four in the morning. Four men came out, one of them paid Brix some money. When they were gone, Miles looked in a window. The place was loaded to the rafters with goods."

"The stuff being stolen on the docks. Just like he said."

Spade smiled thinly.

"The overhead loading door doesn't have a window. The door beside it has a window, but it is covered with butcher paper on the inside. The other windows are ten feet off the ground and covered on the inside with butcher paper too. Yesterday Miles told me he saw another payoff to Brix the night before. Through one of those windows."

"Which are all covered with butcher paper."

"Yeah. Miles also described the man he said was paying Robbie Brix for information about the goods that later were disappearing. Harry Brisbane, right down to the Aussie accent. Except Miles couldn't have seen him paying anybody any money on Green Street. Harry's been laid up at home for two weeks with a broken foot, and never heard of anybody named Robbie Brix."

"You trust Brisbane?"

"He's a straight shooter. And the warehouse is owned by the Shipowners' and Merchants' Tugboat Company and they haven't leased it out to anyone else."

"But they're one of your clients. It just doesn't figure."

"There's a way it does. Through the Blue Book and Miles."

Wise blew out a breath and scratched his head. Flakes of dandruff settled on his shoulders. "I told you not to take him on as a partner. Are you going to confront him with it?"

"No. I'll just try to keep him off anything that might hurt Spade and Archer, then kick him out at the end of our year." Spade shook his head. "In business with him for less than a week, and I find out he's a son of a bitch."

At the Continental office Spade asked for Mickey Linehan. The op was out in the field, but he'd left an envelope. In Bush's Coffee Shop in the 700 block of Market, Spade got a grilled-cheese sandwich and black coffee, ate and drank while scanning the single sheet of paper with Linehan's scrawl on it.

Effie Perine said, "Miss Choi called asking for a report."

"Tell her to come by first thing in the morning." He

hooked a hip over the corner of Effie Perine's desk. "How straight do you think she's being with us?"

"She acts as if she's telling you everything you need to know, but—but she's—"

"—not your typical Chinese woman? Almost more like a white woman?" When she nodded, he said, "Do you know any agents out at the immigration station on Angel Island?"

"I was in grammar school with an American-born Chinese boy named Ray Chong Fat who's a translator out there."

"See can he find out if Mai-lin passed through the station in the last year or so, how long she was detained and questioned. She says she's been here for maybe a month, but was that when she got to Angel Island or when she was cleared for entry into San Francisco? For the Chinese, clearance can take weeks, months."

Effie Perine was making pothooks in her notebook. "You think she's lying about who she is and how she got here, Sam?"

"I don't think anything yet. I just need to know." He stood up. "Ask Chong Fat about the Reverend Sabbath Zhu Pomeroy too. Being a clergyman, he wouldn't have had any trouble getting in. But there'd still have to be a record of his entry."

35

Ah, the Money

Spade's suit coat was over the back of his chair. Morning sunlight laid a bar of filtered gold across the desktop. Mai-lin Choi came in, much more Chinese than on her first visit. Gone was the haughtiness of face, the sternness of eye. She gestured to emphasize her clothing.

"You like?" she asked in a singsong voice.

She wore the sort of loose-fitting washable frock that a maid could buy for sixty-nine cents. Her shapeless slippers would make plop-plop sounds as she walked. The jacket she draped over the back of the chair was dark, warm, shapeless, standard dress for cold foggy days on upper Grant Avenue.

"Soon I will be going to talk to people in Chinatown. If I am small and humble with eyes downcast, dressed cheaply, they will feel at ease and talk to me. Otherwise . . ."

"Otherwise," Spade said in a passable falsetto, "no savvy."

She seemed to suddenly tire of the game.

"What do you have to tell me?" she asked.

"Nothing on Charles Boothe yet. But Fritz Lea spent six years in Joliet prison in Illinois, nineteen fourteen through nineteen nineteen, for a phony timber-stock scam. He next surfaced working a bank fraud in New York in nineteen twenty-two. It was nol-prossed, lack of evidence. In nineteen twenty-six he was indicted in Los Angeles on a counterfeit bearer-bond scheme that was again dismissed for lack of evidence. Who are you going to be talking to in Chinatown?"

"Methodists whose parents helped my real father when he came to San Francisco the first time. They were children then, but I am hoping they will remember personal anecdotes about him."

Spade leaned back in his swivel chair, hands interlocked behind his head. He appeared totally at ease.

"Why are you looking for Boothe and Lea eighteen years later?"

She checked the wall clock behind Miles Archer's unoccupied desk, looked at Spade out of the corners of her slightly slanted eyes. "Look at the time! I must go."

Spade nodded pleasantly as she started to rise.

"I'll have Effie return your retainer on your way out."

She settled back in her chair. "Because of the money. I shall remain until I find it, or find out there is none."

"Ah," said Spade, "the money," as if they had already been discussing it. "How much money?"

"A great deal, raised for my father's . . . political aims."

"I have a banker friend who could check up on it for us." Spade chuckled. "Give him one look at you, he'd do anything for you. He's a romantic."

"It will not be in a bank. It will be in cash."

"Buried treasure?" asked Spade in a joking voice.

"Perhaps even that."

Spade frowned, stubbed out a cigarette.

"What do you mean by a great deal of money?"

"Perhaps as much as a quarter of a million American."

"And your father died in Peking three years ago."

"You are indeed clever of mind, Mr. Spade. And yes, my father was indeed the great Chinese patriot Sun Yat-sen." Her eyes flashed. "Liang Qichao had defected to reformism, and the young radicals, who had despised my father, then made him their standard-bearer."

"Let's go talk with these people of yours in Chinatown."

"Tomorrow," she said. "I will ask Reverend Zhu, their pastor, to accompany us. He will have influence with them."

Spade bowed her out of the office, stopped beside Effie Perine's desk. "Now she claims that her real father was Sun Yat-sen. Tomorrow I meet the famous Reverend Sabbath Zhu Pomeroy."

"Why is he so important?"

"I don't know, sweetheart. I have a feeling about him. Meanwhile, ring up Ralph Toomey at Matson Shipping, tell him I need an up-to-date list of the goods stolen on the docks in the past month." As she got busy with the telephone Spade said, "Have we heard anything from Miles today?"

She held up a finger, said, "Mr. Spade would like an

appointment with Mr. Toomey at his earliest convenience." She covered the mouthpiece, to Spade said, "Nothing so far," uncovered the mouthpiece, said, "A half hour would be perfect."

"When Miles calls in, don't tell him about my appointment with Toomey."

Ralph Toomey's ornate corner office at Matson Shipping looked kitty-corner across the 200 block of Market to the old Hansford Building. Dominating the office was a huge rolltop desk pockmarked with green-felt-lined pigeonholes. In a corner of the room was a green *secrétaire* with an inlaid top.

Toomey got out of his big leather chair to shake Spade's hand and gesture him into an armchair, also leather, that smelled of saddle soap. Toomey was in his sixties, white-haired, well barbered, his nails manicured, with a broad, bony face, an unforgiving mouth, and direct blue eyes. He had captained his own five-master around the Horn before the turn of the century, was still thick in the arms and broad in the shoulders, and was not at all dwarfed by his massive padded swivel chair.

"How is Miles working out, Spade?"

"He may have a line on where the stolen goods are being stored. That's why I want that list. Do you have ideas of who the thieves might be? Union agitators, maybe?"

"Personally, I don't care who they are, just so long as you stop them without any publicity." He shrugged his big shoulders. "At this point that is paramount. No publicity. Of course the Longshoremen's Association, the Blue Book people, would love it to be Harry Brisbane and his ilk, but I don't think so."

Spade put a hint of skepticism in his voice. "Why's that?"

"Harry was a crewman on one of the last ships I captained. Just a kid then, but an honest kid. They tried to bribe him in twenty-four, but he wasn't having any of that."

"Who was it offered him the money?"

"I don't remember. Probably Stan Hagar. He's Blue Book union heart and soul. Hates Harry Brisbane and the I.L.A. union." Toomey shoved an envelope across the desk. "Here's your list of stolen goods."

36

Bound Feet, Natural Feet

Sam Spade was on his way out the door at 7 in the morning when his phone rang. He went back inside to pick it up and answered it standing. Effie Perine sounded sleepy but smug.

"The *Angel Island* is leaving for the immigration station from the Nippon Yusen Kaisha Line Pier Twenty-four at eight thirty. Ray Chong Fat has fixed it so they'll think you're a customs official named Nick Charles who needs a translator."

"Thanks, sweetheart. I'll bring a bulging briefcase and try to look official."

Spade changed into a heavy coat and pulled on a woolen knit cap. Twenty minutes later he was walking onto Pier 24 at the foot of Harrison.

Two dozen Japanese men and women were boarding the 144-foot steamer. Spade towered over most of them by nearly a foot. At the head of the gangplank an officious man with a clipboard singled him out.

"State your name and business."

"Nick Charles," said Spade. "Special customs agent to—"

"Oh, sure." The man made a check beside an item on his clipboard. "A translator named Ray Chong Fat will be waiting for you at the immigration station."

It was a short trip; Angel Island lies in Richardson Bay between Tiburon and San Francisco, an irregular rocky oval covered with trees and vegetation and rimmed with pale sandy beaches. Spade stood at the railing, rolling and smoking cigarettes and watching the island materialize out of the fog.

After the luggage was stored in the shed at the end of the long curving immigration pier at China Cove, the passengers trooped toward the administration building, set back and up from the beach. A slender black-haired dish-faced Chinese man Effie Perine's age fell into step with Spade.

"Mr. Charles? Ray Chong Fat. I hope I can translate those documents for you." He lowered his voice. "You're helping a paper daughter named Mai-lin Choi who passed through here?"

"If she did."

"She did. I was the translator at her interrogations."

The immigration station was a vast complex of fifty buildings, dominated by a sprawling two-story administration building, with tan walls and a peaked tile roof. Farther up the slope were the detention barracks, the power plant, and the hospital.

The day was gray, blustering, the fog still swirling, the wind off the bay stabbing at their backs as they walked. As they mounted the steps of the administration building, Chong Fat shivered in his skimpy Immigration Service uniform and said abruptly, "Thirty percent of all Chinese immigrants are deported without ever setting foot in America."

"So seventy percent make it in. Not bad odds."

The administration building smelled of damp paper and stale coffee and disinfectant. It was cold and echoing, with linoleum-covered floors and rows of tiny cubicles. In one, a dull-eyed emaciated Chinese youth in a rumpled jacket and unmatched pants was sitting in a hard-backed chair at a glass-topped table. Across from him were two middle-aged Americans in dark suits and ties, one balding with glasses, the other black haired with a small precise mustache. No one was speaking.

Chong Fat led Spade up creaking wooden stairs to a small office on the second floor. He sat down behind the desk while Spade drew up a chair across from him. Chong Fat gestured at Spade's briefcase, spoke almost in a whisper.

"You brought papers to spread across the desk?"

"Sure. Did you find any record of the Reverend Sabbath Zhu Pomeroy ever passing through?"

"No record," said Chong Fat, still low voiced.

He opened the bottom drawer of his desk and brought out a folder, took out a bulky transcript marked "Mai-lin Choi." As Spade half-hid it among his jumble of meaningless papers on the desk, he said loudly, "I hope you can translate this for me."

Spade started reading the transcript, making squiggles

on a pad to make it look like he was taking notes as Chong Fat talked in a high, hesitant voice to sound like he was translating into English the characters he was reading in Chinese.

Spade read:

How many steps are there to the front door of your house?

Three.

Who lives opposite your house?

Chin Doo-yik. He lives with his wife.

Describe his wife.

Ng Chee, natural feet.

Didn't that man have children?

No.

How many houses in your row?

Four.

Who lives in the third house in the second row of houses?

Leong Yik-gai.

What clan does he belong to?

I never heard his family name.

Do you expect us to believe you lived in that village and don't know the clan names of the other people living there?

Not Leong Yik-gai's. He never told anyone his family name. He is always away somewhere. He has a wife, one son, and a daughter living in that house.

Describe his wife.

Woo Fong. Bound feet.

Spade finished, slid the transcript back to Chong Fat, who returned it to its folder and quickly put it back in the drawer.

"Thank you very much, Mr. Chong Fat," said Spade in a loud, hearty voice, gathering up his meaningless papers. "You have saved the Customs Service a week of hard work."

When Spade entered the office, Effie Perine was still there even though it was well after 6 o'clock. She was all business.

"Mai-lin and Reverend Zhu will meet you at St. John's Methodist Church, Washington and Stockton, tomorrow at one p.m."

"Good. Those interrogations out on Angel Island are mainly nonsense—who lived in the fourth house in your row, did his wife have bound feet or natural feet?"

"They weren't able to trap her or confuse her?"

"They never came close. She's smart and quick-witted enough to be Sun Yat-sen's daughter. Everything she told us checks out. We can't say the same for Zhu. No record."

"You said clergymen come and go as they like."

"He still would have had to pass through Immigration and Customs. So he either got here illegally or was born here. When Miles comes in tomorrow, tell him to meet me at the Green Street warehouse at midnight. Tonight, grab your coat, I'll buy you dinner at Julius Castle. Anything you want on the menu."

37

Reverend Pastor Sabbath Zhu

Spade climbed up Washington from Grant Avenue to Stockton Street on the upper edge of Chinatown. Late-fall sunshine flooded the street. St. John's Methodist Church was sheathed in shingles, topped with a witch-hat shingle tower. Mai-lin Choi and a slender, slightly stooped whipcord man wearing a minister's dark suit awaited Spade between carved ornamental wooden gates.

"Mr. Spade," said Mai-lin formally, "this is the Reverend Pastor Sabbath Zhu Pomeroy. Reverend Zhu, Mr. Samuel Spade."

They shook hands. Zhu's long fingers were bony but strong. His mixed blood was most apparent in his shiny black hair and in the hint of a slant in dark eyes behind thick horn-rimmed glasses. He peered at Spade for a long, intent moment.

"I recommended you to Miss Choi for your competence as a detective, not for your truthfulness or sense of honor."

"Yeah. Well, thanks." Spade gestured at the little church behind them. "You're the pastor here?"

"Oh, no, assistant pastor only. And only very recently that. I chose it as our meeting place because it is here that I first heard Sun Yat-sen speak."

Mai-lin gave a visible start. "You met my father?"

"Only heard him speak. It was enough. Let us go inside."

Light from the tall windows flooded the interior. At the front were the pulpit, the organ, and two tiers of risers for the choir at Sunday services. Pastor Zhu gestured Mai-lin into a pew halfway up the broad central aisle, slid in beside her. Spade stood in the aisle facing them, his back to the altar, one hand resting on the back of the pew ahead of theirs.

"After my ordination I first was sent to one of the Chinese churches in the valley. Then, eventually, I was assigned here. It was the fulfillment of all my dreams."

"Because you heard Sun Yat-sen speak here?"

"Exactly. He arrived here on April sixth, nineteen oh four, traveling under false papers that declared him to have been born in Hawaii and thus eligible for American citizenship."

Mai-lin said hotly, "Employees of the Customs Service who were members of the Society to Protect the Emperor recognized my father and denounced him. He was detained for several weeks."

Reverend Zhu said, "It was cooperation between the Chinese pastor of this little Methodist church and his local converts, along with the efforts of the head of a local Triad, that brought enough pressure to finally get Sun Yat-sen admitted."

The door at their backs opened. An aged Chinese woman, carrying bags and sacks and made shapeless by a black coat, came past them to edge her way into the front pew on the opposite side. She sat down wearily, distributing her bags around her.

"They had a 'grand meeting' at this church. Your father spoke. I was here, a boy of nine, right in this very pew." Zhu began to declaim in a booming orator's voice that made the old woman turn painfully to look at him, then away. " 'America, we need your help because you are the pioneers of Western civilization. Because you are a Christian nation. Because we intend to model our new government after yours. Above all, because you are the champions of liberty and democracy.' "

Mai-lin was silent, as if transfixed by her father's words. Spade's face had become almost stupid in its lack of expression.

Before the quake Grant had been known as Dupont Gai, Street of a Thousand Lanterns. The two-block climb from the Bush Street Gate to California was then lined with gambling clubs and brothels with half-opened window shutters through which scantily clad Caucasian whores raucously called their prices at passersby. The cribs had burned in the '06 fire; they had been replaced by bazaars and restaurants and import houses and warehouses.

On the southeast and southwest corners of Grant and California were the Sing Fat Company and its competitor, the Sing Chong Company. Both were four-storied, with ornate balconies and decorations and pagoda-style towers.

"Sing Fat means Living Riches," said Sabbath Zhu, "and Sing Chong, Living Prosperity."

In a white-tiled butcher shop in the next block an aged Chinese man with a wispy Confucius goatee and timeless eyes was using a gleaming cleaver to section a whole pig roasted to a deep mahogany color. On hooks behind his head hung a dozen smoked ducks.

The next building was the Chow Chong Trading Company. Its spotless windows featured carved ivory and teak statues, porcelain bowls and vases, bronze temple bells. The display cases were filled with silk, lacquer, embroidery, and cloisonné. The air was heavy with sandalwood and camphorwood. A dozen Westerners were shopping, browsing, buying.

A woman in a form-fitting floor-length silk gown approached them. She had a serene narrow face, hair that could have been lacquered itself, and dignity in her bearing.

Mai-lin spoke to her in Cantonese. Her face suddenly became animated. She replied excitedly, with many hand gestures. She looked over at Reverend Zhu, seemed to study him deeply, then bowed even more deeply, started to go on in Chinese.

Reverend Zhu said in a gentle voice, "Please, in English." He gestured at Spade. "So our Western guest will be able to follow the conversation."

She switched to only very slightly singsong English.

"I am Moon-fong Li. You honor me by your presence."

She led them past a silk curtain and around silk-paneled

screens to a small room, seated them around a hardwood table. An aged retainer in traditional dress brought a delicate teapot and four exquisite handleless bowls on doughnutlike saucers. Moon-fong Li went to the door with him, stood with her hand on his arm, speaking earnestly in low tones. He bowed, departed. She returned to fill their cups with steaming tea, spring-water-clear, pale amber, delicate of taste.

"When your father was released from detention in nineteen oh four he was taken directly to my parents' home under cover of night. My brother, Yee-chum Li, was twelve. I was eight."

A sudden youthful smile lit up Moon-fong Li's features, momentarily replacing dignity with delight.

"When Sun Yat-sen had to move about Chinatown we always had to make sure he was well hidden in various parishioners' homes. It was great fun for us as little children, even though we felt the weight of responsibility because our parents told us that Sun Yat-sen would be the savior of our homeland."

"Why did he have to hide out?" asked Spade, sipping tea. "He had officially been admitted to the United States."

Mai-lin said, "He was being dogged by imperial agents of the Manchus." To Moon-fong Li she said, "Did you meet my father again upon his return to San Francisco in nineteen ten?"

"No, but my brother did. He was eighteen then, a man."

Reverend Zhu said, "Am I correct in my belief that your father had to counter the fund-raising activies of Kang Youwei, his rival for the loyalty of the American Cantonese?"

"Yes." Mai-lin turned to Spade. "Kang Youwei was the founder of the Society to Protect the Emperor. It was his people who denounced my father to Immigration in nineteen oh four. They did not wish to unseat the Manchu dynasty, but to preserve it."

Moon-fong Li said, "I took the liberty of sending our retainer to my brother's restaurant to tell him you might wish to speak with him. Yee-chum Li's on Waverly Place."

The scents of ginger, hot peppers, and herbs followed them up Sacramento Street. Outside an import shop they had to step around a wet wooden tub filled with fuzzy-looking sea snails.

At the corner of Waverly Place, Spade, Mai-lin, and Pastor Zhu went down a set of worn steps to a basement. A black-spotted inset mirror above the heavy double doors reflected their yellowish distorted images. When the moon-faced girl of five who stood on the cashier's stool behind a glass-topped counter saw them she leaped down and ran to the back of the restaurant.

Within moments a woman who was obviously her mother came from the kitchen, drying her hands on a dish towel. She stopped before them, bowed to Mai-lin, spoke in English.

"Daughter of Sun Yat-sen, we are honored by your presence."

Mai-lin answered in Cantonese, also bowing. The woman looked keenly at Reverend Zhu, after a moment bowed, bowed to Spade, and turned to the little girl.

"Sweet Flower, go tell your father that Mai-lin Choi is here with two others."

The girl scampered off. The woman threaded her way across the white tiled floor between round close-set tables jammed with Chinese men and women using chopsticks to shovel rice into their mouths from white porcelain bowls held just below their chins. The low-ceilinged room rang with the clatter of cutlery and high-pitched conversations in Cantonese.

She ushered them into a booth with curtains that could be closed for privacy. A skinny waiter with buck teeth in a seamed face brought a pot of green tea and small white handleless cups with green gilt-outlined dragons writhing around their sides. He departed, pulling the curtains closed behind him.

"You see how they acknowledge my father and honor his memory?" asked Mai-lin with pride in her voice.

Rings squealed on a brass rod as the curtain was drawn back. The waiter set down steaming bowls of chicken clear soup, platters of startlingly green *chow yuk*, pork fried rice, sweet-and-sour pork, and almond duck steaming under its almond-dusted sauce.

The curtain was drawn shut again. They picked up their chopsticks. Mai-lin started to speak, but Spade stopped her with a tiny shake of his head. He made sure their conversation was limited to the niceties observed among people who have been thrown together for a common cause but are essentially strangers.

As they were finishing, the skinny waiter appeared to clear the table and bring a fresh pot of tea and delicate almond cakes. He left the curtain open. A slender, muscular Chinese man about Spade's age appeared. The family resemblance to Moon-fong Li was unmistakable: high cheekbones, a well-shaped mouth, an almost aquiline nose, piercing jet-black eyes under heavy brows. He was handsome in the way that his sister was beautiful.

"I am Yee-chum Li. Welcome to my eating establishment." He nodded slightly to Pastor Zhu. He slid in beside Spade; the curtain was pulled closed by unseen hands. Yee-chum fixed Mai-lin with an almost hypnotic gaze. "I revered your father. He was one of the few great men I have known in my lifetime."

"Your sister said that you met with him when he returned to Chinatown in nineteen ten," said Mai-lin.

"Yes. What do you know of his activities at that time?"

"I know my father was involved with two men, Charles Boothe and Fritz Lea. I know Boothe was a banker and Lea an adventurer. I know they were trying to raise money for an army. Beyond that I know very little. I seek knowledge."

"I warned your father about Boothe and Lea, but I was only eighteen and my voice was not heard."

Mai-lin poured tea for all of them. Reverend Zhu asked, "Warned Sun Yat-sen about them why?"

"Lea at first was a 'general' in the entourage of Kang Youwei, Sun's rival, and inspected and trained cadets across the United States. He dreamed of bringing down the government of China, taking over, and dividing the spoils. So when Kang's fortunes began to wane in nineteen oh nine, Lea co-opted Sun Yat-sen."

Spade leaned back, took out papers and tobacco, raised

his eyebrows. Yee-chum nodded. Spade started making a cigarette.

"Sun Yat-sen couldn't see that for himself?"

"His idealism blinded him. Their plan was simple—on paper. 'General' Fritz Lea and 'President' Sun Yat-sen brought in a retired banker named Charles Boothe because he had links to military circles in New York whose members had weapons." He focused on Mai-lin. "These arms would be stockpiled in western Guangdong Province until the insurrection occurred. Lea would be commander in chief; Boothe, 'exclusive financial agent for overseas,' would raise the money as loans from his banker associates in New York."

"How much money?" asked Spade.

"They calculated a budget of three and a half million dollars American."

"On what collateral?"

"A special role for investors would be reserved in the economic reconstruction of China. They would be rewarded by the future republican regime as customs commissioners and postal administrators, by concessions of commercial monopolies, and with mining rights in Manchuria."

"And they all lived happily ever after," grunted Spade.

Mai-lin was confused. "But if they had it all set up—"

"Boothe couldn't raise the money," said Yee-chum. "After that he just disappeared."

"What about Fritz Lea?" asked Mai-lin.

"He turned up in London after the revolution, when your father was seeking the support of America and the European powers so he would have Western backing to impose his own authority on his compatriots. Lea acted as an intermediary between Sun and the International Banking Consortium to divert funds intended for the Manchu dynasty to the new republic."

"Did it work?" asked Spade.

"No. They remained neutral. But just the rumors that Sun had been in touch with Western leaders was enough to get him elected president, and he proclaimed a new government, the Republic of China, on January first, nineteen twelve. For forty-five days he headed the provisional government at Nanking, then stepped aside for the former imperial general Yuan Shikai."

"And Fritz Lea?"

"He too dropped out of sight." He turned to Mai-lin. "Your father's republic was all too soon replaced by a military dictatorship, then by Chiang Kai-shek. That was the end of your father's dream. I hope that I have been able to help you understand him better, Miss Choi."

"I feel more confused than ever."

They departed Yee-chum Li's restaurant and the three of them stood on the corner of Waverly Place. Reverend Zhu offered his hand to each of the other two in turn, said, "I must return to my pastoral duties." He headed up Sacramento, leaving them alone.

After dark Chinatown wore a different, slightly sinister aspect. The fog was swirling, the wind cold; the streetlights were haloed, their illumination dimmed. Only the sound of heels on the pavement betrayed the presence of hurrying pedestrians. A group of adventurous tourists, overcoats clutched about them, was being told lies by their guide, about the mysterious labyrinths below the Chinatown streets.

Spade said, "I'll walk you back to your room."

Mai-lin walked slowly, watching her feet. "Why did you not want us to talk about Lea and Boothe while we ate?"

"Did you notice the old waiter came to whisk our plates away just when we were finished eating? There's a narrow passageway behind the booths. Someone can stand there and hear things you might not want him to hear."

A few drops of rain splatted down. A blue-denimed waiter hurried by with someone's hot dinner from some restaurant.

"Tell me again how Zhu got in touch with you," said Spade.

"He heard from the Methodist church in Hawaii that I was coming to look for Boothe and Lea and asked if he could help me in any way." She looked over at him. "Why do I trust you even when you're trying to turn me against Moon-fong Li and Yee-chum Li and even Reverend Sabbath Zhu himself?"

"Maybe it's because you trust everyone. Or maybe it's because I don't trust anyone," said Spade. "Good night, Mai-lin."

38

I'm Working for You, Remember?

Spade doglegged over to Green from Sansome in the rain. As he turned into the Green Street stub, a car swooshed by, splattering him with muddy water. Miles Archer's sedan was parked on Green, empty. Spade climbed up to the warehouse loading dock. The wind-danced streetlight skittered his shadow in shifting praying mantis shapes against the red brick wall. Just at midnight Archer's dark, heavy shape materialized from the shadows to trudge up the concrete steps.

"You had to pick the worst damn storm of the year for it," Archer complained in his rather hoarse voice.

"I have a list of the stolen goods from Toomey at Matson," said Spade. "We'll do an inventory of whatever we find in the warehouse. Hold the light."

Archer shone the hand torch on the heavy brass padlock on the overhead door. The third key Spade tried worked. He laid the open lock on the concrete.

They heaved the overhead up enough to slide underneath

it, let it drop back. Inside was utter blackness and relative silence. Archer swept the torch around. The warehouse was crammed to the rafters with cartons, crates, boxes, and barrels.

"Didn't I tell you?" he chortled in coarse delight.

Spade gave half the list to Archer, tossed his raincoat over a barrel of molasses, compared the numbers on the barrel with those on his list; made a check mark. Seventy minutes later he had checked every item on his list. Archer emerged from behind a tall stack of wooden crates of industrial nuts and bolts, flush faced and with a rip in the knee of his trousers.

"Damned nail!" But he held up his list in triumph. "Every one of them, Sam. It'll be all over the papers. Spade and Archer bust dockside theft ring led by lefty union agitator."

"I'm not sure our clients want publicity. And I'm not sure union agitators are behind it."

"Our clients'd be fools not to, it's what they hired us for. And I saw the Aussie guy paying off Brix myself. Twice."

"So you say, Miles. So you say."

By 7:30 in the morning the rain had blown by, taking the fog with it and leaving choppy water and blue skies and bright sunlight behind. Spade pushed open the heavy warped hardwood door of the cavernous concrete-block building on Pier 19 that housed the so-called Blue Book union.

Inside were half a dozen desks messy with paperwork, dirt-grimed windows that looked dimly out across the bay toward the army garrison on Alcatraz. Heavy-bodied men in rough clothes crowded the room, all talking and laughing at once. Others, in suits and ties, tried to work at the desks despite the din of the longshoremen's voices. The air was heavy with cigar smoke and the faint but harsh smell of cheap booze.

Spade leaned over a littered desk where a hulk-shouldered man in a woolen tweed suit was counting money into a green tin box.

"Stan Hagar around?"

The money counter looked up. His nose had been bent to one side by a board or a brick. His face was heavy and needed a shave. It would always need a shave. His eyes were brown, dead.

"Who's askin'?"

"Sam Spade. I want to see him on business."

The union man tossed the last of the money into the box, closed the lid. Picked up a half-smoked cigar smoldering in a brass bowl he was using as an ashtray. He stuck the stogie between thick lips that wore a permanent sneer.

"What kinda business?"

Spade leaned close to him. "My own."

The cigar chomper shrugged. "In back. Corner office."

Most of the offices were little more than cubicles with interior windows and glass panels in the doors. Spade could see Hagar alone in a large corner office that actually had a window, talking on the phone. He went in without knocking, shut the door behind him. Hagar looked up in surprise mixed with annoyance.

"What the hell do you think you're . . . Oh. You. Spade."

As the detective sat down in the room's spare chair, Hagar said into the telephone, "I'll call you back," and hung up.

Hagar had worked the docks and showed it in a knuckle-scarred face, scarred-knuckled hands, and a heavy body running to fat now that he was behind a desk. But there was slyness there.

"What're ya doin' here, Spade?"

"I'm working for you, remember? I'm here to report."

"I deal with Miles Archer. He should be here, not you."

"That would be clever since he's undercover on the docks." Spade leaned across the desk. "Last night we confirmed where the stolen goods are being warehoused."

"Good! We told Miles what we wanted done and he's done it. A damned good man. He gets his bonus when he puts the finger on Harry Brisbane as the man behind the thefts."

"Yes, the bonus," said Spade thoughtfully. He stood. "I wouldn't move too quick on this, Hagar. Miles might report to you, but I report to the Industrial Association."

Ralph Toomey stood up behind his big rolltop desk.

"My secretary tells me you have something to report."

Spade's face was flat, his eyes hooded. "You hired me to find out who was stealing on the docks and to put a stop to it. Without publicity, you said. I'm doing it—my own way."

Toomey sat back down, abstractedly waving him to the leather armchair across the desk from his own.

"I know you're an independent son of a bitch, Spade. But

the Industrial Association *is* footing the bills for Spade and Archer." He frowned, twiddled a pencil between his fingers. "That list of goods I gave you help?"

"Broke the case. Last night Miles and I went into a warehouse on Green Street. The goods are there. They checked against the list."

Toomey leaned forward, suddenly smiling. "That's good work, Spade. I like it."

"So Miles gets his bonus."

"What bonus?" demanded Toomey. "For what?"

"Stan Hagar said something about it, that's all."

"You talked with Hagar?" demanded Toomey. "Is that wise? You're supposed to be undercover."

Spade shrugged.

"The case is finished, Toomey. Hagar says he has verbal descriptions that match Harry, right down to the Aussie accent, of him paying money to a known Communist agitator and being at the warehouse on at least two occasions in the past week."

Toomey said, "I wouldn't have thought that Harry would—"

"Nor would he. He's been laid up at home for three weeks with a broken foot. The warehouse is owned by the Shipowners' and Merchants' Tugboat Company. I'm assuming that you don't know Hagar set up the dock-pilferage thing to frame Harry Brisbane to take the fall as the ringleader of the thieves."

"I sure as hell didn't until you walked in, and I'm not sure I know it now." Toomey was starting to get red in the face. His big hands twitched into loose fists. "And I don't know what the hell you think you're getting at, Spade. Shipowners' and Merchants' are members of our Industrial Association. They would not store stolen goods in their warehouse—"

"I checked with Charles Barber, who's on their board of directors. The warehouse had been standing empty for months. But before he went with the Blue Book, Hagar was Shipowners' and Merchants' office manager. My take is that he lined up some Blue Book longshoremen he trusted to start organized pilfering on the docks after hours and had them store the goods in the Green Street warehouse without the Shipowners' and Merchants' Tugboat people knowing about it. Then he came to the Industrial Association with a sad tale of massive thievery on the docks."

Spade paused to start rolling a cigarette. Toomey stared at him, then lit a cigar, laid it smoldering on his ashtray, and crossed to the green *secrétaire* in the corner. He returned with two snifters of cognac.

"Success to crime," said Spade. They toasted, drank. Reawakened anger made Toomey slam a fist on the desk.

"Came to *me*, Spade! Asked *me* to hire private detectives to look into it since we didn't want any publicity. And then recommended Miles Archer as a good man to go undercover. So Archer was in on it from the start."

"No." Spade told his lie with a face totally devoid of animation. "Miles is a good detective but he hates Commies, so Hagar was able to lead him around by the nose."

Toomey drained his snifter. "Well, by God, I'm going to blow 'em out of the water!"

"What about the publicity?"

Toomey slumped back in his big leather swivel, looking deflated. For the first time he used Spade's first name.

"What do I do, Sam? If this should get to the newspapers, the Industrial Association will be torn apart."

"You pay Spade and Archer for our investigative work. I keep my mouth shut; I make sure Miles keeps his mouth shut. You have Stan Hagar in and tell him he shuts down his bogus theft ring just as quietly as he set it up and gets the stolen goods back to their owners the same way. Quietly. Once the newspapers forget about thievery on the docks, you get Hagar fired."

When Spade got back to his office, Effie Perine told him, "Henny Barber called. He thinks he's located Charles Boothe."

39

Horse Liniment

They'd taken the Golden Gate auto ferry from the Hyde Street pier to Sausalito, had driven north to San Rafael, then on to the little town of Fairfax cupped in the wooded hills a few miles to the west. The top of Henny's Austin was down; Spade had the open backseat of the little upright saloon car to himself. Mai-lin was huddled close to Henny in the too-big leather coat he gallantly had given her.

At 3 p.m., Henny stopped at the south end of Pastori Road, one hundred yards from the railroad station. Ahead was a wooden bridge over a meandering stream, flanked by white wooden slat fences like those at horse ranches. At the far end was a gate.

"Used to be Pastori's Hotel," said Spade. "Built around an outdoor dining area with the big oak tree in the middle of it. Once they winched a piano up into the tree and Irving Berlin climbed up and played it for one of their dances. Three years ago the Emporium department store bought it up to turn it into a country club for its employees."

"That's how I found Charles Boothe," said Henny. "I was at lunch with Pater at the Bohemian Club. The manager of the Emporium heard us mention Boothe and told us a retired banker named Charles Boothe was accountant for their country club."

They used the turnaround in front of the main building, stopped, and Spade got out. The grounds were beautifully landscaped, with a manicured lawn perfect for croquette matches. Whiskey jays squawked raucously in the flanking hardwoods.

"You folks wait here for me," said Spade.

A pleasant-faced woman in her forties, hair cut short in the current fashion and a sheaf of menus under her arm, greeted Spade in the open, airy front dining room. The room was bright with ferns and round paper Chinese lanterns.

"May I help you?"

"I'm looking for your accountant."

"Mr. Boothe?" She consulted an enameled Ball watch on a chain around her neck. "He's probably in his cabin." She raised her voice. "Hank? Do you know if Charles is around?"

Hank was in his forties, bearded, dressed casually.

"Left ten minutes ago, Mrs. Hendrix." He looked at Spade without enthusiasm. "Charlie doesn't like to be bothered."

"We're a little protective of Charles," said Mrs. Hendrix. "He's got a stiff leg, and for a time he was . . ."

"A boozer?" asked Spade.

"Oh, no, nothing like that," she lied. She led Spade out

the rear entrance. Bees buzzed lazily in honeysuckle vines draped to the ground. She pointed past a row of buildings. "The cottage at the far end. You can drive down there."

The little cabin was of the same architecture as the main building, with two white-framed windows on each side and one in the rear. Low hedges shielded it, shade trees overhung it. The three of them crowded onto the narrow-roofed front veranda. Spade knocked on the door. There was no response.

"Mr. Boothe?"

After a long pause there was the sound of approaching uneven footsteps. The door opened.

Boothe was in his late sixties, as tall as Spade. His face would have once been rubicund, but now his nose was W. C. Fields's, bulbous and red veined; his watery blue eyes behind rimless glasses had no answers, only questions. His free hand held an ebony cane. One leg was obviously stiff.

"Yes?"

Mai-lin stepped forward, bowed slightly to him.

"You were an associate of my father, Sun Yat-sen."

"Even if true, there's nothing to talk about."

Boothe started to close the door, but Spade pushed past him into the cabin's spacious main room. It had a round table, four chairs, and a double daybed that would open out into a bed at night. Beside the daybed was a floor lamp with an oval shade on a swivel that could serve as a reading lamp, and a bookcase crammed with adventure novels, mostly for kids.

Boothe stood stiffly, his back to the table. Spade chuckled.

"*A Child's Garden of Verses*?"

"The books came with the cabin," said Boothe quickly. "A woman and her two little daughters lived here before me."

"Mmm-hmm. Let's talk about Sun Yat-sen's money."

Strangely, Spade's words seemed to lessen Boothe's hostility.

"A young journalist from one of the San Francisco papers came round shortly after Sun Yat-sen's death. He thought there might be a story in it. There wasn't. Apart from him, nobody's wanted to talk about those fund-raising days for years."

"What was his name? What did he look like?"

"Slender. Dark hair. Fine features." Boothe made a dismissive gesture. "There really was no story. I was unable to raise the money that Sun needed. It all came to naught."

"Unable to raise *all* of the money," said Spade.

"I don't know what you mean." Boothe glanced toward Mai-lin. "I'm sorry, but your father was an impossible man. He did not ever really trust Fritz and myself."

"He was wise not to," said Spade.

"What ever happened to Lea?" asked Henny.

Boothe's eyes went vague. "I have no idea."

Mai-lin was disbelieving. "Are you saying you didn't know that he turned up after the revolution, in nineteen twelve, in London?"

"Oh, I knew that of course." He gave a wry drinker's chuckle. "Then I lost track of him, lost a leg, lost interest."

"Miss Choi has it on good authority that you raised a quarter of a million bucks that's never been accounted for."

"Errant nonsense! The Emporium paid a quarter million to Adele Pastori for this property in nineteen twenty-five, and that was one of the largest real estate transactions in Marin County's history." His mouth tightened. "What good authority?"

Mai-lin said, "A few years ago the pastor of my Methodist congregation in Hawaii received a communication from the pastor of St. John's Church in Chinatown. It told of a rumor that in nineteen ten a quarter of a million dollars had been raised for my father's cause by you and Mr. Lea but was never turned over to him."

"It's all lies. Nothing but damnable lies."

"Maybe a drink would help you remember." Spade stood up abruptly. "We're through here."

A silent Henny drove up Main Street, recently renamed Broadway, in the gathering dusk. The water cart had been by, sprinkling the road and laying the dust. Mai-lin was huddled beside Henny as if exhausted.

"Stop here," said Spade.

Across the street, at 19 Broadway, warm light came through the windows of the Fairfax Hotel and Restaurant. Henny twisted around on the car seat to face Spade.

"I don't approve of some of the things you said and did back there, Mr. Spade. You were very unpleasant and—"

"I'm doing what she hired me to do. Ask her."

"It's all so . . . mixed up." Mai-lin put a hand on Henny's

arm. "I went to Mr. Spade because he is the kind of man who can find out for me those things I thought I needed to know."

Henny looked sheepish. "Heck, I'm sorry, Mr. Spade."

Spade got out, said, "Go back to the city; I'll catch the train to Sausalito."

He crossed the ill-lit street to the two-story brick building. Light from the hotel lobby fell on a man of twenty-five leaning against the corner of the entryway in shirtsleeves. He had wise guy eyes and black hair slicked back with a lot of pomade.

Spade said, "Last time I saw you was in Wop Healy's joint."

"It got a little too hot for me over there across the bay."

"I need a bottle of horse liniment, Slick."

"Whiskey or rye? It all comes out of the same bathtub."

"Just so it's got alcohol in it."

40

Buried Treasure?

Spade went back across the bridge and walked on the grassy verge of the road. There was no moon. Light came from Boothe's cabin through lowered shades. Spade's skeleton key silently opened the back door. On his way through the kitchen he picked up two water glasses from the sideboard.

Boothe was lying fully clothed on the daybed, his stiff leg stretched out straight. He was reading a newspaper by the light of the floor lamp.

Spade said cheerily, "Young Spade, bearing booze."

He set down the glasses on the table, set a bottle of whiskey beside them. Boothe struggled to a sitting position.

"I—I don't drink," he faltered, his eyes on the bottle.

"Sure you don't." Spade sat, poured whiskey into the glasses. Boothe maneuvered himself into a chair.

Spade pushed a glass toward him. "I need the whole story. "About the money. About Fritz Lea. About Sun Yatsen."

They drank, Boothe greedily. Light came immediately into his eyes. He sighed, smacked his lips.

"I've spent a lot of years trying to drown the memories of our lost treasure."

"We've got all night."

"It didn't take all night, but it took the bottle and the best part of four hours to get his story. He's a foxy old gent."

It was 8 in the morning. Spade was in his swivel chair, Effie Perine was in the armchair across from him. He tossed papers and tobacco pouch on the desk, leaned back with his hands clasped behind his head while she made him a cigarette.

"He finally admitted that, yes, money was raised and, yes, it was indeed a quarter of a million."

"Do you believe him?"

"I think I do," he said softly. "A quarter million was nowhere near enough to fund Sun Yat-sen's revolution, so they didn't tell him about it. They just banked it for themselves."

"Mai-lin was so sure it wasn't in any bank."

"In a way she's right. In nineteen twelve, before he went to London, Lea pulled the money from the bank and buried it. Literally. He didn't trust Boothe to leave it alone until he got back. He wouldn't say where he'd hidden it."

"I guess he never did get back," she mused softly.

"Maybe before nineteen fourteen, when he went to jail. Anyway, Boothe says he never saw him again, never knew where he hid the money."

The sound of the hall door opening brought Effie Perine to her feet. Spade said, "Of course everything Boothe told me last night might be a pack of lies."

Spade was stubbing out his cigarette when she returned.

"There's a man says his name is Magnus Lindholm and he wants to consult with you. He's a giant."

"A giant? Send him in, darling."

She opened the door and stood in the opening with her hand still on the knob. "Won't you come in, Mr. Lindholm?"

Lindholm was indeed a giant, seven feet tall, with a massive square head and dark, quick eyes. He wore a dark brown woolen worsted suit and was removing a sand-colored Bond Street hat with one ham-size hand as he came in.

"What can I do for you, Mr. Lindholm?"

Lindholm filled the oaken armchair beside the desk. The upper half of his heavy face was ruddy and jovial, the lower half set, almost concrete colored, the mouth a hard line.

"I have been in your beautiful city for a week, Mr. Spade, seeking word of some . . . associates, yes, that is the word, associates of mine in a, shall we say, venture, whom I believe planned to come here from . . ." He looked keenly at Spade. "I have heard that you are a man who is unusually well-informed about what goes on in San Francisco."

Spade opened his hands in a deprecating manner, saying nothing quite forcefully. Lindholm nodded as if he had spoken.

"I have found no trace of my associates."

Spade's face became gravely attentive. His voice was husky. "And you wish to hire me to . . . what? Find them?"

"Perhaps that. Or perhaps a man like yourself has already been approached by them on this matter?"

His voice made it a question. Spade smiled reprovingly. The telephone rang once before it was picked up by Effie Perine in the outer office. Neither man paid any attention to it.

"There's nothing in your idea that I might already have run across them." Spade drew a pad toward himself, picked up a pencil. "But if they're here, I can find them."

Lindholm pushed himself upright, using his hands on the arms of the chair as well as his legs. He took out a wallet with cyrillic letters embossed in the leather and laid three twenty-dollar bills on the desktop. He gave a slight bow.

"As a consultation fee. I will be in touch."

The huge man turned and left the office. Spade followed him out to the reception room and Effie Perine.

"He left without a word. Should I open a file on him?"

"He's involved in some shady enterprise with some other shady characters who plan to cut him out of things. Or maybe the enterprise is theirs alone. He thought I might have run across them. When he realized I hadn't he decided he'd said too much. Did you notice anything else odd about him, apart from his size?"

"The skin color of the upper and lower halves of his face didn't match."

"Yeah, ruddy above, almost gray below. Recent razor nicks from shaving off a thick beard to make it difficult for anyone who knew him to identify him. No, no file on him. His name isn't Lindholm and he's no Swede and he won't be back." Spade pointed at the phone. "Anything important?"

"Miles is on his way in."

Miles Archer stood at the corner of Spade's desk, hands in the pockets of his brown woolen pants, teetering slightly on his heels, a dissatisfied look on his face. Finally he went over to his own desk and sat down facing Spade.

"Well, you called that one right, Sam."

"What do you mean, Miles?" Spade was too busy rolling a cigarette to look up. Archer took out his own pack.

"I did damn good work on that Green Street warehouse, and what did it get me? No publicity. Nothing in the newspapers. And then when I went to make my final report to Stan Hagar at the Longshoremen's Association, he just said the matter was closed."

"You're going to get your bonus, aren't you?"

Miles started slightly at mention of the bonus. When Spade said nothing more about it he added quickly, obliquely, "Well, yeah, but with the publicity we'd get—"

"So what are you bellyaching about?" Both men lit up. "I told you the Industrial Association wanted two things: the looting on the docks stopped. We stopped it—you stopped it. And they wanted it kept under wraps. It is. Dead and buried. Between you and me, Miles, it was a setup from the beginning."

Archer looked suddenly uneasy. "A setup?"

"Stan Hagar set up raids on the Industrial Association's warehouses so Harry Brisbane would get blamed for them.

Spade and Archer was hired as window dressing. But the big boys downtown got wind of the scheme and put a stop to it. Right now we're sitting pretty. We did what we were hired to do. We'll get our money, and in a month or two Hagar will be gone." He stubbed out his half-smoked cigarette. "Along with anyone they find out was playing his games along with him."

Miles Archer went silent again.

"Meanwhile, I need to get a line on Mai-lin Choi's 'spiritual adviser,' calls himself Reverend Sabbath Zhu Pomeroy."

"Half-breed, with a name like that?"

"Probably," said Spade with apparent indifference. "Zhu is in his thirties, five eight, one hundred forty, thin face, sleepy-looking dark eyes just slightly slanted, heavy eyeglasses with black horn-rims. Shiny black hair. Formerly assigned to some Methodist Chinese church in the Valley." Again a thoughtful pause. "After all that night work I thought you might want to get out of town, into the country for a couple—three days, make a round of the Valley towns, see what you can dig up on him."

"Yeah, good idea." Archer's eyes lit up. "Expenses?"

"Within reason."

Archer was energized. He ground out his cigarette, stood. "You'll see me back here Friday with the goods."

"That's swell, Miles. I knew I could count on you."

Spade remained behind his desk after Archer's departure, his lip slightly curled. Then he went through the reception area and on out, telling Effie Perine as he passed by her desk that he was going to St. John's Methodist Church in Chinatown.

41

I've Got a Business to Run

Henny Barber had Mai-lin Choi out on the dance floor in the crowded New Shanghai Café on Grant Avenue, whirling her around and around to the music of the live band. He was dressed in a custom-tailored suit, she in a silk party dress. Spade, seated alone at their table, noted with a wry grin that Henny was the better dancer of the two. The number ended; they returned flushed and laughing. Henny leaned across the table to Spade.

"So Boothe says he doesn't know where Lea hid the money."

"Yeah, if you believe him." Spade looked at Mai-lin. "What does Reverend Zhu think about it all, Miss Choi?"

"He feels if there was any money, it will never be found."

"We're not going to give up so easily," declaimed Henny.

The fog was in, haloing the streetlights, dulling the night sounds of the city. Spade got off a streetcar at California and

Locust on the edge of Laurel Heights, walked up a slanting half block to a narrow row house. Vague light showed through the lowered shades of the front room windows.

Spade stood looking moodily at the house, then climbed the three steps to the stoop. He rang the bell. The door opened, Iva Archer's backlit face peered out at him. Her soft red lips parted in a smile.

"Come in, quickly, Sam. The neighbors."

She drew him inside, raised her face hungrily for his kiss. She wore a rose-colored crepe de chine negligee open enough to show a silk chemise cut low in the bodice to emphasize her bosom.

Spade took off topcoat and hat, tossed them on the couch. "I could use a drink."

"There's one waiting—in the bedroom." She led him toward the rear of the house, talking rapidly, breathlessly. "You were so clever to dream up some meaningless out-of-town investigation to keep Miles away for two days and nights!"

They went into the bedroom; she shut the door behind them. Candles glowed on the dresser and on the bedside table.

She turned to him, already opening her negligee.

Spade had his chair turned toward the window so he could smoke a cigarette while gazing across the narrow court beside the Hunter-Dulin building. The door was flung open and Dundy came in wearing a black overcoat, his black derby jammed down tight on his head. Tom Polhaus came in behind him, half a head taller than his superior, filling the doorway.

Spade lounged back in his swivel chair. "Why don't you act like a gentleman, Dundy, and take off your hat?"

"We won't be here that long, Spade." Dundy's eyes were alight. "You're coming with us over to Marin County."

"The last time you hauled me across the bay it all came to naught for you."

Dundy crowded up to the desk. Tom followed, slower, shaking his head as he usually did at these encounters.

"There's been a death at the Emporium Country Club over in Fairfax. Their accountant, a fellow named Charles Boothe. Don't try to tell me you didn't know him, because—"

"I knew him."

"Get your hat. You're coming with us."

Spade winked at Tom Polhaus. "Why don't you tell your boyfriend he needs a warrant to take me anywhere."

"Aw, c'mon, Sam, we're just—"

"When and how did Boothe die?"

"Sometime last night," said Polhaus. "The housekeeper at the administration building, a Mrs. Hendrix, looked through his window and saw him lying on the floor and called the Fairfax town cop. He called us and asked us to bring you over there."

"That's when. How?"

"Someone was roughing him up and his heart gave out."

Dundy snapped, "The town cop, Andy Peri, dug up a Slick Hansen who sold you a bottle of bootleg night before last, and Mrs. Hendrix said that on that same night you'd been drinking with Boothe. I can get a material-witness warrant—"

But Spade had come out from behind the desk.

"See how easy it is when you ask nice, Lieutenant?"

They were waiting on the front veranda of the Emporium Country Club when the Fairfax policeman, Andrew Peri, arrived on a motorcycle. He was in uniform, complete with a badge and a Sam Browne belt across his chest, his pant legs protected by shiny leggings. He had a square face with a stern mouth and a cop's eyes under his uniform cap. He took Spade to a table away from the others.

"I figured I had to talk with you, Mr. Spade. You're the only stranger who spoke with Boothe recently that anyone here knows about, and you were with him night before last."

"You don't have to handle this bird with kid gloves," said Dundy, hustling over to their table. "If he cracks wise, I'll take over and get what we need out of him."

"Thanks for getting Mr. Spade here, Lieutenant, but I think I can handle it." To Spade he said, "I talked with the sheriff before you folks got here, and he told me you'd helped him out on a couple of cases and let him get the credit. I got no reason to think you came back again last night, but I gotta ask."

"Sure you do. I was dining and dancing with a client and his lady friend at the New Shanghai Café in Chinatown."

"That seems straight enough. Give me their names, then let's go over and view the body and the crime scene."

. . .

A dozen residents of the country club were milling around outside Boothe's cabin. On the veranda the pleasant-faced Mrs. Hendrix, pale and all but wringing her hands, was obviously glad to be relieved of her watchdog duty.

Inside, there was an unpleasant scorched smell on the air. One of the chairs was overturned by the table, with a big serving spoon beside it. The body of Charles Boothe was sprawled near the bed. He was shoeless, with a sock on his right foot. His left arm was outstretched above his head, pointing toward the bookshelf. Half a dozen books had been pulled out and were scattered about on the floor.

"Looks like he was attacked over near the table," rumbled Tom Polhaus. "After the attacker left he must of come around enough to crawl to the bookshelf to try and get to his feet."

"Not on that foot," said Spade.

"Good God in heaven!" cried Mrs. Hendrix, who had ventured in through the front door.

The bottom of Boothe's bare left foot was blackened and blistered around ovals of angry red raw flesh. Dundy went down on one knee to get at a book wedged under the body. He turned the book upside down, open, and shook it vigorously. No papers fell out. He snorted with laughter as he tossed it on the bed.

"Hell, just a kid's adventure story. *Treasure Island.*"

Tom Polhaus also leafed quickly through it, as if looking for handwritten notations in the margins, then dropped it on the bed. From outside came the sound of an approaching vehicle. A long shiny black Buick sedan with side curtains pulled up.

"Coroner's here," said Peri. "Guess you all better clear out so him and me can get on with our official duties."

Spade casually picked up *Treasure Island* and walked out, pausing a dozen yards away from the cabin to put it under his arm and work on a cigarette. Tom Polhaus came up behind him.

"Ain't that evidence, Sam?"

"Of what? I loved this story when I was a kid, thought I'd read it again." He chuckled sardonically and held the book out to Polhaus. "But of course if it's *evidence* . . ."

"Aw hell, Sam," said Tom. An almost crafty light entered his eyes. "What were you over here to talk with Boothe about?"

"Nothing that was going to get him killed." He clapped Polhaus on the shoulder. "I've got a business to run, Tom. Take me back to the city and I'll buy you pickled pigs' feet at Big John's Hof Brau."

42

Death by Fire

On Friday morning Spade looked up, stopped leafing through *Treasure Island,* and said offhandedly, "Hello, Miles. When did you get back?"

"Late last night." Archer went to his desk, sat down, said, "I've gotta do my expense account on the trip."

"Try to hold it down on the bribes, booze, and biddies."

"You kidding?" Archer guffawed. "Over in those Valley towns you can't sin if you want to. Anyway, Zhu turned up in Sacramento maybe three years ago with a diploma from an outfit advertising in the back of a magazine, saying he was a minister of God."

"Aimee Semple McPherson, look out," chuckled Spade.

"The Chinese Methodist church in Fresno took him on as assistant pastor. He stayed a year. He looks clean to me."

"Good. He has a lot of influence on our client; I just wanted to make sure he's a right ghee, that's all."

Spade got his hat, stopped at Effie Perine's desk.

"Call Doc Naughton out at the U.C. Med School, sweetheart."

She picked up the phone. "Do I tell him where it hurts?"

"Just tell him I'm curious."

Spade walked up Parnassus to the Hooper Foundation for Medical Research. The sky was gray and the wind whipped the tails of his overcoat. He had to hold his hat on his head, had to chafe his hands together after entering the imposing granite building.

James Naughton met Spade in the doctors' lounge and poured coffee. He was a big man with ice-chip blue eyes, a Guards mustache, and a marked British accent. He radiated authority and confidence.

"I suggested we meet here, Samuel, because I have surgery in a few minutes and Effie said you were suffering from nothing more dangerous than a terminal case of medical curiosity."

Spade said, "I seem to remember, from that time I took that wart off your back, that cosmetic surgery is your field."

"Took the wart off my back?" Naughton chuckled. "A good way to describe excising a blackmailer. So?"

"I seem to remember you telling me that the ancient Egyptians reconstructed lips, noses, and ears with skin grafts and that the ancient Greeks and Romans perfected the technique to include eyelids."

"You've got a good memory, Samuel. A first-century Roman physician named Aulus Cornelius Celsus did indeed report making excisions in the skin of the eyelids to relax them. During the Middle Ages plastic surgery was banned as unethical and godless, but during the Renaissance many of those ancient surgical procedures and techiques were rediscovered."

Naughton checked his watch.

"In eighteen eighteen a German doctor, Karl Ferdinand von Graefe, called operations to repair deformities caused by cancer in the eyelids blepharoplasty. He laid the foundations for the work done by surgeons like myself on men disfigured in the Big War."

"You ever get asked to try and change a Chinese woman's eyelids to make her look less Asian and more Western?"

Naughton leaned back, shook his head. "No. Chinese American women are generally too conservative to want something like that. But two years ago in Boston a Japanese man in love with a girl from Iowa wanted a doctor to Westernize his features so he'd be acceptable to the girl's good God-fearing conservative Midwest folks. The doc cut the eye corners so the slant was gone and tightened the man's pendulous lower lip."

Spade started to dig out tobacco and papers, thought better of it, drank coffee instead. "How'd it work out for them?"

"The patient changed his name to William White and married his true love."

"One more question, Doc. Could a white woman, say, have that surgery done in reverse? Get an operation to make her look like she was Chinese? Or half Chinese? From Hawaii maybe?"

"Intriguing. Just a matter of removing the superior palpebral fold of the Caucasian eyelid to give the eye the slanted look of the typical Chinese." He checked his watch a final time, said "Damn," then said, "I met a doctor from Sacramento at a medical convention three years ago who said he had a Caucasian patient wanted him to do something like that."

"What was the doctor's name?" asked Spade quickly.

"I don't remember. He died in a fire a few months later."

Spade climbed the sweeping marble staircase to the second floor of San Francisco's Main Library, across the Civic Center Plaza from City Hall. In the newspapers and periodicals room he told a sweet-faced lady librarian whose name plate read THERESA MCGOVERN, "I'm interested in out-of-town newspapers."

"Current newspapers are on the racks along the walls. If you need back issues I can bring them to you. Library patrons aren't allowed in the periodicals stacks."

"I'm looking for the death of a Sacramento-area doctor by fire during the last three months of nineteen twenty-five or maybe early nineteen twenty-six."

She came back scant minutes later with a sheaf of folded newspapers. She shook her head sadly.

"The poor man. A wife and family and a good practice, then to die when some arsonist burned his office to the ground."

Spade thanked her, then added, "You make it look so

easy that maybe you can dig up some information on one other thing."

"You just name it," smiled Theresa.

"Red Rock Island."

Effie Perine was bent over her desk, studying the horoscope in one of the afternoon newspapers.

"I see a handsome stranger in your life," said Spade.

She tossed the paper aside with a rueful grin. "Don't I wish." She opened her pad. "Tom Polhaus left word that the autopsy on Charles Boothe showed his heart gave out when he was being tortured." She shivered. "A nasty way to go, Sam."

"Yeah. Call Mai-lin, darling, set up an appointment here for tomorrow morning. Tell her that dead men sometimes speak."

"Meaning what?"

"Meaning Charles Boothe left me a message." As she reached for her phone, he added, "I have to go over to Marin. Cook up something for Miles to do so he won't come barging into the office tomorrow morning."

Afternoon fog flowed down over the brushy hills that ringed Sausalito to bring cold, wet air and cut off the weak winter sunshine. Benny Ruiz was at the Sausalito yacht harbor sitting on the hatch cover of his fishing boat, the *Portagee,* using a long curved needle to repair a fishnet. Half a dozen crab pots were stacked on the deck. The boat smelled of fish scales and tar and, very faintly, bootleg booze from Canada.

A smile lit up Benny's round, slightly concave face. His heavy lips opened in a smile.

"Hey, Sam!" He was wearing his usual black sweater and black peacoat. A Greek fisherman's cap was tipped back on his head. "You got any more English gold you want found?"

"Fresh out, Benny." Spade put his backside against the gunwale, gestured at the net. "No more bootlegging?"

Benny put down his needle.

"The competition's gotten so fierce that a lot of us Portagees are going back to fishing almost full-time. Don't pay so good, but it ain't so hard on the nerves."

A seagull swooped down to land on the top of the cabin. Benny threw a scrap of rope at him.

"You know the waters around Red Rock Island, Benny?"

"Back of my hand. It's only twenty minutes from here even for this old scow." Benny laid an affectionate hand on the hatch cover. "When I was a kid we'd go out there moonlit nights, try to shoot us some rabbits. Thing we could never figure out, how did they get there in the first place? It's really deep water out there, maybe fifty, sixty feet—I took soundings once."

"There any rabbits left?"

"Not many." Benny tossed aside the net. "No foxes or nothing can get at them, but there's not much vegetation for 'em to eat, and only rainwater or fog or dew on the rocks for 'em to drink. Only other wildlife is seabirds and bats that hang around those old manganese mining tunnels."

"I need you to take me out there tomorrow night, late. Don't let anybody know about it, Benny. Not *anybody.*"

"Anybody asks, I'm going out after a load of hootch."

It was 1 a.m. Sam Spade was merely a bulky shape in Effie Perine's chair. The flexible arm of her adjustable desk lamp was twisted so its circle of light in the otherwise dark office illuminated a smoldering cigarette, a butt-heaped ashtray, *Treasure Island,* its front endpaper skillfully and carefully laid open, and Spade's big hands holding a folded, soiled, amateurishly drawn map.

The hands laid down the map and picked up the ornate Greek dagger Effie Perine used as a letter opener. The right hand began pressing the blunted bronze point against the left palm, idly at first, then hard. The point was so rounded it did not make the slightest indentation. The right thumb tested what should have been the cutting edge of the dagger's thick six-inch tapered almost-oval blade. It drew no blood.

Spade dumped the ashtray, folded the map, and put it into his suit-coat pocket. He slid the dagger into its symbol-laden scabbard and thrust it into the pocket with the map. His movements brought his thoughtful face into the oval of light. He picked up *Treasure Island,* turned out the light, and left.

43

Red Rock Island

Effie Perine closed the door and said, "Miss Choi is here. She's not alone. Henny Barber is with her."

"That boy is plenty smitten. Sabbath Zhu?"

"No Sabbath Zhu."

"Then by all means have them in, sweetheart. And sit in yourself. Don't bother with your shorthand pad."

"So that's the way it is."

"That's the way it is."

Henny Barber said almost aggressively, "That Fairfax policeman came around asking all sorts of impertinent questions about Charles Boothe's death. He said nothing about a message. Why haven't we heard anything about it until now? Mai-lin has the right to know everything."

"Henny. Please." Her tone was of fond exasperation. She leaned forward intently. "Mr. Spade, did our going there that day have anything to with . . . what happened to Mr. Boothe?"

"Hard to say one way or the other. Nobody followed us there, that's for sure." His voice became ironic. "So, no, I'd say you can't take the blame for that one."

"Thank God." She leaned back, looking suddenly exhausted.

"He knew that I didn't believe him when he said he didn't know where Lea had hidden the money he pulled from the bank. So I thought the books pulled out of the bookcase and scattered around on the floor were some sort of message. They weren't. But one of them was under his body, clutched in his hand."

"That was the message?"

"Not quite." He looked at each of them in turn. "You know anything about Red Rock Island?"

"No," said Mai-lin in a puzzled voice.

"Yes," said Effie Perine. "It's a six-acre knob of dirt and rock in the bay off the Richmond shoreline, eight miles from Fisherman's Wharf. We had a picnic there once. My father said Russian and Aleut fur hunters after sea otter used to camp there in the early eighteen hundreds."

"Manganese," said Henny suddenly. "Wasn't it found to be rich in manganese? That's why it's called Red Rock. And didn't speculators dig all sorts of tunnels and mine a lot of ore?"

"Two hundred tons," said Spade. "And Norwegian and Swedish sailors loaded their ships with it, calling it ballast. Only when they got back to Europe they sold it to paint manufacturers. Our government owned Red Rock then and put a stop to it."

"What does this have to do with Charles Boothe?"

"Everything, Henny. The early Spanish explorers called it Moleta Island after the pigment in the rock. In eighteen twenty-seven Captain Frederick Beechey of the Royal Navy charted it as Molate Island—he got the Spaniards' name for it wrong. Then it was called Golden Rock because of legends that pirates had buried their treasure there. Then—"

"And then later it was called Treasure Island because of those same legends!" exclaimed Effie Perine.

Spade had gotten elaborately busy constructing a cigarette.

"The book Boothe was holding on to was Robert Louis Stevenson's *Treasure Island.* That's the clue Boothe managed to leave for me."

"So the money is buried on Red Rock," said Mai-lin.

"Don't get your hopes up. It's a long shot at best."

"And there have to be dozens of tunnels on that island," said Henny in a dispirited voice.

"Except that Dundy did his usual slipshod investigation of the murder," said Spade. "He saw it was a kid's adventure book and dismissed it. But Boothe had hidden a map of Red Rock between the front cover and the endpaper. With a tunnel marked."

Henny was on his feet. "Where's the map?"

"In my safe," said Spade. "And there it stays until tomorrow night. And then it'll be just Mai-lin and me." He studied the girl's face intently. "Just us, Mai-lin. You don't tell anyone else. Not *anyone.* You got that?"

After a long pause she said, "I've got it, Mr. Spade."

. . .

Effie Perine returned to Spade's office after seeing the couple out. "What do you really think of it all, Sam?"

"I think there's nothing there to find. Boothe probably made the fake map to sell but never got any takers. Or maybe Fritz Lea lied to Boothe. Or maybe dug it up himself. Or maybe a weekend treasure hunter found it. Anyway, I don't believe there's any pot of gold at the end of this particular rainbow."

She stuck a cigarette between his lips, lit it with the desk lighter. "Then why did you say you'd take her out there?"

"She's my client. This is what she wants."

"Do you think she'll tell Sabbath Zhu about it?"

"I hope not. Zhu came up clean in Miles's investigation, but I still don't trust that bird."

"Miles or Zhu?"

"Miles I trust as an op. Zhu I don't trust at all."

"Be careful, Sam. I—I have a bad feeling about this, like I did when Penny . . ." A shiver ran through her slim body. "You aren't planning something tricky and . . . dangerous, are you?"

"I'm a big boy now," said Spade. "I know what I'm doing."

Thick ropes of white and silent fog were rolling in from the Pacific through the Golden Gate. Alcatraz was gone, as were Sausalito and the lights marking the East Bay towns of Berkeley, Emeryville, and Oakland. The air was wet, heavy, cold.

Spade stood wide legged on a slatted wooden dock at the end of Gas House Cove in the Marina Yacht Harbor. He wore a woolen cap, a waterproof coat, waterproof pants tucked into vulcanized boots. Water slopped up between the slats and over his boots.

The headlights of the few passing cars on Marina Boulevard were haloed in mist, their sounds muted. Henny Barber's Austin turned off Laguna Street and stopped above the pier. The windshield was closed; Spade could just make out the two dark shapes close together on the front seat. At the same moment came the slow chug-chug-chug of Benny Ruiz's fishing boat. Spade caught the line Benny tossed and tied it around the hand railing with a slipknot that could be undone with a sharp jerk.

"Good timing," he called and jumped down into the boat.

By the light of the metal-caged bulb at the head of the ramp, Henny and Mai-lin edged cautiously down toward the *Portagee,* Henny with an arm hooked through hers as if he had already found his precious treasure. They were bundled up in heavy slickers, Mai-lin's with an attached hood.

Spade held out a hand to help her down off the dock. He said to Henny, "See you back here in two or three hours," but Henny was already crowding on behind Mai-lin.

"Not on your life. I'm coming with." Mai-lin had moved off a few feet, staring out into the fog, subdued, only her small face visible within the encircling rain hood. Henny lowered his voice. "I don't care about the treasure, only about Mai-lin."

"What about your folks?"

"What about them? They'll accept her, or I'll talk Aunt Ev into opening a branch bank in Hong Kong."

Spade raised his voice. "Mai-lin." As she came back toward them he jerked the mooring line to undo the knot. Benny backed the boat off. "Did you tell Sabbath Zhu about tonight?"

"You don't have the right to ask her that," said Henny.

Ruiz swung the *Portagee*'s prow toward the narrow yacht harbor entrance. The dock disappeared into the mist behind them, leaving only the telltale glow of the caged bulb above the ramp.

Mai-lin raised her head. The imperious daughter of Sun Yat-sen was staring at Spade through dark slanted eyes.

"Sabbath Zhu was a great help to me. I had to tell him. What harm is done? I know you do not trust him, but he did not even want to come. He does not approve of what we are doing."

"A fool for a client," said Spade in apparent bitterness.

44

Chapter and Verse

Benny was in the wheelhouse flanked by Mai-lin and Henny, his broad, coarse face underlit by the binnacle light, his eyes probing the opaque gray blanket of fog. Spade was forward, checking the gear he'd be taking ashore.

From every direction came the warning cries of the ferries and tugs braving the fog. Underlying all of them was the periodic baying of the Alcatraz foghorn.

"The hound of the Baskervilles," said Henny.

Mai-lin shivered, asked Benny, "How are you able to tell where you're going when you can't see?"

"The bells," said Benny. "The whistles. The horns. I can tell them apart the same way that Henny can tell a ten-buck bill from a fifty. I started in on my old man's fishing boat when I was twelve. I know this bay." Off to their right a foghorn bellowed mournfully. "You can't see it, but that's Alcatraz."

Spade looked in at them, his big hands gripped the frame

on either side of the doorway. His face was beaded with moisture.

"All set," he told them.

"Red Rock," said Benny.

They could hear waves breaking almost gently against an invisible foreshore. The engine was already in neutral: they were drifting with the tide. Henny, holding Mai-lin's arm again, said in a low voice, "I think I can see the shape of the island."

"You'd make a good bootlegger," said Ruiz.

Spade's muffled voice came from the prow. "Your romantic adventure. Next best thing to stowing away to the South Seas."

"Better," said Henny, pulling Mai-lin closer to him.

"Now that we're here," she said in a subdued voice, "I almost wish we weren't."

The craft turned toward the darker shadow of Red Rock, now visible through the fog. Spade lit the carbide lamp Benny had supplied. It was a compact model with folding handles and a seven-inch highly polished nickel-plated reflector, better out here in the fog than any flashlight or hand torch.

The prow grated gently on gravel. Spade swung his legs over the gunwale, dropped down onto sand hard packed by the waves. He reached back in for shovel and lamp, stepped free of the boat.

Then he put a boot against the prow and shoved, hard, swinging the boat at an angle to the shore. At the same time Benny put the engine in gear to an outraged shout from

Henny Barber. Spade turned the carbide lamp their way. Henny was dragging a bewildered Mai-lin forward, but it was too late. The fog closed in around their shadowy figures, and they were gone.

A half an hour later Spade was shining his light into a tunnel mouth when a sardonic voice spoke from behind him.

"We meet again, Spade." He started to spin toward the voice. It warned, "Slowly. Very slowly."

Spade obeyed, turning slowly, hands out well from his sides. His lamp showed him Sabbath Zhu. In Zhu's hand was a Colt 1911 automatic, most of its bluing worn off by the years.

"I can't believe she told you we were coming out here," Spade said in a disgusted voice.

"She trusts me. I thought she would be with you; I could square accounts with everyone at once." Already his slightly singsong Chinese accent was slipping, as if he knew it no longer mattered. His thick glasses glinted with his head jerk. "Put the shovel down. Carefully. Slowly." Spade did. "Good. Now set the lamp on that rock . . . Good."

He continued his instructions. "Lay the map on the ground with a small rock on it to hold it down . . . Move back ten feet . . . Shed the heavy coat, roll up the sleeves of your shirt, empty your pockets on top of the discarded coat . . .

"No weapons of any sort, not even a pocketknife," Sabbath Zhu marveled. "A sad mistake on your part."

"I don't like guns. They go off at the wrong time or not at all. All I thought I'd need was a shovel and the map."

Zhu was studying the map while keeping an eye on Spade. He crinkled the paper, said almost abstractedly, "Boothe's?"

"He'd hidden it between the front cover and the endpaper of Stevenson's *Treasure Island.* It was found under his body."

"And the police missed it?"

"Dundy, what d'ya expect? Why don't you take off those specs? They're just clear glass anyway."

"You're right." Zhu tossed aside the eyeglasses, rubbed his delicately slanted eyes. "I won't be needing them anymore after tonight. When did you first become suspicious of me?"

"The first time Mai-lin mentioned Sabbath Zhu, spiritual adviser. I wondered why you'd recommended me to her even though you thought I was of questionable honesty."

"I knew too much about you for a man who'd never met you?"

"Or too little. At the Chinatown Methodist church you said you were assistant pastor but you didn't take us into a meeting room. With Moon-fong Li and Yee-chum it became obvious you didn't know more than a few words of Cantonese. They were members of your supposed church, yet they didn't know you but were too polite to say so. I checked with the pastor of St. John's. He'd never heard of you. You never came through the Angel Island Immigration Station, so you were American born."

Zhu gave an airy shrug. "None of it matters anymore now. Reverend Pastor Sabbath Zhu will mysteriously disappear.

Along with Sam Spade, of course. I'll find a doctor to reverse the blepharoplasty and then—"

"Then kill him, like you did the doctor in Sacramento."

That seemed to shake him slightly. "You've been busy."

"Yeah. Chapter and verse." Spade added without apparent emotion, "Back in nineteen twenty-one St. Clair McPhee masterminded the *San Anselmo* gold-bullion robbery and disappeared with seventy-five thousand dollars in British pounds after murdering four men in Sausalito. In nineteen twenty-five Devlin St. James murdered Collin Eberhard and Penny Chiotras and went on the run. He disappeared from an eastbound train from Oakland. One of the stops was Sacramento, and St. James had run his scam on Cal-Cit Bank from Sacramento. When I started to suspect that Sabbath Zhu was also St. Clair McPhee and Devlin St. James I sent my partner to Sacramento to snoop around."

"You are quick, aren't you?" Zhu said with admiration.

"Not quick enough." Spade's voice was rueful. "Always some religious connection. St. Clair. St. James. Sabbath Zhu."

"My old man was a tent-show minister in the Midwest. Guy C. Menafee, rector, *di*rector, and *pro*tector." Sudden hatred flooded his voice. "The sanctimonious bastard."

Spade ignored this. "When I found the map in *Treasure Island,* I knew the reporter who interviewed Boothe after Sun's death in nineteen twenty-five had to be you. I figure that's where you first sniffed out that quarter million. When I found out about the dead doctor in Sacramento, I wanted to take you apart, see what made you tick." Bitterness entered his voice. "I didn't know Mai-lin was going to spill her guts to you."

"You should have." He gave a short laugh. "Her spiritual adviser, remember? Why do you think I recommended you to Mai-lin in the first place? Because I knew if any man could find out where Lea and Boothe had hidden Sun Yat-sen's money, it would be you. Now, at long last, I get to take *you* apart and see what makes *you* tick." He made an abrupt gesture with the pistol. "Pick up your shovel. I'll follow with the lantern."

The tunnel was hewn through the rock, twisting and turning, going up and then down, following the vein of manganese deep into Red Rock's belly. It was wide enough and deep enough so they could move through it upright. The walls dripped with moisture. The light drove black clouds of chittering bats out of the tunnel past them.

Beyond an abrupt right-angle turn, the lamp showed a very slight dip in the tunnel floor, as if someone had dug there not too many years before.

Zhu exclaimed from behind Spade, "Stop here!"

Spade stuck his shovel upright in the depression. Zhu placed the lamp on a convenient knob of rock, staying far enough back so he could not be hit with the shovel, could not have a shovelful of earth thrown into his face.

"What are you waiting for?" he demanded hoarsely. "Dig!"

Spade was staring at him keenly. "You've got it," he said.

"Gold fever. Greed. And more. The killing lust. I saw a lot of it in the war. Men who like to kill. What if the map's a phony, Zhu? What if there is no treasure?"

"Then you'll just be digging your own grave."

"Won't I be doing that anyway?"

His thin lips curled. "Of course. To repay me for seven long years of frustration caused by your meddling."

"Dig your own hole," Spade said.

Zhu brought up his .45. "Don't they say that where there's life, there's hope?"

Spade dug. The dirt was moist, loose, easily shoveled. What rocks there were came free easily, to be tossed on the growing pile to one side of the hole.

Once Zhu said, "Be sure to dig it wide enough and long enough for a grave."

"Go to hell," said Spade.

But he dug on, chest deep in the hole. Even in shirt-sleeves, he was caked with dirt, and sweat ran down his face in rivulets, gleaming in the light of the lantern that would stay alive on one charge of carbide for four hours. They had been on the island for less than three.

Spade drove his shovel down again—to the clank of metal on metal. With a surprised exclamation, he dug feverishly, throwing dirt in every direction. Then he dropped to his knees, almost out of Zhu's sight, digging like a dog with his hands.

"Jesus!" he exclaimed. "It's a chest! It's got to be the quarter million dollars!" His arms were buried almost to the elbows in the dirt. He panted, "I . . . never actually thought . . ."

Zhu set the lamp on the pile of dirt, dropped to his knees to stare down at Spade.

"Let me see it. Let me see the money!"

Spade leaned back. The lamp threw his shadow huge and black and cruel against the side of the hole. The chest could be seen, half uncovered, but its tipped-back lid kept Zhu from seeing what was within. Spade's hands reached down into it.

"Here's your treasure," said Spade.

He sprang erect, driving with both feet against the bottom of the hole, his right arm slamming hard against Zhu's lower belly what he had buried in the chest two nights before. The arm ripped upward in a disemboweling thrust. Before any blood could get through Zhu's thick clothing, Spade had stepped aside so the stricken man's body could roll in on top of the chest.

Zhu ended up on his back, his terrified eyes staring up at Spade through the gloom of the grave.

"For Penny," said Spade. "And for all the others."

Zhu's mouth worked as if he had something vital to say. But life left his body before he could speak.

Spade filled in the hole, tromped down the earth over it. Then he burned the map.

45

I Was Counting on It

"So you're saying there was no treasure," said Sid Wise.

Spade, Mai-lin, and Henny were grouped around the lawyer's big desk. Crystal-clear winter sunlight through the windows laid a white-gold oblong across the stacked files on the blotter. Henny was sitting very close to Mai-lin, their hands touching. Spade, lounged back in his chair, was placidly smoking a cigarette. He shrugged, then jabbed the cigarette toward them.

"I don't know. But I warned you. I told you I thought there was no buried money, that there never had been."

Henny grunted. "Even so, that was a crummy trick you played on us, stranding us on the boat that way."

"Benny said he entertained you with bootleg stories." Spade reached inside his breast pocket, took out a folded sheet of old, crisp paper. He held it out. "Here's Boothe's map, Mai-lin. You can keep it as a souvenir." To Henny he added, "Of your great adventure. Or you can go back to Red Rock with it."

Mai-lin picked up the map, stared at it, then went to tear it in half. But Henny took it from her hands.

"If there is a treasure out there you should have it."

Mai-lin shrugged, then said to Spade contritely, "I'm sorry I told Sabbath Zhu about Red Rock, even though I knew he had no intention of going there. I know it made you very angry."

"I was counting on it," said Spade obscurely.

"How do you really feel about there being no money, Miss Choi?"

She smiled at Sid Wise.

"When I realized it had all been a—a sort of dream, I felt only relief. My father repudiated me, never gave me anything. I thought finding the money would . . ." She shook her head. "But I've realized that I don't need anything from him."

"But if it's there we'll find it," insisted Henny. "And if it isn't"—he almost preened—"you'll always have me."

"Who supported you down through the years?" asked Wise.

"My father's brother. Not through any affection—he hardly knew me. He financed most of my father's ventures too, during the early years. Then my father's son from his first marriage took over. Again, I was a family duty for a Chinese Christian."

They all fell suddenly silent at the same time. Sid Wise patted his files with open palms.

"Then I think we're through here. No legal entanglements and I've got a pile of work to do, so . . ."

They were all on their feet. Shook hands all around. As

they started out, Wise said casually, "Oh, Sam, I need to talk to you for just a minute about the Creighton case."

Spade came back in, shut the door, sat down again in his favorite chair. He started making another cigarette.

Wise said, "You can fob off a story about a map between the endpapers of a book to those children, but I know different."

"How's that?" asked Spade without much interest.

"I happened to run into Tom Polhaus in court yesterday," said Wise in a careful voice. "He told me how Dundy tossed *Treasure Island* aside and how he himself went through the book page by page looking for marks or notations. He didn't find anything."

"That still doesn't mean there wasn't a map hidden in it."

Wise stared at him keenly for a long moment.

"You're a very different man from that twenty-seven-year-old kid who shoved a crumpled-up newspaper into my hand in our old office building over Remedial Loans. Harder. Colder."

"A lot has happened to both of us, Sid. We grew up."

"Sure, but." Sid Wise paused. "I don't know what happened out there on Red Rock the other night, but—"

"I didn't find any treasure."

"You found something." Wise was silent while he trimmed and lit a cigar. "What do you think will happen with the girl?"

"She'll be fine. She's got Henny Barber."

"What will his folks say about him and a Chinese girl?"

"They'll come around. She's beautiful and smart—smart as a Greek girl, and that's plenty smart. She's of good blood, even if from the wrong side of the bed. She'll make Henny the kind of wife an important banker needs. Maybe they'll go to Hong Kong and open a branch bank like he keeps talking about. Or they'll take the map to Red Rock Island and maybe find a treasure."

"I guess you're right." Studying his cigar, Wise added, "But what if they follow that map and find something buried besides Sun Yat-sen's money?"

Spade chuckled. "Maybe there were two maps. Maybe there was one hidden in *Treasure Island*, the one they have now, and maybe there was another map, a fake one, somebody else made."

Sid Wise's sharp features became very tight. Then he nodded. He had to clear his throat before speaking.

"Then you don't think Sabbath Zhu will make any trouble?"

"I think Sabbath Zhu has already moved on."

When Spade came into the office the next morning, Effie Perine gave him a strange look. But all she said was, "How did the conference go at Sid's office yesterday?"

"Everyone healthy, wealthy, and wise. Any messages?"

Instead of answering, she said, "And what did you do to my knife? I almost cut myself opening the mail yesterday."

"Which knife?"

"You know very well which knife." She ruefully displayed it. "The Greek knife that . . ." She fumbled her words for a moment, then rallied. "That Penny gave me all those years ago."

Spade shrugged. "I just sharpened it up a bit. They always say a dull knife is more dangerous than a sharp one."

She thrust it under his nose.

"What's this smear on the blade?"

"Rust."

"It's a bronze blade. Bronze doesn't rust."

"Then it's paint."

"You know very well it isn't."

He shrugged again, started toward his office, paused.

"What I do know, Effie, is that Penny, if she were still around, wouldn't mind a little rust on the blade of that knife."

He went into his office and shut the door.

A half hour later, Spade was smoking behind his desk when Effie Perine came in. He looked up at her.

"Yes, sweetheart?"

She finished shutting the door behind her, leaned against it, and said, "There's a girl wants to see you. Her name's Wonderly."

"A customer?"

"I guess so. You'll want to see her anyway: she's a knockout."

"Shoo her in, darling," said Spade. "Shoo her in."

Acknowledgments

Always first in my acknowledgments is Dori, wife, lover, best friend, forever my first and last reader, editor, critic, and collaborator. She inspires me to write and always knows when I am going astray—and always knows how to fix it.

Henry Morrison, canny friend and adviser and my agent for over forty years, came up with countless suggestions for the book. He loved the idea of it, so he prodded and poked and cajoled and even swore to push me through to those two magic words, *the end.*

Rick Layman is our foremost Hammett scholar and historian. Without his friendship, enthusiasm, and expertise and his *Discovering "The Maltese Falcon" and Sam Spade* to use as my primary source material, I could not have written *Spade & Archer.*

Jo Marshall, Dashiell Hammett's only surviving daughter, in 2006 said "Yes!" to a prequel to *The Maltese Falcon.* Jo gave me not only her blessings and inspiration but also the idea (and the research) for much of part III of the novel.

Vince Emory let me write the introduction to Hammett's *Lost Stories,* then shared his vast knowledge of San Francisco and Hammett with me. A history of the coroner's office from 1850 to 1960 gave me the idea for part II. Vince and Rita are rare friends.

Acknowledgments

Theresa McGovern, research librarian at the Fairfax Library, once again filled every goofy research demand I made on her. She even gave up a weekend to find out about secretaries' salaries in the 1920s. Dori and I treasure her friendship.

Again, the entire staff at the Fairfax Library helped with the project whenever they could. Especially Shereen Ash, who found me the history of the Bohemian Club and put me in touch with the club's historian. Librarians are wonderful people!

Jo Marshall's children, Julie Rivett and Evan Marshall, gave me advice and information about their grandfather, Dashiell Hammett. Their enthusiasm and support for the project have been a great inspiration to me.

Sonny Mehta, chairman and editor in chief at Knopf, gave his blessing to the project. And my editors, Diana Coglianese at Knopf and Zachary Wagman at Vintage Books, did a marvelous line edit of the manuscript and had countless suggestions that made *Spade & Archer* a much better (and shorter!) book.

The late Matt Bruccoli, a friend of many years and our best Hemingway-Fitzgerald scholar, gave me the background for Spade's service in World War I. Matt was wildly enthusiastic about *Spade & Archer.* Matt, I so wish you'd had a chance to read it.

Last, but certainly not least, Dori's and my dear friend Bill Richardson got me unprecedented access to the Bohemian Club and walked me through everything I needed for the scenes I wanted to set there. We owe you and Betsy a great dinner, Bill!

ALSO BY DASHIELL HAMMETT

THE CONTINENTAL OP

Short, thick-bodied, mulishly stubborn, and indifferent to pain, Dashiell Hammett's Continental Op was the prototype for generations of tough-guy detectives. In these stories the Op unravels a murder with too many clues and tangles with a crooked-eared gunman called the Whosis Kid.

Crime Fiction/978-0-679-72258-8

THE GLASS KEY

In this tour de force of detective fiction, Paul Madvig aspires to something better: the heiress to a dynasty of political purebreds. Did he want her badly enough to commit murder, or is one of his numerous enemies trying to frame him?

Crime Fiction/978-0-679-72262-5

THE MALTESE FALCON

A treasure worth killing for. Sam Spade, a slightly shopworn private eye with his own solitary code of ethics. A grifter named Joel Cairo, a fat man named Gutman, and Brigid O'Shaughnessy, a beautiful and treacherous woman. These are the ingredients of a novel that has haunted three generations of readers.

Crime Fiction/978-0-679-72264-9

THE THIN MAN

Nick and Nora Charles are Dashiell Hammett's most enchanting creations, a rich, glamorous couple who solve homicides in between wisecracks and martinis.

Crime Fiction/978-0-679-72263-2

ALSO AVAILABLE

The Big Knockover, 978-0-679-72259-5
The Dain Curse, 978-0-679-72260-1
Nightmare Town, 978-0-375-70102-3
Red Harvest, 978-0-679-72261-8
Woman in the Dark, 978-0-679-72265-3